The Bookmaker
from Rabaul

The Bookmaker
from Rabaul

*A fictionalised account of
true events*

Peter Bowes

For Parker

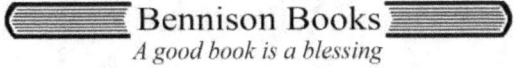
Bennison Books
A good book is a blessing

Bennison Books Contemporary Classics
ISBN: 978-0-9954302-1-1

I have, I am aware, told this story in a very rambling way so that it may be difficult for anyone to find their path through what may be a sort of maze. I cannot help it. I have stuck to my idea of being in a country cottage with a silent listener, hearing between the gusts of the wind and amidst the noises of the distant sea, the story as it comes. And, when one discusses an affair — a long, sad affair — one goes back, one goes forward. One remembers points that one has forgotten and one explains them all the more minutely since one recognises that one has forgotten to mention them in their proper places and that one may have given, by omitting them, a false impression. I console myself with thinking that this is a real story and that, after all, real stories are probably told best in the way a person telling a story would tell them. They will then seem most real.

The Good Soldier, Ford Madox Ford

*I sent my soul through the Invisible,
Some letter that After-life to spell:
And by and by my Soul return'd to me,
And answer'd "I myself am Heav'n and Hell"*

The Rubaiyat of Omar Khayyam
Fitzgerald version

Also by Peter Bowes

Bloodlines
Lineage

His short vignettes in Bloodlines are visceral, teeth rattling, funny and even true, and they stretch from then to now and this horizon to that, from the poetic to the poignant to the hilarious. ~ Sean Doherty author of *My Brother's Keeper* and *MP: The Life of Michael Peterson* published by HarperCollins.

The Cuckoo-Shrike

This fellow comes by twice a day, depending on the sun's position in the large glass pane that protects us from summer's northeasters.

Coracina novaehollandiae

He flies up to the glass about thirty or forty times, flutters up and knocks it softly with his beak. Then he retires to a branch of the durobby tree that grows close by.

Sometimes he manages to fly over the top of the glass and into the atrium where we sit watching him. And, of course, the bafflement continues. Now he's fluttering up to the inside of the glass and tapping it with his beak.

It doesn't matter which side he's on, the problem remains the same.

There's only himself on the other side.

~ PB

Though heaven and earth were blent together, though all the lustre of the stars went out, I would wait in your path, O beloved, and ask of you why you have taken away my life.

The Rubaiyat of Omar Khayyam
McCarthy version

Is This the Man?

DS Leane was asking a question.

He spoke again.

'Do you know this man?'

The detectives had dusty shoes and the one called Brown a ragged edge to one of his trouser cuffs.

'No.'

'Would you please look at the bust? Is this man Alfred Baxter?'

'No.'

Leane exchanged glances with Canney.

'Mrs Beecham?'

Tangiers, 1938

They were bare-chested. The slighter, bespectacled man's face had burnt a sharp red in the Moroccan sun; a wide-brimmed black hat protected his taller companion.

Both men were looking over the hotel parapet down onto the Grand Socco where a procession of donkeys was being led through the crowds to the dockside warehouses, all double-loaded with hessian bags of kief brought down from the Atlas Mountains overnight and destined for Spain.

A young girl from a café across the square brought them a small plate of hashish *galletas* and a stone pot of cream with their coffee. She had surprised them on the first morning when she pushed aside the curtain that served as a door and brought her tray into the rooftop bedroom they shared, and from that day the Englishman called her Mata Hari because she knew their secrets.

The windless morning promised another hot day.

'The war will change everything.'

Pym gestured at the Mediterranean's distant, tranquil

surface.

'This ...'

He turned to his companion, who had just picked up one of the flat biscuits and split it with his thumbnail.

'Us.'

Seed

Moscow, 1941

The lecturer had an Albanian name: Otto Troseth ... Trozyth? He mentioned it as the six recruits settled into their seats in the small windowless classroom, young men and women, pale from their long weeks of learning the operational intricacies of a dozen different cipher machines. Trozyth wished them good afternoon. The two women smiled at him, the men remained impassive.

He held up a small soft-covered book and wondered, as he did with all his classes, how many of them had ever finished a book they didn't *have* to read.

'This book contains seventy-five quatrains, seven to nine words per line, twenty-five to thirty letters on each line.'

Otto opened the lid of his desk, took out another five copies and walked around distributing them.

'In each book you will find a sheet of paper with two typed stanzas.'

He waited until everybody had found and read them.

I, a fugitive caravanserai,
crept silently east.

That yellow, departed hand,
be with me again.
Thou seed.

'If I were to write a covert message using this book, wherein I described my present situation, my method of travel and destination, would you agree that the first verse is sufficient?'

No one spoke.

'Well? Somebody speak up please.'

One of the women looked around before slowly raising her hand.

'Yes?'

'I am a fugitive. I am coming east.'

'What is your name?'

'Yana.'

'What else do you know of your fugitive, Yana?'

The young woman bent her head and read the verse again, then spoke without looking up.

'He is travelling overland under forged identification

papers, perhaps by train. Nobody knows where he has gone.'

Otto took a piece of chalk from his pocket and turned to the blackboard.

'Which words did you use to arrive at those considerations, Yana?'

'I. Fugitive. Caravanserai. Crept. Silently. East.'

Otto wrote the six words on the board.

'Explain how the word *crept* metamorphoses into *forged identification* to the class, all of whom seem to be struck dumb.'

Otto had little time for the thick-minded and wasted no effort with them. He turned and looked at the young woman.

'*Forged identification*. How did that come into being, Yana?'

'Anyone who travels with proper papers does so openly; it is another matter for someone on forged papers.'

Otto smiled

'They creep from place to place?'

'Yes, sir, that is my interpretation.'

'Then I hope you never have to travel under such a burden. Why don't his superiors know of his movements?'

'He has kept silent.'

Trozyth looked over at the other students until one met his glance and raised his hand.

'Yes?'

'I am familiar with the book, but not those lines.'

'Your name?'

'Oskar.'

Otto faced the board and chalked a line of characters, speaking as he wrote.

LIV 1 1 XXIV 3 1 XXXV 1 7 XVI 1 5

'There are enough words in the *Rubaiyat* to satisfy any message.'

He turned around, placed the chalk on his desk and looked at each student in turn; he had no doubt some would fall asleep if he allowed it.

'Oskar, what is the fifth word on the first line of verse sixteen in the book you have on your desk?'

Oskar picked up the book and flicked through the

pages.

'Caravanserai.'

'What does the word represent, now that Yana has broken the code?'

Oskar and Yana exchanged a quick glance.

'An agent, in flight.'

Otto looked over at Yana.

'What of the second stanza?'

'It is a response: I will be where we last met. All is well.'

'Where will they meet?'

'Hong Kong, China.'

'China?'

'They are the yellow people.'

'All is well?'

'Seed.'

She was worth all the hundreds who passed through his classes.

'What if all is not well?'

'There would be no seed.'

Otto allowed a small triumphal surge to quicken his blood before looking away from the girl's face and back at the class.

'Perhaps you could explain?'

'A seed grows; its absence means nothing will come of a meeting.'

Exodus

Hong Kong, 1941

The correspondent had arrived in Hong Kong with orders to retrieve a package from the Russian legation's safety room, now being emptied. It was to have been picked up and taken to Australia by a regular courier but the recent and rapid course of the war had hurried the exodus from the island. The courier had abandoned the city and an orderly search of his rooms took fifteen minutes to come up with nothing. He had gone.

The correspondent knew where to go and was in and out of the building quickly. His escape from the colony now depended on a merchant steamer, the *Cycle*, docked a few miles east and no doubt anxious to be away from the air battles drifting over the city. The roads along the waterfront were choked with emigrants and expatriates, the footpaths piled with abandoned possessions, the air steaming with panic. The Japanese were already in Kowloon, almost at the edge of Victoria Harbour, and the only escape from Hong Kong Island was by boat.

George Lorrimer had been sitting on two stacked wooden crates behind the kitchen window of an empty

Hong Kong office suite for two days. He was uncomfortable and had no electricity to boil water for the coffee he kept in a tin in his camera case. Perch jobs, he hated them.

This was not the first time Frank Delaney had given him the key to these rooms. They were across the road from the Russian legation and the cigarette butts he'd ground onto the floor earlier in the year were still there, as were the exposed nail heads on the crates and the cockroach husks in the cupboards.

When he slid open the window above the sink, the uproarious clamour of engines and voices from the street filled the room. The roads were chaotic, the noise of the traffic pierced by the continual wailing of older Chinese women among the crowds, lamenting their doomed right to live in Hong Kong: the Jewel. The Japanese would be cruel and brutal and here in days.

Lorrimer rested his camera on the work surface to his left together with his notepad and pencil. The enamel sink, directly beneath his chin, had a blackened and ungated cavity at its centre and at times a low grumble came from its depths, as if from some internal shifting of organs, issuing soft gusts of foul wet air into his face as he watched the doorway across the street.

He shook three Lucky Strike cigarettes out of his packet and arranged them next to his camera, then took a silver Zippo lighter from his trouser pocket and laid it alongside them. Three cigarettes for a three-hour shift before a break outside in fresher air.

A noise in the corridor and Lorrimer turned to see a shadow pass beneath the door.

He got up from his seat and quietly crossed the room, opened the door and stepped out into a deserted hallway that stretched fifty feet one way and fifty feet the other. He looked to his left and right then came back inside, closed and locked the door, resumed his seat, took up his first cigarette, lit it, put the lighter back into his pocket, picked up his camera and focused it on the legation entrance.

'Who do you want?' he had asked Delaney. 'They'll be coming in and out like it's a Woolworths store.'

'Anyone with a white face.'

On the second day, Lorrimer saw two men inside the lobby exchanging a package before they separated and left the building.

Both were wearing hats; one slightly built, dressed in suit and tie and wearing glasses, the other broad-shouldered and squat; a seaman, wearing a pea-jacket, dungarees and heavy boots.

He weighed it up: follow the package, or the man who had sent it on its way.

Lorrimer was used to the crowded Hong Kong streets and sometimes tried his hand at trailing a local man who looked to be in a hurry. But following one black-crowned head into these confounding mazes of alleyways and streets had proved impossible; at times he had to stop, stranded and directionless in the dark and almost subterranean depths of the city, among a silent people who looked at him without overt curiosity, assuming the oriental stillness of temple cats to watch him until he was gone.

He skirted the crowded footpaths by walking in the gutter and looked for a man wearing a hat in a crowd of hatless Chinese. One small boy coming towards him slipped away from his mother's hand, walked onto the road in front of Lorrimer and stopped to stare at him. Lorrimer stepped around the child and was startled by the impatient bleat of a car horn; he turned to watch a silver chauffeur-driven Rolls-Royce pass slowly by with two women in the back seat, one smoking, both wearing hats. One of the women turned her head to look at Lorrimer as he stood in the gutter on the other side of her window. She glanced up into his eyes from beneath the brim of her hat.

Two blocks on he had him. One block further and Lorrimer watched as Oskar Rostov walked to a dockside gate, produced a piece of paper and handed it to a uniformed officer who stamped it, passed it back and let him through.

Rostov walked in the direction of three steamers tied bow to stern along the wooden dock, all with their gangways down, crowded with lines of slowly climbing evacuees. Small groups stood about the dockside, families, some in tears as they embraced each other. Rostov moved through them quickly; oblivious to the women's despair as they held their husbands; the men were certain to be imprisoned for the duration of the war after giving up their berths to allow more women and children to flee.

Lorrimer passed through the gate using one of Delaney's police dockets and watched Rostov join a gangway that led to the upper deck of the *Cycle*. He was the only passenger without a suitcase.

Raffles Hotel

Lorrimer's military flight out of Hong Kong landed at Sembawang RAAF base in Singapore where US Embassy official Frank Delaney met him and took his films away to be developed.

Three hours later they were sharing a bottle of malt whisky in Delaney's suite at the Raffles Hotel where they toasted the grand old city – now under air attack again – as it flashed and shook under high-explosive thunder and lightning.

Delaney's manila folder contained Lorrimer's Hong Kong collection: over one hundred and fifty photos. Delaney also had a list of names and the two men sat around the bottle and played match-up. Faces and names, faces and code names, faces and double names.

Lorrimer picked through the pictures, now scattered across the table, until he came up with the man in glasses coming out of the legation and another of him standing at the back of a line of people looking over the side of a merchant steamer.

'*This* guy ... and he had a friend ...'

He picked through the images again.

'*Here* – the pair of them had a little meeting in the lobby before they came out into the sunshine.'

Delaney took the three photos and arranged them either side of his glass as Lorrimer got up and wandered over to the suite's harbour view windows.

'What's the big fire out there, Frank?'

'Naval base, the Nips knocked it off this morning.'

'When are you getting out?'

'Tomorrow, sailing to Bombay; do you want a berth?'

Lorrimer stood with his hands on his hips, gazing out of the window at the fires raging throughout the city. He watched a canvas-topped jeep career into the hotel driveway and park in a flowerbed; four men in air force blue exited at the double and disappeared up the front steps and into the building. Australian fighter pilots. He'd seen them when he landed in Sembawang and walked through the aircraft revetments.

'I might try the RAAF base, see if I can talk my way onto an aircraft going south.'

'Here we go,' said Delaney. 'Oskar.'

'Which one?'

'The small guy with glasses.'

'How about the solid one?'

'Who's he? Door security?'

'They didn't have any.'

'Don't know him.'

'Who's Oskar?'

'Regular spook on a Russian diplomatic passport, came through here a few times before these guys interrupted,' Delaney gestured at the distant thunder.

'Oskar our name or his?'

'His, Oskar with a K, last name Rostov.'

'Is *that* real?'

'One day you might get to ask him.'

They worked for another hour without success before wrapping it up; the bombardment had ceased, leaving the city glittering with fire.

Lorrimer finished his drink, gathered his photographs and prepared to leave.

'Before you go, George.'

Delaney tore a page from his notebook and wrote down a name and phone number.

'The local MPs have locked up a guy they caught talking to the Japs; with a bit of luck they've got his transmitters as well.'

He handed the piece of paper to Lorrimer.

'Ask for Sergeant Parker.'

'Anyone had a good look at them?'

'One was disguised as a typewriter and the other concealed in a field communication set.'

'Who is he?'

'Patrick Heenan. Tell Parker I sent you.'

A gunshot sounded beneath them, a quick flat report followed by a muted cheer. Lorrimer walked over to the door and listened.

'What's down one floor?'

'The bar, runs along the front of the building.'

'Aussies.'

Lorrimer walked back and shook Delaney's hand.

'They could be my ticket out. See you on the other side, Frank.'

Delaney watched as he slipped through the door.

The empty corridor was hung with softly lit chandeliers and carpeted with oriental rugs laid on fawn and tan tiles; the rooms along its length were vacant, their doors open; housemaids had cleaned them before being told to go home. Lorrimer poked his head into a large suite on his way past, expecting to see a bowl of orchids and welcome note from a management anxious to please its all-conquering guests. In less than forty-eight hours the Japanese were expected to be in control of the island and resident in its best hotels.

He heard men singing to his left as he came down the grand staircase, and turned towards an open door as they started the second verse.

Lorrimer walked into a dimly lit, richly ornate room with all its furniture stacked against the walls. The airmen were standing at the far end of a long and otherwise deserted bar, drinking and gazing out through the windows at the smoke-covered city, a whiff of cordite mingling with their cigar smoke. One looked over as Lorrimer approached and smiled broadly.

'Care for a drink? The staff have kindly left the bar open.'

Lorrimer joined them without argument; they were all wearing pistols.

An hour later, duty called the airmen via the bar phone. After leaving a few dollars for the drinks, the group was met at the hotel forecourt by five armed Singaporean policemen who had responded to an emergency call from the hotel's general manager. The manager stood with the police, shouting and waving his finger at the airmen as they walked down the hotel steps.

Lorrimer wasn't surprised; one of the airmen had shot the padlock off the liquor cabinet.

The Singaporeans stopped their complaining when His Grace, as the sharpshooter was known, pulled a handsome alligator skin wallet from his trousers. The son of a wealthy Sydney retailer, he had embarked for Singapore with twenty gold sovereigns sown into a money belt which he had promised his father he would double or, at worst, keep. His wealth had been forgiven by his fellow officers because of his flying skills.

Lorrimer accepted their offer of a seat in the jeep and a billet at the Sembawang airfield for the night. When the driver asked how he planned to escape the Japanese, Lorrimer smiled at the pilots who sat either side of him in the back seat.

'Anyone taking passengers?'

The four pilots conferred as they travelled through the city, past smouldering buildings and around great mounds of rubble. The driver asked Lorrimer what he weighed, another his height. The sharpshooter asked if Lorrimer was willing to pay for the flight and after a short negotiation he agreed to fit the American into his aircraft for the price of four crates of Johnny Walker Scotch Whisky he had planned to liberate from the

Sembawang Officers' Mess.

The Execution

Lorrimer rang Parker the next morning, mentioned Delaney and asked if the transmitters could be brought to the docks with the prisoner. He was told the machines and the prisoner would be at Dock G2 Kepple Harbour that morning at ten o'clock sharp.

Patrick Heenan, a former captain of the 16th Punjab Regiment, was a hard and resolute soldier who for days had resisted his interrogators with bitter insolence. The military police had been left unchecked in their treatment of him and with the occupation of Singapore only days away they dispensed with formality and cut cards for the executioner's job. Heenan was the only man left in their cells and the station was to be evacuated.

Lorrimer arrived at the dock entrance in time to see a dark Wolseley sedan roll to a halt some one hundred yards along the wooden jetty. He coasted to a standstill alongside it and watched as two non-coms dragged Heenan from the car and stood him at the jetty edge. He was barefoot and ragged from the beatings.

The sergeant stayed inside the car a moment to remove his cap and flashes, the custom being that a soldier should not be in full uniform during a summary execution.

He took out his revolver, an unreliable Enfield, and loaded the chamber with two bullets. Climbing out of the car, he noticed Lorrimer and nodded. Lorrimer walked over.

'Parker?'

'You the Yank who phoned?'

'That's me. Where are the transmitters?'

'Gone. Everyone's stealing everything. Sorry.'

Lorrimer stepped back.

Heenan was held facing the strait as tumult reigned in the distance; dozens of merchant ships were underway through a heaving carpet of smaller boats and sampans, some jostling hard to keep close to any gangways that might still be lowered.

The sergeant walked around and faced his prisoner.

'Patrick, my lad.'

Heenan lifted his head.

'Have you a last request? Something you'd like to go out on? A smoke, perhaps?'

Heenan swayed in the soldiers' grip

Parker winked at his two companions, walked behind Heenan and shot him once in the back of the head from a range of six inches. Heenan toppled into the water and Parker stepped to the edge of the dock, took careful aim with his pistol and popped the second bullet between his shoulders.

The car was pushed in after him on the sergeant's order. He saw no sense in leaving the Japanese a good vehicle in which to tour their new city.

Leaving Singapore

L orrimer left Singapore that afternoon strapped behind a pilot's seat, only just managing to keep the contents of his stomach down as His Grace calmly weaved the Buffalo fighter through the pillars of smoke that rose from the city.

The Japanese caught up with them at Batavia airstrip. Both men were sitting in a hangar drinking coffee when they heard the sudden roar of fast-approaching low-level aircraft. Grace put his coffee down, stood and walked towards the open hangar doors.

'Shit. *Zeros.*'

He turned to Lorrimer who was already running, hands clamped over his head, towards the back door of the hangar and the sheltering jungle beyond.

Four Japanese fighters swept low over the strip, strafing the stationary aircraft. A shrieking arc of high-calibre bullets punctured the fuselage of Grace's Buffalo fighter and smashed through the cockpit. By the time the Japanese pilots returned for a second attack thirty seconds later, Grace had joined Lorrimer to watch from beneath the forest canopy.

Lorrimer took out a packet of cigarettes, lit one with a shaking hand and looked over at the heavy roils of black smoke rising above the hangar roof.

'What does the RAAF do next?'

Grace looked at his watch.

'Give these fellows a couple of minutes to buzz off then we'll go and find a hotel.'

Lorrimer laughed.

'That's a great idea, but how are we going to get back to Australia?'

Grace walked out from under the forest canopy and looked at the sky.

'I'd say we're all clear.'

He turned back to Lorrimer.

'Coming?'

Tosya

The sea off Hong Kong drowned dozens during the furious typhoon seasons and now the Japanese were killing as many every day as their aircraft slowly traversed the sea lanes, targeting the larger ships with their bombs. The British did not have enough anti-aircraft guns to seriously deter them and a few sharpshooters on the Victoria Peak crags pot-shotted away during the daylight hours in the hope of hitting an aircraft.

After two weeks' travel across the South China Sea to Java on a sailing lugger, Keyannik was put ashore in Anyar from where he planned to travel to Batavia by road. The coastal town was overcome with displaced settlers and expatriate families who had fled from Singapore and Medan by sea and were all waiting for transport to Batavia. A Javanese headman had offered the women and children shelter in a longhouse, leaving the men to stand around on the beach, talking and smoking, looking for any movement on the horizon and listening for the sound of aircraft. The air was heavy and humid and night promised waves of mosquitoes from the coastal swamp.

Columns of smoke had been rising in the hills all week as the jungles let slip men intent on assisting with the expulsion of the European settlers. Javanese natives, many under the influence of local Japanese sympathisers, surrounded the plantation buildings at night, stamping and shouting outside the windows and doors, waiting for the bravest to bound up to the entranceway and throw his fire.

Some of the larger coffee estates had the remains of great firepits dug into their lawns where the owners had burned whatever they could not carry away. The women had worked their way through their wardrobes, taking scissors to the clothes that could not be packed.

Treasures were buried among the graves in long-prepared brick crypts and nothing was left for the Japanese.

Keyannik paid for a seat in the back of an open truck already crowded with families; the children stared as he carried his seabag aboard, sat down and folded his short, thick arms. The man sitting opposite glanced at Keyannik's face, then looked down at his pea jacket, heavy dungarees and work boots before returning to study his pale Slavic features. He met Keyannik's impassive eyes and looked away.

The trip to Batavia took four hours, stopping once to pick up an elderly villager whose legs and feet were wrapped in soiled and bloodstained bandages. Keyannik helped lift the old man aboard and settle him on the tray-bed among their feet where he lay mute and suffering as the truck continued its journey.

Once in the city, Keyannik made his way to the waterfront and found lodgings in a seaman's mission where he remained until obtaining work as stoker aboard the Brisbane bound steamer, *Maiwarra*.

From Brisbane he travelled to Sydney in a train compartment with five other men; a dark-eyed man who sat with his silence all around him, a jovial buffoon who laughed at his own jokes until he fell asleep and a trio on their way south to enlist, claiming the food was better in the New South Wales recruitment camps.

Keyannik stayed awake while the others around him slept, filling the compartment with their spent air. He left his seat at dawn and stood at a window to look out at the dry fields and blownabout homes, their sun-warped timber walls slanting this way and that.

Children, half-glimpsed, played their melancholy games in the dusty streets as the train closed on the city, crashing past soot-blackened tenements and diseased yards of ruined iron machinery and discarded timber, rows of flatbed trucks with their snouts bared and innards removed.

A man leaning up against the wall of a foundry in a patch of early sunlight with his hands in his pockets and his face up to the sky. Another, dark-skinned, hurled a bottle at the carriages as they passed by his littered humpy.

The staff at the information kiosk at Sydney Central Station had been directing men to the enlistment centres for months; men who had travelled hundreds of miles from the interior to sign up, some with faces burnt to leather by the sun. Goldminers, opal diggers, drovers and blacktrackers; men with a registry of thieving and killing skills cached in the cunning behind their eyes and boys without the years to grow a beard.

Keyannik disappeared among them.

He found a public phone and rang the number he'd been given in Hong Kong; when asked his business he said the package had arrived and would be delivered tomorrow when he found a way to get there. That done, he walked to nearby Haymarket in search of better clothes; the glimpses he had caught of himself in shop windows were of a bearded, menacing vagrant clutching a greasy swag of belongings to his chest.

Keyannik entered the main market hall and walked with the crowds until he came to an aisle of rag traders. He picked through their bins buying a jacket from one and two pairs of trousers from another; an old stallholder told him that underwear and socks could only be bought new, and in another part of town. She pointed to a corner of the market where Keyannik could buy a second-hand hat. The only one that fitted was a leather trilby.

Ed Baxter

E d Baxter was sitting on the back stoop with his son Tim watching the little boy as he pushed his miniature cars off the bottom step and onto the ground. Every time one tumbled over, Tim looked up at his father and chuckled. Ed thought he had signs of the wrecking yard about him already.

He leant over to put his hand on the boy's head and gave it a soft caress.

'Don't grow up too quick while I'm gone, will you?'

Tim pushed another car off the step.

'And stay out of under the house.'

Ed turned the boy's face up so they could look at each other.

'Spiders *bite*.'

Tim turned back to his cars and pushed two over at the same time.

The little boy was almost two. He had a keen understanding of where the best hiding places in the back garden were and had recently developed an interest in the darker recesses under the house. Ed stood, picked him up and walked back inside.

Ellse was in their bedroom, crying. She had been busy all morning with his breakfast and final packing, spartan as it was. The list Ed had been given by the army was just enough for a weekend's camping.

She had been dreading this day.

Many of the homes in the street had waved their men away to the war and now Ed had enlisted when he could have stayed out of it as a mechanic, a protected wartime trade. His obstinacy had infuriated her and they argued at both ends of the day, breakfast and dinner.

Ed was thirty-eight and they had been married for ten years; his side of the bed would be empty for months, perhaps years. There would be no one beside her at night when she might wake, frightened by her premonitions or a noise outside the house, and Tim would miss the foolish goings-on that often had him chasing his father through the house, both of them on hands and knees.

The firing ranges on the nearby South Maroubra headland had been rattling with gunfire for years as recruits filed through the redoubts, waiting their turn at the targets. On clear days Ellse could hear men shouting and the faint shriek of cease-fire whistles. Sometimes she sat on her front porch listening and wondering if the sound of real fighting was any different.

Ellse had washed, ironed and put away his clothes and hung his working jackets and trousers in the spare bedroom wardrobe. They would have to be aired every couple of weeks to cope with the long disuse. Ed had rubbed a final coat of polish into his work boots and buffed them to a fair shine before stuffing them with crushed newspaper and putting them on the floor by her bedroom dresser.

'I want to see them in the morning,' she had said one night when all was soft between them, 'and every evening, last thing before the light goes off.'

Until then, she had insisted he leave his boots by the back door and for ten working years Ed had stowed them in a tin chest with his wet weather gear

Ellse reached up, touched his head and traced the small red scar on his neck; two months ago Ed had been trying to subdue an enraged man at a union meeting and had come home while she slept, bleeding from a police baton's blow. He'd cleaned himself up before coming to bed, leaving a bloodied towel on top of the laundry tub.

Earlier that morning he had finally locked up the corrugated iron shed where he kept his spare bikes and workbenches and Ellse asked him to bring in his enamel mug and put it with the teapot. Ed liked a brew-up when the mechanics of a bike needed some thought, black with two sugars and a seat on the bench outside his shed in the sun where he sat, supped and pondered.

Ed put the boy down, cupped his wife's face and kissed both her cheeks; they were wet with tears and she looked at him hoping he might yet change his mind, proud as she was, and knowing that he would not.

'Nothing silly from you, Ed,' she warned him again, 'leave the younger men to the weapons.'

Ed took the boy's hand and they walked to the front door and out onto the porch. He squatted down, took Tim into his arms and hugged him for the couple of seconds he was allowed before the little boy began to squirm. Then Ed stood and embraced his wife.

'I can't tell you not to worry, Ellse, but you're not to. I'm too old to be sent fighting.'

She stood listening in the open doorway until the sound of his bike was lost in the rumble of surf breaking not two hundred yards away.

Cowra Training Camp

Cowra, 1942

The Army Training camp on Darby's Falls Road was a two-hundred-acre swathe of farmland and forest that echoed day and night to the chatter and bang of gunfire and the earthy bombardments of grenades tossed into slit trenches. Recruits were shouted off their buses on arrival, threatened and abused as they milled about, bullied into untidy lines and marched briskly and without rhythm to the barber and quartermaster where they were stripped of hair and identity, then issued regulation khaki kit together with hats: great shady lids of rabbit skin curled up on one side like a breaking wave, fastened and festooned with the crown.

Then, pale-headed and regimentally brutalised, they were doubled out into the sunshine holding their bundles, marched to the armoury and handed bayonets and World War One issue Lee Enfield bolt-action .303 rifles.

'If I find a mark on the stock when you come back from the range,' warned the sergeant-quartermaster as he handed over the much-used rifles, 'I'll ram the fucken thing up your arse.'

A veteran of the Great War told the recruits how to overcome superior numbers of the enemy in trench fighting situations or a blind alley in a French village.

'If you turn a corner and run into a pack of the bastards, keep both your eyes open, point and snap shoot, count the shots, and reload after six.'

'Rush him,' the pot-bellied corporal yelled at them on the training field, 'and stab him, anywhere. If his muscles spasm or you hit bone and the bayonet sticks, fire a round into him and wrench it out. Then look around for another one.'

They ran at suspended bags of sand screaming obscenities and stabbed and stabbed.

Leave was granted at the end of the training month and a great stream of men dressed in sharply pressed khaki and highly polished boots exited through the camp gates in a rush for the buses, jostling and chaffing at each other as they climbed in, one month in camp and fit enough to burst out of their shirts. City boys, hardened up and indoctrinated in the ways of war, eager for a day in town on the drink.

Cowra's cafés were the soldiers' first call, where they feasted on breakfasts double the size the army offered. All the café booths were packed with uniformed men eating purposefully and silently, too busy chewing to talk, cushioning their stomachs for the day ahead.

Doug McCimber was among them, snarfing down a

steak as big as his four-and-a-half-fingered hand.

An itinerant drover from Chillagoe possessing small patience with the world's more belligerent inhabitants, McCimber was known throughout the cattle towns of Queensland as Chat, Havachat being considered too unwieldy.

He lounged in a corner of the bar at the Imperial Hotel later that morning with Ed Baxter, listening to the races. Chat had his smokes, a local form guide, a schooner and a double tot of OP rum set out on the bar in front of him, a widower's picnic. He and Ed were the oldest recruits in camp and shared a mutual desire to avoid the more serious conflict as the Japanese moved south towards Darwin.

'You don't have to be Einstein to know that by staying with this mob of no-hopers you'll be up to your arse in mud in two months.'

Chat gestured at the boisterous young soldiers around them.

'And getting dry fucken gulched by the Nips every time you stop for a piss.'

Chat knew of a plan to station men at the Top End near Darwin.

'I'm told they work in small patrols in the rivers up there, six blokes in a couple of canoes with guns and radios, hunting the Nips. You're not going to compare that to humping a rifle through the jungle and being chased by one, are you? And there's Darwin just around the corner on weekends; a bloke would need his head examined not to put his hand up for that caper.'

As McCimber took a mouthful of beer, Ed noticed his right hand was missing a finger. Doug caught his glance and putting the glass down, waggled his shortened digit in the air.

'Lost it mustering cattle. I was tying the bloody mare to a post when the bloody dog barked right under its belly. Up goes her bloody head and the end of my finger got squeezed off like a melon pip. The fat-arsed recruiting bastard didn't want to sign me up until I threatened to thump him.'

He glanced at Baxter.

'What d'you reckon?'

'I reckon it's hard to tell between your bullshit and the real thing. Who's in charge?'

'The boss of the outfit is Bill Stanner. He's got a few uniforms in camp signing blokes up. Have a think about it, Ed; if I get a post they'll give me a train ticket to get up there; if you get one, you can ride that noisy fucken bike of yours all the way up to Darwin.'

'That bit I don't mind,' replied Baxter, 'but the only reason he'll want me is because I'm handy around machinery. You're the Hopalong bloody Cassidy; I'll be stuck in the heat with my head up a truck's arse, as usual.'

'You'll love it, you grumpy old bastard, so you're comin', no fucken arguments. I've already told 'em about you anyway.'

Ed laughed at the bandy old codger sitting beside him.

'I'm not sleeping in the same tent as you, Chat. That's if they take on a bloke without a trigger finger who probably talks in his sleep.'

A fight started nearby and both men took their drinks and stood by the wall away from the ruckus. Chat drained his schooner.

'Some blokes can't wait.'

Mordecai

Timber Creek, 1942

'It's a taipan,' said Col.

Ed took a step closer. The old Aboriginal was sitting by a campfire with the head of a dead snake gripped between his teeth.

Ed grunted.

'Brown snake, I reckon.'

Ed Baxter and Col Martin, both recently arrived at the Nackeroos base camp in the Northern Territory, had been told by the CO to stow their kit in a spare tent and do a little sightseeing before the light faded. They came across the Aboriginal humpy at the edge of the army encampment and Ed thought this fellow was the blackest a man could ever be.

The old man placed his fingers in the slit he had cut around the snake's neck and began to peel the skin off until it all came away. Then he took the head out of his mouth, picked up a sharpened sapling and slid it into the snake's mouth, eased it all the way through to the tail, gave it a twist and held it over the coals. He looked over at the two men watching him.

'You blokes fancy some fresh tucker?'

Blacktracker Mordecai was one of the many local tribesmen hired by Bill Stanner to help search for signs of Japanese infiltration, and in his spare time he taught Baxter how to trail a man over ground that looked as if it had lain undisturbed for centuries. The old man would search out some high feature, a barren hump of earth capped with sunbaked rock, sometimes carved by an ancient hand into the likeness of an animal, and sit there with his eyes roaming over the landscape of scattered dwarf trees, stony plains and distant purple ranges.

Mordecai passed his great Jawoyn hand over a scrabble of scattered ground, pausing at a thin twig of paperbark crushed at one end. He called to Baxter.

'Here,' he said, 'somethin' steppin' light but steppin' here, coming by here. See?'

Ed looked.

'Two days since any wind up here to blow away. That's how old be this fella passin' by.'

'Jap man?'

A deep chuckle as the old man rose effortlessly from his haunches, thirty years older than Baxter and not a grunt of discomfort.

'Wallaby, Boss, rock wallaby. On their way to water, over there.'

He pointed to the south, where the desolate plains ended in an abrupt uprising of cliffs.

Ed thought it clever to try a game on Mordecai: a scuffmark on an exposed boulder, some crushed leaf litter a step or two away, a small disturbance in the red earth.

They squatted under the sun, snaffing away at the bush flies like intent old men bent over a found gold nugget.

Mordecai observed the disturbance that Baxter had led him to; bent low and blew away the top layer of earth, then a little more, until the small, crushed end of a cigarette became visible.

He picked up the smoke, held it under his nose and took a long, slow inhalation before hissing the air back out between his teeth.

Mordecai breathed out a rumble of laughter.

'This here is a Capstan, Ed, white Aussie smoke. The Jap smokes jungle leaf. You so good at this malarkey, you pullin' me leg now are you, Boss?'

Hoover

Sydney, 1943

When General Douglas MacArthur planned his five lines of command for the South West Pacific Area he was obliged to include the Allies in three, a portion far too generous in his estimation. The Sixth United States Army had another and he kept the fifth for himself. MacArthur called it the US Army Forces in The Far East. Submerged within its many Allied relationships was an Australian Army Signals and Intelligence operation, unofficially linked with the FBI and a secret American decryption station housed in a war-requisitioned ladies' school in Arlington, Virginia: a secluded campus of elegant buildings six miles from Washington D.C., surrounded by a hundred acres of woodlands and newly secured with two miles of barbed wire fencing and two guarded security gates.

The unofficial status of this link between the FBI and Australia was made necessary by J. Edgar Hoover's mistrust of the British Secret Service, born of his unshakable conviction that half of them reported to the Russians.

'How can they be other than disaffected?' Hoover

argued more than once to his inner circle.

'They've had the privilege of an English public school education, all attended Oxford or Cambridge attempting law or literature – and were seen sitting up like monkeys in the front row of Communist Party meetings, *regularly*.''

He argued – insisted – that agent George Lorrimer return to Australia, asserting that the Australian agency responsible for material destined for America be co-managed by the United States Department of Justice.

David Mansard-Pym, an Englishman stationed at Arlington with responsibility for the Australian signals operation, suggested to Hoover that the FBI's case management and surveillance techniques might unnecessarily impinge on the smooth running of the Australian cable intercept and signals operations. He had taken the final call but nothing he said could abate Edgar Hoover's relentless, wordy obduracy.

'We have a situation, for instance, here in America, David, where an ex-slaughterhouse labourer and decorated veteran of the Spanish Civil war was found to have his very large unofficial hands all over the distribution of a cache of extremely sensitive, top secret information. Some of which could only have come from cables intercepted at the Gawler station.'

Phone calls from the director of the FBI were punishing.

'Your very own successes are to blame for my instruction to include Lorrimer, so object all you want if it pleases you. George Lorrimer is on the payroll and your man on station will now have to work with him as well as manage his tea ladies.'

'He is not trained in our particular field,' Pym responded, when finally given an opportunity to speak.

'Lorrimer is a clandestine operator, the file you sent me says as much, or as little.'

'Is this all you intend to do, David, manage a classroom of women who spend their days at cipher machines, then go home in the hope that all goes well with the rest of the war?'

Pym's man on station was John Xavier Bingham, controller of the Gawler cable station in South Australia and director of the East Coast Signals and Intelligence Office, housed in Sydney's Grace Building. He and Bingham had been colleagues for centuries and Pym was in Bingham's office when he took the call from America.

'You're leaving it to me to speak to John about this?'

'We've already spoken. I was hoping he'd pick up the phone before you did. Is he there?'

'No, he's gone to his club for a swim.'

'Not a swimmer yourself, David? I thought you might

at least have had a dip at Bondi.'

'The water you are throwing me in looks to be deep enough, Mr Hoover. Bondi will have to wait. What are we to expect when Lorrimer arrives, the massed deployment of listening devices? Men in overcoats and hats shadowing men in overcoats and hats?'

Pym looked around the walls of Bingham's requisitioned office; they were stripped of pictures, the bookshelves emptied. He laughed. Lorrimer would find it difficult hiding a bug in here.

'Laughing at your own jokes?'

'No, something just occurred. What do you know of John, now you have conscripted him, am I privy to that?'

'Enough,' said Hoover, who made it his business to know of everybody. 'Archaeologist, Military Cross at Ypres, add to that a couple of mentions, the ability to throw a bomb and an enterprising mind. Do you want my view, David, on what makes men like him and George Lorrimer better ... no, more effective than you in these times?'

'I can hardly hang up the phone, Mr Hoover.'

'They have no past worth remembering.'

Hoover laughed, his contralto peals echoing in the earpiece.

Pym waited.

'When did you arrive in Australia?'

'An hour ago.'

'And John is flying out to Washington tomorrow. Has he told you?'

'He mentioned something on the phone the other day; as I said, he's at his club.'

'We want him for a few days, his tea ladies are yours.

Pym didn't reply, his eyes travelled over the empty walls and bookcases again.

'David, are we clear on this?'

'Yes, Mr Hoover. Quite clear.'

The Cryptologist

Arlington, 2 April 1943

Meredith Gardner liked to make use of the outdoors, particularly when the sky was clear and he could walk his visitors through the woodlands and fields that surrounded the Arlington school buildings.

He asked Lorrimer how many types of birdsong he could hear and they stopped beneath the trees, waiting for the birds to resume their calling.

Lorrimer counted five but could identify only two; Gardner counted nine and knew them all.

'We're forever listening to radio transmissions,' he explained, 'getting behind the static that masks everything, so I like to think they gave us the school and its birds as compensation. What do you think, George? Perhaps we could use birdsong for codes in the next war. What tunes we could all play to each other!'

He plunged both his hands into his pockets and jingled some loose change.

'Tell it to me in one chapter, beginning, middle and end.'

'Meyer Lansky was a fully paid-up member of the Mafia,' Lorrimer began. 'I met him when he was doing some work with Charlie Haffenden, Commander Charlie Haffenden of the US Navy. This was after a big troop ship was sabotaged in Manhattan and Haffenden needed help from the Italian longshoremen in watching the waterfront. Meyer was their front man.'

'Lansky is a Jewish name,' said Gardner. 'Did that bother them?'

'When you're as smart as Lansky everybody listens.'

Gardner scratched at the unruly thatch of black hair that overgrew his forehead.

'I should read the newspapers, George, all this has passed me by.'

'Relax, Meredith, they missed it too.'

The men had reached the school buildings but neither was ready to give up the sunshine. Gardner suggested they walk around the rear of the main building and see what was edible in the kitchen's vegetable garden. Lorrimer took out a cigarette, lit it and offered the pack to Gardner.

'At the same time as all this was happening,' George continued, 'Lansky was running illegal casinos in

Atlantic City just down the road, and the stuff, I was told, the money, was kept in suitcases on a farm back in the hills.'

Gardner was an easy listener, and he stooped a little to hear better as they ambled along the shaded path.

'Meyer's problem was he could only use the money if he got it out of the country. Cuba wanted some casinos so he transported his cash over there and started building them. That lit up a big button on J. Edgar's desk, we tapped a few of Lansky's phones, I got lucky.'

'You're from Chicago, aren't you, George?'

Lorrimer laughed.

'OK, what borough?'

'Keep talking, I'll have you at the end.'

Gardner finished his cigarette, ground it out under his shoe, then picked up the butt and put it into the cuff of his trousers. He brushed his hands and looked at George a little sadly.

'A small-town habit, they don't like butts left on the street. You were saying?'

Lorrimer pinched his butt out with his thumb and forefinger and flicked it into the underbrush.

'We knew that Lansky shipped the money out of

Florida. There are plenty of places for a fishing boat to get in and out on the west coast but the only way to organise it was on the phone.

'He also had to avoid a thousand loose hoods roaming the country looking for an opportunity to grab his money while it was on the highway. Those guys travelled in armed caravans. So he worked out a system.' Lorrimer laughed. 'Where have you heard that before? … Anyway, say he was taking his money to Tampa. There's no way he's going to say that word over the phone when he's talking to his skipper, so he's got to change it to something else and make sure the skipper knows how to change it back, because that's where his boat is needed.

'T is number 20 in the alphabet, A is number 1, M is 13, that routine, five numbers for T A M P A.

'There was always more for him to say, like what day and what time, et cetera, and when he was done writing it up he would do the numbers for the whole message, letter by letter. This was his first string of numbers.'

Lorrimer paused, hoping he hadn't lost Gardner, who waved him on.

'Say fifty-five numbers, however many words there were in the text. Next, he'd ring down to the roulette table and get someone to give him the next fifty-five win numbers.

'Lansky wrote the numbers up under his first string and

then added the two together.'

'An interim key!' Gardner shoved his hands back into his pockets and turned to Lorrimer.

'Lansky re-invented it ... I'm sorry, George, how did he get the message to the boat?'

'It wasn't a big deal. Lansky had someone call the skipper and give him the third string. Later on, Lansky would call the skipper to check he had gotten the first call, and then he'd give him the win numbers. Bingo: T A M P A, or wherever. Nobody got it. The guy was a genius, but he never knew we were listening on both phones. So not so clever.'

Lorrimer spread his arms wide.

'That's it.'

'South Side.'

They rounded the main building and came upon a raised bed with trellises of tomatoes and sweet peas. Gardner picked a couple of berry tomatoes and put them in his pocket.

A Washington Dinner

Lorrimer took a cab across town from his Georgetown hotel and walked into the grand lobby of the Mayflower Hotel fifteen minutes later, found a chair with a clear view of the busy reception desk and waited. They had arranged to meet in the lobby at 6pm. Lorrimer was five minutes early.

Bingham had been described to him as tall and grey-haired with the upright demeanor of an army officer. He was also said to have a soft voice and the self-deprecating sense of humour of a man who would rather stay in the background. Ten minutes later, Lorrimer watched him approach the desk, speak to one of the staff then turn and search the room in a slow sweep.

Lorrimer lifted his hand when Bingham's eyes met his and Bingham smiled. He left the desk and walked over.

'George Lorrimer?'

Lorrimer stood and extended his hand.

'John Bingham.'

Bingham's palm was dry and hard, and he smiled again as they shook hands.

'Lovely city, I could walk around it all day.'

'Are you still okay for dinner?'

'All the readier, George, lead on.'

Half an hour later, Bingham and Lorrimer were comfortably seated at a table in the rear of a busy Chinese restaurant in Washington DC. Thanks to Lorrimer's fluent Cantonese greeting, the startled owner had immediately arranged a royal passage through the restaurant to a more secluded table adjacent to a family of seven who had just started their meal.

Lorrimer took the proffered menu, gave Bingham a glint of a smile and mouthed the word *expenses*.

As they ate, a woman at the next table with vermillion streaks in her hair lifted a small child down from her lap, placed him on the floor and turned to look at Bingham as she straightened up in her chair. Lorrimer watched as her eyes ran from Bingham's face to his hands.

'You're getting the once-over from the next table.'

Bingham looked over.

'She probably thinks I could do with a haircut.'

Bingham told Lorrimer that he'd flown to and from Adelaide in eleven different aircraft over the past four years, usually on a collapsible metal seat the size of a waiter's dish strapped to a couple of steel thwarts bolted onto the fuselage.

'Horrendous bloody racket,' he said, 'deafening, and then you're expected to don the earphones and listen to whispers.'

Lorrimer gently tapped away the crust that protected his crabmeat.

'Keeping everybody happy down under, with me on the way?'

'She has diamonds on two of her fingers, an emerald cluster on a third. Add to that an inscribed golden bangle fastened around her right ankle.'

Lorrimer sat up and looked around.

'Who?'

'The lady who gave me the once-over; I'm picking up a few of the FBI's surveillance skills and I'm not keeping anyone happy. Now I must have another phone, a special one, so we can communicate … securely.'

Lorrimer grunted.

'Any stamp collectors in your family, George?'

'My brother, when we were kids.'

'Close, were you, like brothers?'

'Joined sideways.'

'What happened when you walked in and talked to him while he was at his table with his books and glue, small, sticky-sided patches of paper, brushes and chemicals for removing excess ink on the postmarks, reference books, carefully arrayed lines of stamps in order, ready to be set in their place. Did he like to chat?'

'No, it got so he locked the door.'

'Well, there you go, George, there's not a lot of difference between your brother and me. What's his name?'

'Mike.'

'I'm considering doing the same bloody thing.'

Lorrimer tilted the brass plate that held his crab's empty carapace and inspected its cavity for missed gobbets of flesh.

'You know,' Bingham said as more food was arranged before them, 'somebody mentioned your name last night.'

'Who?'

'Meredith Gardner.'

'Lovely guy.'

A small Asian child walked over to their table, stopped at its edge and gazed at them. Bingham smiled down at the youngster.

'Do you know the lore behind the shape of Chinese eyes, George?'

Lorrimer guessed some mischief and remained mute.

'No?'

'All I can do is their menus, go ahead.'

'Anthropologists say it was the closed squint of an Arctic people who, when driven south by the ice, had their eyes opened by the colours of China.'

'Very poetical, JB, you should write a book.'

The child blinked once, turned and walked away.

'Another beer?'

Bingham shook his head.

'Brandy.'

Lorrimer smoked as their table was cleared.

'Meredith Gardner. No way you can cut short Meredith and be happy so that's what he got called: Meredith. I know women that name. He'd heard about the casino code the Mafia were using in Florida and found out it was me who was listening in when they were using it. I told Gardner and he had it figured it out in two seconds.'

'But you had it first.'

'I was lucky.'

Buford and Stace

Sydney, 1943

L orrimer knocked on the inner door, waited two seconds, heard a call from inside and entered Bingham's spacious office.

John Bingham was standing by a glass-topped table in the middle of the room, sorting manila folders into some kind of working order. He looked up with a grim smile.

'Everyone is to be vetted again.'

He gestured at an open file as he continued working.

'This one was here earlier. Her husband of six months is in New Guinea battling dysentery, stomach worms and the unsettled disposition of his corporal while she's obliged to stay with his parents for financial reasons. They never approved the marriage apparently and now she is in the final stages of a condition that proves them insightful.'

'You get to talk about all that?'

'It's what they talk about, George, and in some

instances, interminably. The listening becomes tedious.'

'I hear a bachelor talking.'

Bingham laughed.

'I'm married to empty rooms and the voice of a race caller; that's almost bigamy.'

The domestic guys we invited over are due, do you want to sit in?'

'Solo on, George, I have a deadline, that's the word they used. I'm to be executed if I don't complete the exercise in thirty-six hours.'

Lorrimer's Australians were Mr Buford and Mr Stace, both senior officers of the Australian Commonwealth Investigation Service. They were waiting for him outside his office.

Lorrimer walked towards them and extended his hand to the biggest.

'George Lorrimer.'

Buford had a ham for a fist and Lorrimer's hand was consumed.

'Buford.' An impassive nod to his colleague. 'He's Stace. We knocked.'

Lorrimer unlocked his office door and showed the investigators inside.

'This is where you work?' Stace looked around the bare office.

John Bingham had an executive's office, but Lorrimer's was a cleared room on the floor above, furnished with a swivel chair on cast-iron legs, a metal desk, and a round pinewood table with three wooden chairs set around its circumference, a manila folder placed before one of them. The single window looked onto the brick wall of a neighbouring building; there was a sink in one corner with a metal cupboard beneath. No filing cabinets, two telephones on the desk.

Lorrimer laughed.

'I leave it like this so I *don't* want to work here.'

The three men sat around the table and chatted about the war, the weather, and the armed marines posted in the lobby and outside the building.

'Waiting for MacArthur?'

'You always know when he's here,' Lorrimer said. 'You can smell his pipe in the lift.'

Buford and Stace exchanged a glance.

'Stupidest thing I ever saw, that corncob. Bloke looks like an idiot.'

'Hard to argue with that.'

Stace pulled a tin of cigarettes from his coat pocket.

'Do you want to get the show on the road?'

Lorrimer got up from the table, walked across the room and took an ashtray from the cupboard. He sat back down, slid the ashtray to Stace and pushed the manila folder to Buford.

'Anyone in here you know?'

Buford opened the file, took out the first four photographs and fanned them on the table.

'How many more in there?'

'Fourteen, all male, some we know, some we don't.'

Buford removed the remaining photos from the file, added them to the four, squared them off and examined each one before putting it face down. He laid one aside.

'Oskar.'

He continued with his scrutiny before taking another photo and putting it aside with the first.

'And again.'

When he was done, he slid both photographs across

the table to Stace, opened his briefcase and took out a leather folder. He placed it on the table.

Stace arranged the photos side by side and pointed his forefinger at Buford's folder. Buford flicked through the contents before taking out a photo and passing it over. Stace gave it a brief glance before looking up at his colleague.

'This the most recent?'

'Last week, the bloke never sleeps.'

Stace pushed it over to Lorrimer.

Rostov, photographed at night, standing in a queue under a lit marquee.

'This is Sydney?'

'Last time we looked.'

'And this is where?'

The Roosevelt Club,' said Stace, 'owned by Mr Sammy Lee. He has to turn them back at the door.'

Lorrimer sat back in his chair, smiling.

'Don't tell me, American bourbon, a swing band and a dance floor.'

'That's what the lucky ones who get in say; the queues

are a block long.'

'I've got someone else you might know,' said Lorrimer, 'a smaller guy, built like a wrestler.'

Lorrimer picked through his photographs until he found Tosya Keyannik stepping into the Hong Kong sunshine, Oskar's shape in the shadows behind him.

'Who's he?'

Lorrimer shook his head.

'Still looking.'

'Do they know each other?'

Lorrimer shrugged.

'They came out of the same building.'

'What about Oskar?' said Lorrimer. 'Does he travel?'

'In and out.' Stace picked up the photo of Rostov aboard the *Cycle*.

'Nobody looks happy about going sailing. Where's this?'

'Hong Kong. They were leaving under pressure.'

Buford looked at his watch and began to collect his photos.

'Are we about done?'

Lorrimer picked up the photograph of Rostov; he was fifth in a queue that started under the marquee lights then trailed into shadow.

'What makes him so interesting?'

'Two things: he's a Tass stooge and he's a queer.'

Buford held his hand out for the photo, put it into his file and looked ready to leave.

Lorrimer smiled.

'Good of you gentlemen to take the time today. I appreciate it.'

'We do what we're told,' said Stace. 'We didn't expect an American.'

Both men stood to leave.

'One last thing: where does Oskar work? Canberra? Sydney?'

Buford glanced at his colleague before answering.

'Sydney. He has a flat in Potts Point, two minutes away from that frenzy at Kings Cross.'

'Married?'

Stace barked out a laugh.

'When did that make any difference? He shows up with Mrs Rostov on his chess nights. Sometimes she works in Canberra.'

Lorrimer led the two CIS men out, thanking them again for their co-operation. He locked the door and rang Frank Delaney's office at the US Embassy in Canberra.

Two Telephone Calls

Sydney, 1943

John Bingham was the custodian of a glittering network of friends and colleagues whose names and last known telephone numbers he kept in a small service diary. He leafed through the pages, stopping when he found the dusty gleam of Major Bill Stanner.

Bill, the Australian anthropologist and linguist, the journalist, flautist and speechwriter, and the admired Commander of the 2/1 Northern Observation Unit, a remote intelligence gathering branch of the Australian Army.

They had horses in common: Bill rode them and Bingham bet on them.

Bingham telephoned Stanner and asked if he could remember a man from his unit, name of Baxter, first name, Alfred, known to all as Ed. Bingham didn't mention the copy of Baxter's war record and intelligence assessment in front of him.

'An older man, Bill, married, about 36. Engineer-cum-mechanic. Probably the only one of your bunch who didn't go to Darwin on leave and frighten the horses.'

Stanner did recall Ed. Preferred riding his motorbike about on the myriad dirt tracks that surrounded the Timber Creek base or expeditioning into the wide unknown with Mordecai. Ed, the shop steward socialist, and Mordecai, the untaught Walpiri Jesuit.

Bingham looked through his notes after Stanner rang off. Alfred Baxter: member of the Australian Military Forces, currently posted to the Australian Water Transport Company, allied to the Small Ships Company and under the overall command of General Douglas MacArthur. Almost everybody under the same roof.

Ed Baxter, a qualified mechanic and former shop floor organiser of a tram and busways union. Detained for assault at a union meeting on one occasion but no record of a conviction. A motorbike rider of proven merit, having won several New South Wales and Queensland provincial races. Married with one child and living in Maroubra.

Ed was currently stationed at the Georges Head end of a submarine prevention barrier, a heavy contraption of gates, booms and chains that restricted the entry of all shipping to the inner Sydney Harbour.

'He'll have a look at it,' Stanner said when he rang back a day later. 'Ed's a man of few words and will need convincing but he should be fine for whatever you have in mind. He asked if it was a uniform job, service-orientated if you know what I mean, or something different.'

'What did you tell him?'

'To expect anything.'

Bingham thanked him, put the phone down and walked over to the window overlooking York Street. It was lined with traffic and warm in the midday sunshine. His club pool was only twenty minutes away; the war could wait.

Seeing the Americans

Ed Baxter left home the next day dressed for church, his wife having ironed almost everything he owned before laying it all on the bed and picking what he should wear. He was to look smart, nothing like the mechanic who usually rode away from the house in work dungarees and worn army boots.

Like many Sydney women, Ellse Baxter knew of the Grace Building and the outrageous prices the ground floor department store charged for French perfume and American nylon stockings. The advertisements Grace Brothers ran in the papers evoked another world where svelte young men wearing tuxedos admired beautiful women hour-glassed into billowing frocks and balancing on high heels while an invisible wind played the devil and exposed their long, nylon-clad legs.

Her parting words to Ed were to be sure to take any samples he might be offered on his way through to see the Americans upstairs.

Ed rode into the city more slowly than usual, parked his motorbike across the road from the Grace Building, walked into the lobby and waited for someone to tap him on the shoulder.

Lorrimer watched as the mechanic walked off a small square on the marble floor, hands behind his back. Baxter was not a big man, but his shoulders had breadth and his clasped fingers looked thick. Stanner had described him as dour as all Yorkshire.

The American walked up and held out his hand.

'George Lorrimer. Alfred Baxter?'

'That's me. Ed Baxter.'

'Good to meet you, Ed. Come on up, there's one more to meet.'

They turned and walked through the lobby towards the lifts.

'I saw you ride in; what is it?'

'A Norton.' Baxter looked down at the oil flecks on his trouser legs.

'The wife made me take off the saddlebags for the big occasion, they usually catch any oil spit.'

Bingham was waiting for them in the upper floor lobby. He walked over as Baxter followed Lorrimer out of the lift, shook hands and introduced himself as a representative of the Australian Signals Service, rank of major, and Lorrimer as his US liaison. He asked after

Baxter's health and thanked him for giving them the opportunity to meet.

'This will be a small, official matter, confidential in nature, but not too onerous. Weapons and travel not involved.'

The old diplomat speaking, very silver service. He waved them towards his office door.

Baxter and Lorrimer took seats at the table and waited while Bingham retrieved a file from his desk drawer before joining them. He placed the file in front of him, looked up and gave Baxter his old soldier's smile.

'Shall we commence?'

'It's your show.'

'Fine. Firstly, I must tell you that you're here on the recommended say-so of Major Bill Stanner. We asked for someone who doesn't get dented too often.'

'Bill didn't say much.'

'I didn't tell him what we have in mind. Can we start off by asking a few questions, just to be sure we're all on the right track?'

'Fire away.'

Bingham looked over at Lorrimer.

'How many boats come in through the nets each day, Ed, what's an average?'

'Twenty or more, sometimes just a couple. What are we talking about? Naval?'

'Merchant.'

'Half that.'

'Do they all stop; the net opening and closing for each one?'

Baxter laughed.

'Even the Manly Ferry. They scrape each boat's arse on the way in just in case there's a Jap sub trying to sneak in under its shadow.'

'Even the navy?'

'*All* craft.'

'Does anyone from your base go aboard the merchants while they're waiting outside?'

'All the time.'

'For what purpose?'

'Bringing blokes ashore, taking blokes to the boats, our tenders are in and out all day.'

'How about you?'

'Every steamer needs an engineer's certificate before it can come inside, and nobody is allowed to dump old boats in the harbour anymore.'

'Meaning you get to look around?'

'Yep, if the skipper doesn't like it he turns his tub around and goes somewhere else.'

'You look at their papers?'

'Yes.'

'Crew lists?'

'If I want to. Every boat has to have a qualified engineer aboard and sometimes I like to see who puts their hand up. Make sure it isn't the cook.'

'What about passenger lists?'

'Sometimes we'll check passenger names against an alien list, but not often.'

George gave Bingham an enquiring look, received no response and turned back to Ed.

'What do you do when a passenger is on the list?'

'Make a note and make sure the CO knows about him as soon as I get back to base.'

'What does he do?'

Ed shrugged.

There was a discreet knock on the door and Lorrimer walked over to open it. A thin-faced tea lady stood behind a trolley, her hands and fingers jittering about as she asked how the visitor would like his tea. How many sugars? Milk?

They watched in silence as she served them and waited until the door closed behind her.

'Ed,' said Bingham, 'did the Nackeroos use carrier pigeons?'

'We had a few.'

'Who wrote the messages?'

'Me, when I was on base.'

'How's that?' Lorrimer asked. 'It doesn't sound like your type of work.'

'I draw. It's my hobby. The OIC made an executive decision and I got the job. It was just one-time coding written on cigarette paper, stuffed into a tube and tied to a pigeon's leg. Somebody tickled the bird's arse and away it went.'

'What about radio?'

'It didn't always work up there.'

Bingham opened the file, took out a photograph and passed it to Ed.

'You two know each other?'

'Pete Musgrave.' Ed looked at Lorrimer in surprise.

'He's had a chip on his shoulder about Yanks ever since the Battle of Brisbane.'

Lorrimer held up his hands in surrender.

'The Major recruited him. I wasn't even in the country.'

Bingham took the photo back and replaced it in the file.

'Pete's been our Georges Head carrier pigeon for quite some time; putting you in his slot when he's posted out would be seamless, and we wouldn't have to teach you any coding.'

'How did he manage that side of it?' Ed asked. 'He used to make a bloody mess of the pay sheets.'

'It took him a while. He persevered.'

The job, Bingham explained, was to copy names from the crew and passenger lists of certain merchant steamers when they arrived at the nets, then get the information to Lorrimer.

Bingham opened Musgrave's file again, took out a small square of paper and handed it to Baxter. Ed looked down at the script Pete had written.

'That's it?'

'Yes.'

Bingham waited for another question before continuing.

'Musgrave leaves it for his wife; she drops it into a postbox at St Leonards and rings me. I tell George, he picks it up.'

Baxter smiled when he heard Musgrave's wife mentioned.

'Joy's in it too, is she?'

'Intrigue beguiles her.'

'Where does Pete leave it?'

'He'll tell you if you decide to take it on. Whatever they do works well.'

'There's about thirty names on a merchant boat, half of them Malays and Filipinos, do you want them all?'

'No,' replied Lorrimer, 'just Anglo and European.'

Baxter sat back and rubbed his palms together before

folding his arms. He looked from Lorrimer to Bingham, unconvinced.

'That's it?'

'More or less. It's just a simple mailing routine.'

'These merchants you're interested in,' Baxter said, 'how many are there?'

'Four are expected in the next three months. *Maiwarra*, *Daphne*, *Cycle* and one that used to be called *Jestine* – it's apparently undergone a name change and we've lost track of her for now.'

Lorrimer leant over the table. 'Are you just being nosy, Ed, or do I see a glimmer of interest?'

'Maybe. This thing starts when Pete and Joy take their postings north, right?'

'Yes.'

'Have you got someone to do Joy's job?'

'Not yet.'

'And if I say I want to think about it the offer disappears?'

'Into thin air.'

Ed remained silent.

'Well?'

'This *is* for king and country?'

'Yes.'

'There is a document that will need your signature.' Bingham said. 'It should only take a minute or so to read. Allegiance, secrecy, that sort of thing.'

'Fair enough. I'll give it a shot.'

The Journalist

The journalist Alex Barrat lived in one room at the end of a gloomy, uncarpeted corridor in the Centennial Hotel at Woollahra. An aged alcoholic, he freelanced his nuanced observations of the city's nightlife to the Sydney newspapers and his political opinions to the publican and his regulars.

Barrat took the call on a public phone in the saloon bar where he was sitting distempered from the previous night's alcohol, watching Lorraine, his favourite barmaid, switching her glorious way up and down the duckboards as she served the few customers.

'Lorrimer, you say? I knew of a Lorrimer once in Blighty. What can I do you for you, Squire?'

Barrat had a deep voice richly lubricated with phlegm and Corio whisky.

Lorrimer explained he was a writer needing some background on Kings Cross for a novel about the Pacific war; he'd read a few of Barrat's columns.

'It's a bloody shambles,' said Barrat. 'What have you

got in mind?'

'I thought you might know someone who can show me around, and hopefully save me from getting my throat cut.'

'The razor gangs have long gone, now we use guns.'

'So you'd know how to duck a bullet?'

'I might be your man, depending.'

'On what?'

'If properly inclined.'

'Fifty US do the job, plus incidentals?'

Barrat watched Lorraine turn and walk in the opposite direction.

'One hundred, transport provided, incidentals not included.'

'When?'

'Tonight?'

Barrat arrived in a taxi filled with alcohol fumes and driven by a well-muscled tough wearing shirtsleeves and a straw fedora banded in scarlet ribbon. The journalist was in the back, nipping from a silver flask; he waved Lorrimer in.

'Nick,' he said to the driver, 'meet Squire Lorrimer.'

Nick stretched his arm over the front seat as Lorrimer climbed in and gave him a quick, brutal handshake.

'Next time I'll know better,' Lorrimer said as he pulled the car door shut. Nick flashed him a clean, white grin in the mirror. Lorrimer turned to Barrat.

'How do you want to settle this?'

'Up front will be fine.'

Barrat took another nip then offered the flask to Lorrimer, who shook his head, reached into his inside coat pocket and took out a wad of notes. He counted ten and passed them over to Barrat.

'What about Nick?'

Barratt sat up and put the money into his trouser pocket.

'He comes with the job. If you feel you owe him a favour at the end of the night then by all means do what you must.'

They travelled through the city and took a right off William Street before reaching Darlinghurst Road, then another turn into Palmer Street, and another into the darkness of Chapel Lane.

'The only place in Sydney where men are happy to do

all the shopping,' said Barrat as they gazed through the car windows.

Dozens of men, some drinking from bottles, strolled up and down the narrow, dark lane, crowding into illuminated patches where doors had been left open for the light to spill out, and inside, one step down into the stone-walled rooms, women seated on stools or chairs, looking up at the leering faces, waiting for the neediest to come down or the drunkest to be pushed in.

Nick cruised past with his arm out of the car window, listening to the street, acknowledging a call from someone with an upturned thumb.

They turned out of the lane into a broader road and Nick slowed as they approached a brick-faced, two-storey building. The first-floor windows were boarded up and the double-sized front door, reinforced with studded timber beams, was closed.

A man slipped away from the doorway as they passed and Lorrimer caught sight of an eye-level peekaboo slot built into the wooden panels. That too was closed.

'That's the local Tong club, communal slat mattresses, cushions and straw pillows on the ground floor and every time you wake, a woman by your side with another flame and another pipe.'

Barrat turned to Lorrimer.

'The longer you stay the more interesting your dreams

become, but I can't guarantee you'll be out before dawn. The upper rooms have softer beds for those who want some exercise.'

Lorrimer laughed.

'Maybe later.'

Nick pulled the cab into the heavier traffic of William Street again, heading for the top of the Cross.

'Do you have anything particular in mind? There's quite a variety available for the choosing, you know, carte bloody blanche with you Yanks still in town.'

Lorrimer smiled as he looked at the prostitutes loitering on street corners and in doorways.

'I'm here to see all the action, Alex. What about we start with a drink at The Roosevelt?'

Nick drove towards the intersection of William Street and Darlinghurst Road and dropped the two men outside The Roosevelt Nightclub. There was a long queue to the door which Barrat ignored as he led Lorrimer inside.

Sammy Lee met them at the rope. He was a long-armed, large-shouldered man who liked to match the colours of his all-girl dancing troupe with his shirts and dinner jackets; tonight he was burgundy over yellow with a white bow tie.

He looked closely at Barrat.

'You're early, Al.'

Barrat smiled.

'And you look like a piano player at a bar mitzvah, Sammy. This is George, an American observer of base human nature who's in need of a drink or two before we descend into its filthy lair.'

Lee extended his hand to Lorrimer.

'A pleasure,' he gestured in Barrat's direction, 'and don't let that untrustworthy bastard write anything improper about anyone in my place.'

He turned to Barrat.

'Now, Al, can I get you both a drink?'

Lee led the two men over to the bar as a long-legged cigarette girl approached him from the floor. He stopped to listen to her before nodding and looking up. The girl smiled at Lorrimer and Barrat then sashayed back to the tables.

Lee caught the eye of a table waiter and beckoned him over. The waiter, a young man wearing glasses and a foolish moustache, listened to Lee's instructions before putting his tray on the bar and walking off in the direction of the front door.

'The hardest thing to find in this business,' Lee observed, 'is a man who knows how to bounce people without anybody noticing.'

'Somebody want more than cigarettes?' asked Lorrimer.

'Table fourteen, the bow-tie. She's had trouble with his hands, twice.'

Lee waved over the barman.

'George, what's yours?'

'Scotch and soda, no ice.'

'Al?'

'Martini, wave the vermouth bottle in the direction of Italy and no fruit.'

Lee ordered the drinks then turned to look at the busy room, his back against the bar.

'You should convince George to stay. Bob Hope's in town and there's a rumour that I've paid him for a half hour performance later tonight.'

Barrat smiled as he watched the barman reach for a bottle of London Dry Gin.

'George wants to remember everything of the evening, Sammy, a couple of hours in your nightclub might interfere with the process.'

'I'm here all night if you change your mind.'

Lee patted both men on the back, left the bar and walked through the tables towards the front door, stopping to shake a hand, kiss a cheek or exchange a confidential aside with one of his patrons. The bow-tie's seat was empty.

After another drink and as the four-piece band began to crank it up for the coming floorshow they left the club to join the crowds on the footpath and walk along Darlinghurst Road, Barrat stopping here and there at a doorway or to gaze into an alley before going on. Lorrimer turned around once to see a cab parked on the other side of the street with Nick leaning against the nearside door, smoking and watching a couple of girls cross the road.

They passed a narrow, neon-lit entrance crowded with American sailors, and Barrat gestured at a strip of lurid photographs decorating the entrance.

'What do you think?'

Lorrimer nodded and followed Barrat up a steep flight of stairs. Barrat knocked on the only door at the top, paid ten US dollars and they passed into the tobacco fog of a large room. Couples were sitting around a dozen tables, drinking and watching the show onstage. Two naked black men were advancing on a voluptuous white woman who was wearing high heels and nothing else. A wheezy sound system played Benny Goodman's *Goody, Goody* as she retreated from them in faux panic, her hands upraised. They reached for her ankles and up-ended her in a well-practised lift and flip, each removing one of her shoes.

Barrat watched Lorrimer as he looked over the room, table by table. The American turned to him then looked towards the door.

'What happens if I want my money back?'

'They'll help you all the way down the stairs.'

Lorrimer glanced at the stage as the woman gave a squeal.

'The only way I'd stay would be if Goodman was playing in person.'

Barrat led Lorrimer to an anonymous building in a quieter street and after gaining entry with another of Lorrimer's ten dollar bills they passed along a corridor of coloured doors, each with a small lamp attached to its lintel. Some lit, some unlit.

'The unlit doors,' Barrat murmured, 'indicate a vacant coffin-sized cupboard where you can pleasure yourself at the sight of some highly irregular couplings. I believe the red door is most popular.'

He smiled at Lorrimer.

'It has younger participants, the others are rather ... tired.'

They both looked up as a man came out of the red door, hitched up his trousers and winked at them as he passed by.

'Interested?' asked Alex. 'You'll only get five minutes. I can wait here.'

Lorrimer shook his head.

Nick picked them up a hundred feet down the street and Barrat asked him to drive to a private club on Macleay Street, opposite the governor's mansion, where they were admitted by the concierge after the covert exchange of more of Lorrimer's money.

They took the lift to the second floor and were met by a square-faced thug wearing butler's livery who showed them into a large, high-ceilinged room framed on two sides with tall brocade-covered windows. Loungers, palms and clusters of tables and chairs surrounded a parquet dance floor and the fifty or so patrons were all dressed in dinner suits; some at their tables eating, others standing at a long glass-topped bar that ran down the length of one wall.

A pale, long-fingered youth was stroking Gershwin from a piano in the middle of the dance floor for three couples, men sleepwalking in each other's arms as they moved in and out of the light cast by a slowly revolving chandelier.

Rostov was paired among them, leading a partner whose head was resting on his shoulder.

'Drink?'

Lorrimer turned to see Barrat smiling at him.

'Or have I found what you want?'

Potts Point

The two men got out of the taxi, both unsteady, and Lorrimer could hear their laughter as they climbed to the front door of the apartment block, louder as one of them tried several of his keys. He eventually succeeded and the door swung closed behind them.

Nick leaned across and flipped open the glove box, the dim bulb inside illuminating the barrel of a Browning automatic pistol. He glanced up at Lorrimer.

Lorrimer shook his head.

'Not necessary.'

Flat five was on the second floor of a three-storey apartment building; right-side corridor, second door down. Information courtesy of the CIS big man, Buford, who, at the end of Lorrimer's call, invited him to watch a rugby match on Saturday.

They waited for an hour. Nick rolled the radio dial until he found a jazz station and both men sat without speaking, Nick checking his rear view from time to time. Lorrimer eased his camera from its case, screwed the flash into its mount and placed it on the seat beside him. He took a small soft leather pouch from his inside coat pocket, unrolled it and removed two of a set of five surgical-grade steel alloy lock picks. He slid them into his coat's lapel pocket.

'Nice set of tools.'

Lorrimer grunted in reply, put the pouch back, took half a dozen bulbs from his camera case, put them in his coat pocket and picked up the camera.

'Time to go.'

Lorrimer's picks allowed him quickly through the first door and he climbed the carpeted stairs to the second floor two at a time, stopping on the landing for a moment before moving down the passageway.

He squatted at the door of flat five, dealing with his second pin-tumbler lock of the evening and was inside the apartment within a minute.

Lorrimer closed the door and listened; he could hear no murmuring, no laughter. He remained motionless for a full five minutes, waiting for someone to get up and go to the toilet, or resume a conversation.

Sandalwood burning somewhere, its perfume infiltrating the dark hallway.

There were three open doors on his left, two closed on

his right and a double, glass-panelled door at the end of the hallway, open. Lorrimer walked the length of the corridor, stopping to listen at each of the closed doors on his way down and glancing through the open ones.

The first door he opened was to a near-empty room. He closed the door behind him and switched on the light; a table had been pushed under the only window and its surface was littered with camera parts, a tripod, several film canisters and a few sheets of writing paper. Lorrimer walked over and looked out at the darkened harbour, Garden Island navy base in the near foreground. Rostov had found himself a soft perch.

He took two photographs of the table, then a close-up of the top two sheets of paper. He turned the light off, gave his eyes a moment to recover, slowly opened the door and stepped out.

Lorrimer eased into the dark bedroom and stopped when he heard breathing. He could make out a double bed in the middle of the room, two bedside tables, two forms under the sheets.

He slowly walked over and looked down at a man's face. His companion was curled towards the wall. The smell of sandalwood was intense.

The room lit up with the intensity of an explosion before being swallowed into depthless black. Lorrimer's fingers flinched away from the hot glass as he popped the spent globe onto the bedroom floor.

There was a commotion on the bed, another flash, then a man's shrill call, the sound of a fall, another flash; Rostov with a look of anguish rising from the bed with his hands up, trying to shield his face. Lorrimer shoved him back down and shot another globe to keep them both blind.

He backed out of the room, shut the door and was out of the building in fifteen seconds, heading in the direction of the car. Nick spotted him, pulled the taxi out of its slot and gunned down the street to meet him. Lorrimer crossed the road, climbed into the back seat, put his camera beside him and took out his cigarettes and lighter.

'Where to now, Ace?'

Lorrimer smiled broadly through his tobacco smoke.

'The Roosevelt. I heard Bob Hope is on late.'

'How about I join you?'

'How about you don't. Your mother might worry.'

Nick grinned.

'You're the boss.'

A Meeting in a Cathedral

Sydney, 1943

The BRUSA Agreement was intended as an affirmation of the wartime intelligence sharing intentions of Great Britain and the United States. It succeeded the Holden Agreement and allowed the United States of America access to Bletchley Park and Britain access to Arlington.

Once the procedural signing had been formally completed, two dozen members of the representative panel were asked to stand on the steps of the Washington building that hosted the final meeting and have their picture taken for the archives.

US Navy Commander Frank Delaney's presence was the result of J. Edgar Hoover's interventionist skill and intricate knowledge of the details of some of the participants' private affairs, not to mention his unshakable conviction that whatever knowledge Britain picked up in Arlington would eventually find its way to Moscow.

Following the signing, and after a two-day stopover in Hawaii, Delaney flew to Sydney and arrived at the

Manhattan Hotel in Elizabeth Bay in the mid-afternoon. He rang Lorrimer's office from his room and asked if Pym had arrived.

'Been and gone,' Lorrimer replied, 'back in two days.'

'Where to?'

'South Australia. He's gone to meet the Gawler Station tea ladies.'

'Where's the best place to give this BRUSA rundown when he's back? Hoover is wary of walls with ears.'

'I'll ask around; JB should know some place.'

'JB?'

'Bingham. I've heard him called The Fossil, but I'm kinder.'

'What do they call you?'

'Seppo.'

'Seppo?'

'Ask an Aussie, and I have something for you.'

'Good. Where will we meet?'

'Somewhere cool.'

Two hours later, Lorrimer was seated on a bench in the shade of a plane tree as he watched Delaney cross Saint Andrew's Cathedral forecourt, climb the steps and walk through the ornate western doors. He followed Delaney inside, took a seat directly behind him and waited for him to get off his knees.

Delaney pushed himself up with a grunt then leant back over the pew.

'George.'

'Frank, you have a suntan.'

'Don't slap me on the shoulder; I fell asleep on Waikiki and have third degree burns under the shirt. Show me what you've got.'

Lorrimer reached into his coat pocket, took out half a dozen photographs and handed them to Delaney: Rostov in bed asleep, face to camera, someone next to him covered with a sheet. Rostov sitting up, unfocused, mouth open, his naked companion half tumbled out between the bed and the wall. Male. Rostov coming at the camera, full face, panicked, reaching out.

Delaney chortled softly.

'You should do this full-time, George. Who else has seen them?'

'Keep looking.'

The perch in Oskar's second bedroom.

'He's a sport, isn't he?'

Lorrimer took the photos from Delaney and put them back into his coat pocket. Both men stood and made their way down the aisle as the church bells sounded the hour. Delaney turned to Lorrimer.

'Where to from here?'

They continued walking.

'I'd like to know if he's still running couriers.'

'From Hong Kong?'

Lorrimer shrugged.

'Won't know until I find out.'

'Figured out how to do that?'

'I'm going to take him fishing.'

They walked into the hot sunshine and breathed in the diesel mist of the city. The traffic was thick and slow on George Street and the light north-easterly cooling the city beaches had faded to stagnant air two hundred yards from the sea.

'Where are you going to be?' Lorrimer asked.

'Canberra.'

As Lorrimer made his way down Pitt Street towards his office he saw a man writing on the footpath with a large piece of white chalk. People were walking around him as if used to him, some offering him a word.

He rose as Lorrimer approached, pushed the chalk into his trouser pocket, brushed both hands together and looked down at his work, the single word *Eternity* written on the pavement.

MacArthur's Cruiser

The Hawkesbury River, 1943

General MacArthur had been offered the personal use of a Halvorsen cabin cruiser while he was stationed in Sydney, and since his departure to Brisbane it had lain at a mooring in the Pittwater, maintained but idle.

The *Gwen Dundon* was a spacious motor launch with two weather-hardened leather loungers fitted into the stern on either side of a shaded table-sized hatch cover.

The three men had clear weather for their meeting and set off from Palm Beach mid-morning, expecting to arrive at the river township of Brooklyn in two hours. Lorrimer had arranged a taxi to take them back to the city.

Delaney joined Bingham at the wheel as they navigated out of the moorings, away from the boat quays and into the river traffic.

A couple of boys shouted angrily as their small tin coracle was set rocking in the boat's wake and Pym, standing in the stern with his eyes closed, was startled from his introspection by their vociferous expletives.

Delaney laughed.

Bingham steered the boat towards Stokes Point and after loosening enough throttle to lessen the engine noise turned to Delaney.

'You've not met David before?'

'Never had the pleasure, John, and I don't think George has either.'

They rounded Stokes Point and headed west. The Pittwater was windless, a few boats here and there lying stationary in the water; two men on surf skis paddling towards the waves off Box Head.

'No, he hasn't.'

'Any reason?'

'George works for Hoover and Pym's relationship with the FBI is at stalemate.'

Pym joined them forward, took the two steps down into the galley and opened and closed a few cupboard doors. He looked up at Delaney.

'B.R.U.S.A is an acronym for Britain and the United States of America, Frank, is it not?'

'Indeed it is, Dave.'

'David. So you would expect the acronym to read

B.U.S.A, to be accurate, yes?'

'I guess.'

'Then you could take it that the R was a gift from the USA to give the B a little more relevance in the acronym rather than the agreement; is that how you see it, Frank, on the face of it?'

Delaney smiled.

'BRUSA means we have agreed to love each other and share intelligence, David. Britain and the USA. Like a family, we are around the dinner table again *sharing*.'

Pym gave a short laugh.

'Really? Did you bring along a copy of the … what is it? Treaty?'

'Agreement. No.'

'Nothing for us to read?'

Delaney shook his head.

'You've read it?'

'Yes.'

'Do you remember who signed it?'

'No.'

'The last I heard of the family from someone of your ilk,' said Pym as he turned away from Delaney and rootled a bottle of beer from the icebox, 'was that one brother's secret was the other brother's collateral. Where are the bloody glasses?'

'In the drawer, Lord Jim, port side.' Bingham exchanged a grin with Delaney and Pym looked up, irritated.

'Britain and the USA sign an agreement to share intelligence every eighteen bloody months. Now we have BRUSA *and* the FBI? How perfectly adequate for the operation here.'

He took three glasses and a bottle of beer to the table, poured his first and took a large swallow before pouring the others.

'Frank?' He pointed to the beers on the hatch cover.

'This is supposed to be your show, you can play waiter.'

Delaney came down, took two glasses and resumed his spot next to Bingham as the launch slowly motored through swarms of brown watermelon-sized jellyfish. Thousands more drifted underwater in the slow seep of the tide.

'You ever fish this river, John?'

Bingham pointed to the mangroves that lined the riverbank.

'If you can sit in a dinghy under the shade of those mangroves for a couple of hours and don't mind the mosquitoes, gnats and midges, you'll catch dinner.'

Delany shaded his eyes with his hand.

'Anyone live out here?'

'Some, they're as wary as possums in the daytime.'

'Wary?'

'The army, the police.'

They drank and watched the next bend in the river approach.

'How many people do you have, John?'

'Fifteen in Gawler, six in Sydney.'

'Plus who, outside of cables?'

'Two, soon to be replaced.'

'And George?'

'Running his own show, as you know.'

Pym put his glass down on the hatch cover hard enough to have Delaney turn and look at him.

'Yes, Frank, George's show, whatever it is. Because I'm

finding it difficult to accept the BRUSA message of inter-allied trust and sharing while not knowing what your local agenda is.'

Pym sat silently for a moment, wrestling his long fingers together.

'You're nothing but an American apparatchik, Frank,' he said quietly, 'and I have similar grave doubts about George Lorrimer.'

'I'm not here to enlighten you on how the FBI operates, Dave.'

'David.'

'My apologies, *David*. I'm here to formally advise you that the BRUSA Agreement covers existing intelligence arrangements within Australia. The boat ride was John's idea; I could have done this in three minutes in a city park.'

Delaney lifted his glass and drained it.

'That's a good beer. The other matter I can tell you about is that the FBI, with the assistance of the Australian CIS, have exposed a foreign network and identified its Sydney-based controller.'

'And?'

'And what, David?'

'*And*, in the BRUSA protocol of loving and sharing, why don't you tell us who our Russian hobgoblin is, Frank?'

'Oskar Rostov.'

Bingham gave a grunt of acknowledgment.

'I know him. He's the local Tass agent; spying goes with the job.'

'We know, and we've made him aware we know.'

They motored slowly for another hundred feet before Bingham swung the launch's bow towards a distant bend. The river was quiet, with only ululating currawongs echoing among the high eucalyptus.

'Who the hell is that?'

Delaney had slid off his seat and stepped over to the rail; he was pointing to a house-sized boulder embedded in a near vertical slope above the river with a figure standing on its topmost edge, silhouetted against the sky with one leg cocked behind his knee, grasping the upright shaft of a long throwing spear anchored in the dirt by his feet.

The great-great grandson of the warrior Pemulwuy, killed by the English, looked down at the arrowhead of wake and the white-hulled motorboat that cruised at its point, all the while reckoning how far distant he would have to travel to be free of the white gubba faces that peered out at him.

Bingham slowly cruised into the Long Island Channel, named by the American engineers who had built the nearby road and rail crossing. The bridge gave the river a gloomy aspect from the boat, enlivened only by the yells and laughter of the half-dozen boys trying to outdo each other as they leapt and somersaulted into the water from the girders.

Somebody whistled from the shore and Bingham looked over to see a man waving from the end of a jetty, a taxi parked by the sea wall. He called down to Delaney, who was sitting across from Pym sharing another beer, though neither man had spoken to each other since they had seen the Aboriginal.

'Frank?'

'John.'

'How do you like the Hawkesbury?'

Delaney shrugged.

'It's a river.'

Bingham turned the boat towards the shore.

'There's a set of stone steps half-hidden in the mangroves not far from here that always had me wondering, so I rowed in one day and took a walk. Found a deserted home halfway up the hill, among the trees. The owner might have been an anthropologist of sorts, there were spears and skulls in most of the rooms. A collection of bone-tipped arrows around the fireplace: astonishing.'

Bingham throttled the engine back and disengaged the propeller drive.

'It's probably long burned down by the bush fires, which is probably for the best. I found a couple of bodies in a bedroom: the stink and flies were enough to keep me at the door when I opened it. The window had been smashed, broken glass everywhere. Shotgun wounds by the look of it.'

Pym looked up.

'One body curled up on the bed and the other on the floor, both men. What struck me as odd was the jewellery left on the dressing table.'

They drifted the last hundred feet to the jetty.

'I called into town, found the local policeman having a drink at the hotel; said he'd look after it and I left him to it.'

Delaney watched a porpoise glide past the hull as it hunted the inshore fish, its fin cutting a single line through the oiled surface. Pym moved to the stern where he was ill. It was the beer, he said later, and the boat's infernal motion

The Musgraves

Ed Baxter and Pete Musgrave were agreed on one thing: being made a lieutenant meant you no longer had to inch along the inside of a ship's hull on your back, face almost touching the engine's hot metal casing, dragging your tool chest behind you on a length of rope as you pull yourself over the bulkheads' jagged edges.

'The skipper thought I'd died down there once,' Musgrave remarked as they sat together at the bar. 'I was so far up the bow chasing an oil leak I couldn't hear him calling me.'

Baxter had recently joined Musgrave's unit at the Georges Head Water Base and they were drinking in the public bar of the Clifton Gardens Hotel.

Baxter finished his beer and put his glass on the bar.

'Go again?'

Musgrave slid the remains of his beer down his throat, burped softly and placed his glass next to Baxter's.

'I'll force another one down to be sociable.'

Baxter watched the room in the bar mirror; most of the drinkers were servicemen from the base, a few locals sitting around the corner tables and half a dozen women in nurse uniforms. The bar was noisy, the air misted with cigarette smoke.

'Does Joy know anything about the new girl?'

Musgrave waved down a barman, ordered two more schooners, stood, took a few coins from his fob pocket and placed them on the bar.

'Young and unmarried. Could be a problem if Ellse finds out.'

Baxter laughed.

Musgrave took his change and sat back down as they waited for the beer to arrive.

Musgrave had only recently grown a thin black moustache and was finding it difficult to keep from admiring himself in the bar mirror as he smoothed his upper lip.

Baxter glanced at him.

'You'll rub the bloody thing off.'

Musgrave gazed at his reflection more intently.

'Has Bingham given you a code name?'

'No.'

'I would have liked to pick my own but he insisted on doing it himself, said it served as an aide-memoir.'

'Wasn't David Niven was it? Or was that before you grew the moustache?'

Baxter turned on his stool before Musgrave could respond.

'Here we are.'

Joy Musgrave was closely examined by most of the male drinkers who turned in their seats or watched her approach in the mirror. The last time she was seen here she had been brunette; today, she was blonde. A younger, dark-haired woman followed in her wake.

Baxter and Musgrave moved off their stools and made room at the crowded bar.

Joy smiled at both men, and turned to her companion.

'Jessica, meet Ed.'

Ed put out his hand.

'How do you do?'

Jessica took Ed's hand, looked up at him and smiled.

'Very well, thank you. Jess is fine.'

Joy turned to Pete.

'This is Peter, my husband and errant lover. Pete, meet Jess.'

Another smile from Jess, another handshake.

'Drinks,' said Pete. 'Who wants what?'

'Joy?'

'Champagne.'

'Love to, but this is on the Major's ticket.'

Joy touched Jessica's arm.

'We should be working for the Americans.'

'Vodka and ice, please, Pete.'

Musgrave looked at Jessica.

'Brandy and soda, please, with ice.'

'You don't look old enough.'

Both women broke into laughter.

'She's a nurse, Pete, not a bloody Girl Guide.'

The three of them left Musgrave to it and headed for the beer garden.

Their table, like the others in the courtyard, was a rusted veteran of many unsheltered years with a wad of folded newspaper under one leg to make it steady. A collection of faded umbrellas had been stacked against the wall, left for the spiders to colonise, and ferns of all descriptions grew from the cracks in the courtyard's stone walls. Musgrave followed a few minutes later with a tray of drinks and they all sat in silence for a moment.

Musgrave lifted his glass.

'Good luck.'

They raised their glasses over the table and drank.

'The Major sends his regards,' said Musgrave. 'He liked the thought of the handover being done over drinks after sunset; reminded him of better days.'

He looked at Jessica.

'Last chance to opt out, Jess, before your future is hopelessly compromised.'

Jessica smiled.

'I've already signed on the dotted line.'

Somebody dropped a tray of glasses on the floor inside

the bar and was rewarded with a rousing cheer. Musgrave glanced over his shoulder at the open doorway.

'Someone's started early.'

He turned back to Jessica.

'You and Ed need to work out a routine.'

'I invented a marvellous one,' said Joy, 'but old stick-in-the-mud here,' she inclined her head in Pete's direction, 'wouldn't play the game.'

'Write the book, sweetheart,' Pete said, 'put it in there if it hasn't already been done.'

'I'd like to know what it was,' said Jess. 'Ed?'

'All ears.'

Joy smiled at her husband.

'I only wanted his poetry if he saw that I had left him flowers, do you remember, darling?'

Musgrave touched his wife's hand.

'Whatever Omar Khayyam can do ...'

Joy turned to Jessica.

'This from a man who doesn't read poetry.'

Musgrave took his hand away.

'You're a fickle woman, Joy.'

They watched a two-piece band arrive to set up a guitar and accordion.

Musgrave groaned and shifted in his seat.

'I will not stay and listen to one of those wretched squeeze bags.'

'Pete, you're outvoted.' Ed looked at Joy.

'Proceed.'

Joy leaned forward in her chair, pushed her drink to one side and laid her hands on the table. She faced Jessica.

'Jess – put a vase of flowers on the hospital windowsill when you're on duty, just pick some from the garden, then take it away when you go home.'

She turned to Ed.

'You know that concrete fortification wall that runs around the front of the hospital, the one with rifle slots?'

Ed nodded.

'When you have something, put it into one of the slots

and leave a stone on top of the wall, right above the slot – but only on the days you see Jess's flowers.'

'Sounds a pretty tidy scheme to me, why didn't you use it?'

Musgrave finished his beer, put the glass down on the table and gestured that they lean in close.

'Leaving it on the hall table when I come home is a lot tidier.'

Joy withheld a snort.

'He'll never let on about his coding.'

Pete sat back.

'Nobody in head office complained.'

Baxter grunted.

'Not what I heard.'

'Complex, is it, Joy?' asked Jess.

'Ask the expert, I've still got his first attempt in my handbag.'

Musgrave turned his hands up.

'I give up.'

Ed stood and picked up the empty glasses.

'Same all around? Jess?'

'Vodka this time please, Ed, and a touch of soda.'

'Joy?'

'Ditto.'

The women watched as the men left the table, jostling as they both tried to enter the door at the same time. Joy laughed.

'Peas in a bloody pod, those two.'

'What does Pete leave on the hall table?'

'A book inside a sealed envelope.'

Joy reached into her handbag, took out two copies of the *Rubaiyat* and handed them to Jess.

'We're packing up and moving out next week, keep them.'

Jessica opened the softcover and let the pages flicker past her thumb.

'I buy them secondhand. Pete prefers the soft covers, they're smaller.'

Jessica put the smaller book down and opened the

hardcover version.

'Did he use this?'

Joy shrugged.

'I don't know.'

'What about that one?' Jessica nodded at the book on the table.

'He said he'd "buggered it" – I quote.'

Jessica picked it up and studied the front and back covers.

'He said he had to do it again the next day but he needed another book.'

'He couldn't use the same one?'

'Only use a *Rubaiyat* once. Pete told me that's the rule. Apparently, the book must go with the piece of paper, otherwise nobody can make sense of what he's written.'

'Why make it so complicated?'

Joy waited until two American sailors had strolled past their table.

'I asked the Major the same question and he quoted the Bible at me: do not let your left hand know what your right hand is doing. Everything must be kept dreadfully secret.'

Jessica laughed.

'The first thing you must do is get on the Georges Head convalescent hospital roster; I can help you with that. You'll travel out and back in one of the ambulances.'

'How many beds?'

'Twenty, some of the badly wounded convalesce for weeks, others are in and out in a day or two. The place is always busy.'

Joy pointed at the books Jessica was holding.

'I have to give you something.'

Joy took one of the books and searched through her handbag before finding a pencil to write a number on the back cover.

'I put the envelope in a mailbox at St Leonards. You'll need the box number.'

The men returned with the drinks followed by the accordionist and his accompanist who took up their instruments and began to play. Musgrave looked at his wife, slit-eyed.

'I will not stay for this.'

He looked at Baxter and Jess.

'The bar?'

'What about dinner?'

'We'll improvise.'

The Musgraves left first, Pete with a finger buried in his ear.

Jessica showed Ed the books she was holding.

'Souvenirs from Joy; which one do you want?'

Ed shrugged.

'You choose.'

Two Men in a Cemetery

Sydney, August 1944

The regular debriefings between John Bingham and his Arlington colleague sometimes took place at Gore Hill Cemetery next to the Royal North Shore Hospital in St Leonards, where they strolled as slowly as the mourners who sometimes crossed their path.

The conversation had turned to the nurse.

'She recruited herself: rang the switchboard, mentioned one of the tea ladies by name and asked to speak to a Mr Bingham. Said she'd heard he was knowledgeable about security matters. *Knowledgeable!* She didn't say much on the phone, which was encouraging, but there was a pressing message. She must have liked the sound of my voice because we met and talked about it the next day. Here, as a matter of fact.'

'Long way to come for something like that.'

'Ten minutes in the train; the office was stifling.'

Bingham gestured at the four-storey building that

loomed across the road.

'And it was convenient; she works over there.'

'Not going to bump into her today, are we?'

'I don't think so; said she found the place depressing.'

'How did she manage to find *you*? Why didn't she ring the Australian security people, or the local police?'

They were walking alongside a narrow row of small graves: Catholic children who hadn't survived the hospital's care. Bingham counted them again.

'Not much trust there, Pym, thanks to the boyfriend's paranoia over our local intelligence colleagues, and anyway, Australians are taught to be wary of the police from early childhood, apparently, when their fathers used them as lookouts for their two-up games.'

'Two-up?'

'Illegal street gambling – the children are called cockatoos by the spinner if they can spot an inquisitive copper and whistle loudly at the same time. This gives the ringy enough time to hide his kip and the boxer to disperse the punters.'

Pym nodded.

'Which leads to another five questions. Punters I understand.'

'Ask away.'

But Pym remained silent as they walked into a short avenue of tall Norfolk pines.

'Look there, have you ever seen a flying fox?'

Bingham pointed to a grove of trees deeper in the cemetery, their branches partly stripped of leaves and hung with the heavy black animals, a full harvest on every tree.

'Handsome little brutes if you cast their heads in silver.'

'I can smell them from here, disgusting creatures.'

'She got my number from the tearoom; one of the ladies goes to church with her mother. They probably sit around drinking tea after the service, talking about the nation's security.'

'What can she do?'

'Well, that's the fortunate coincidence I'm having to come to terms with. A position is just about to become vacant and she will fit it perfectly.'

'You're becoming as efficient as the Americans.'

'She has yet to meet George.'

'*Young* nurse, is she?'

'Very. Convincing her to separate from the boyfriend was like walking on bloody glass.'

'What about Lorrimer? Do you still have reservations?'

'I'm not allowed to,' said Pym.

A mausoleum dominated the next walkway; a squat, windowless, suburban brick cottage roofed in red tiles with a double front door sheathed in stippled copper. The entrance was secured with two padlocks and a heavy connecting chain; a mature wisteria vine had climbed to the building's eaves and crept under some tiles lifting them from their battens.

'What would you like when it's your turn? Arms crossed and buried on a desolate plain, like the noble Chaldean?'

Pym laughed at the idea.

'None of your wizened skeletons, John. I'm planning on being burned, having my ashes mixed with flour and made into small testicle-sized offerings, then left on a temple rampart in the Himalayas for the vultures.'

'No cortege, no eulogy?'

'For that you need friends and family. What about Lorrimer? You were saying?'

'He verified the nurse's story; boyfriend Millar has a problem with personal surveillance, the CIS are all over him. There are so many of their people in town they're called *sparrows,* and some of them hardly bother with concealment, apparently.

'George was tempted to use his camera. He watched a woman writing her case notes in the street, stuff them into her handbag when her target came out of the toilet and nearly trip over a pram as she scurried after him.'

'What's he like, this man? What is she dealing with?'

'George likened him to a gridiron back.'

The men left the cemetery and crossed the road to a footpath separated from a large, terraced garden by a sandstone wall. Tables and chairs were set up under a copse of Moreton Bay figs and small groups sat about in the shade, visitors with wounded servicemen among them. A few ward beds had been wheeled outside and a woman leant over one, apart from the rest, both she and the patient concealed beneath the brightly coloured umbrella she held in one hand.

Two nurses dressed in crisp blue uniforms and white caps floated from group to group like butterflies drawn to flowers growing in the shade.

Pym stopped and looked over the wall.

'Tell me, John,' he said, 'how do these fellows know what their enemy looks like up there? Don't the Japanese wear the same colour uniform?'

'Hats, Pym,' said Bingham, smiling. 'If they see a man without a hat they shoot him. Australians have a noble concept of war.'

'Without a hat?'

'A *slouch* hat to be precise. Anything else is a fair target, and that, I'm told, is largely drummed into them when they are first given a rifle.'

They walked on under the shade of a giant fig that had littered the street with its dropped fruit, pungent and slippery underfoot.

Bingham thought nobody would notice if they took advantage of one of the hospital's empty benches, and after finding an open gate and entering the grounds both men sat and let the silence settle. A couple of magpies called to each other from the high branches and one glided down to the lawn before stalking towards an uncleared table crowded with scavenging gulls. Pym watched its approach.

'Which do you want to back in this, John?'

Before Bingham could answer the magpie flew at the table, scattering the gulls into panicked flight.

'Avoid the local magpies, Pym, they're bloody lethal.'

They both watched as the bird stepped around the paper plates and littered food.

'Fussy brutes, aren't they?'

Bingham sat back on the bench and closed his eyes as the sun moved from behind a cloud bathing him in warmth. The magpie departed after delivering a long, warbling melody from the back of a chair. Pym laughed.

'J. Edgar Magpie, nobody ever dare disabuse him of his appetites.'

A seagull glided to the abandoned table and began feeding before being joined by two more. Another three flew in to create a squalling jostle and the few remaining scraps of food were scattered about in a fluster of wings and beaks.

A minute passed.

'No wonder the émigrés come here,' said Pym, 'there is no winter.'

Bingham spoke without opening his eyes.

'Jessica told me she compensated for the boyfriend's paranoia by eating too many of the babkas they sold in the coffee shops.

'How long has she been putting up with it?'

'Some years; the problem comes and goes according to the degree of scrutiny, apparently one feeds on the other.'

'What's his sin?'

'He's the sort of galoot who will stand on a soapbox and make sure everyone sees his face and hears his opinion. He's an easy target and the watchers get paid by the hour. It's as simple as that.'

The men left the hospital grounds, crossed back over the road and turned to the distant railway station. Bingham, a cigarette smoker with old army habits, took one from his pack, tore off the filtered end, lit up the ragged half-stump and took a couple of fierce drags before dropping it to the ground and grinding it out under his shoe.

'I should give the bloody things up.'

They walked on before stopping to watch a procession of stately black coaches slowly enter the cemetery fifty feet further down the road.

'I'm sure that one owes me two hundred quid,' Bingham said, pointing to a silk-maned chestnut with a high step.

'Flying bloody Rover!'

Pym spoke as if he didn't hear.

'Are you going to take her on?'

Bingham grunted.

'I'd hire her tomorrow, but everything is done by committee these days.'

Bingham let Pym go on as he stopped on the railway bridge to watch a chain of coal carriages pass beneath, too many to count. A couple of young boys stood by the tracks hoping for a spill of the black nuggets.

They took the train back to the city; Pym was subdued and didn't lift his head as they travelled over the harbour, his preoccupation unshareable.

Maureen and Jessica

Gore Hill Cemetery, July 1944

The only girl Bingham had loved left her Hayward Heath home when she was sixteen to accompany her father who had been posted to Shanghai. Bingham, a shy and gangling youth, walked past her house on his way home from school for two years afterwards, imagining the shadow he sometimes saw in the upstairs back window was Maureen, petite and dark-haired, watching him as he went by.

Bingham wondered, as they walked to the station end of the old carriageway that ran through the centre of the cemetery, if he could be mistaken for Jessica's grandfather. They sat together on one of the stone benches by the entrance gates.

'How much time do you have?'

Jessica looked at her watch.

'Half an hour. I'm due back at two. Don't you take notes for this sort of thing?'

Bingham shook his head.

'Just tell me what's on your mind.'

Jessica took a deep breath, looked down at her nails then clasped her hands.

'I want to work for you.'

'As a nurse?'

'No.'

'Then what?'

'I was told you hired people for work outside of the services.'

'Did they say what the work consisted of?'

'No, just that it helped in the war.'

'Surely nursing is enough.'

Jessica looked up at Bingham.

'It used to be.'

Bingham watched two men enter the cemetery, deep in conversation, one of them glanced at Jessica.

'Did you keep the telephone number?'

Jessica nodded.

'Call tomorrow, they'll give you an appointment.'

'Should I bring anything?'

'No.'

Bingham patted his pockets for a cigarette. 'I'll stay a minute longer.'

The Bookseller

The bookseller Otto preferred to sit for most of the day. His right hip and ankle had never recovered from the fall – the push from behind then an endless tumble down the eight stone steps that led to the London railway platform.

Enduring another winter in Europe would have left him permanently on crutches and incapable of effective work so they prepared his way and sent him to more temperate latitudes.

Now Sydney's winter sun beamed through the bookshop window and warmed him as he sat reading – always needing two cushions to support his back and a low footstool to raise his legs and relieve him of the sciatic pain. These careful arrangements did not incline Otto to rise when customers queried him about the availability of a particular publication and he was given to gesturing in the general direction of its likely location from behind his book-laden counter. Otto had little to do all day but read and tend to his few customers. When tired of the print he closed his eyes and dozed, relying on the doorbell to wake him if anyone entered his dusty shop.

The bookshop occupied the bottom floor of an apartment building in the Haymarket, the shelves as crowded as the railway platforms Otto remembered in Bombay.

A soft-voiced Englishman had begun a series of infrequent exchanges by handing Otto an envelope and asking if he could pass it on to the correspondent Rostov, who was well known about town. The bookseller obliged without any formality or payment; he was known to facilitate relationships that flowered in darkness, illicit or otherwise.

Sometimes, David Pym made a purchase when he was in the shop, a book reader after all, and he could discourse at length about many subjects. He was an attractive, dark-haired man, subtle in his choice of words, and Otto enjoyed the brief company, guarded as it was by their intrigues.

Otto was consulting the book he was expecting to be picked up later in the day, it being a Tuesday, although not before the correspondent had spent ten careful minutes browsing the shelves.

He wrote a few more words onto a slip of paper before turning to another page; the lightly pencilled code written between the lines of the book only ever took a couple of minutes to unravel.

He finished his decryptions and slowly lowered his feet to the floor, gripping both armrests to push himself upright. The ache returned and despite his best efforts he could only shuffle back to the shelves where Pym had left his chalk mark.

The Decision

Sydney, 1944

John Bingham had interviewed dozens of women, a hundred; he had as many personnel files in his cabinet.

Jessica sat with him at the table in his office, his 10am appointment; she was wearing a nurse's uniform with a small frangipani pinned to her coat. Bingham couldn't tell whether the traces of perfume were coming from the flower or her skin.

She waited, hands in her lap. The preliminaries were over. She was to call him Major.

Bingham opened a manila folder and took out two sheets of paper, tapped them square and placed them on the table beside the folder before taking a capped pencil from his suit pocket and laying it alongside.

Jessica saw her name at the top of the first page and the letters TYN, only to look up and find Bingham watching her.

'Is that my reference number?'

'Any other recruit wouldn't be asking; now I'll have to write everything in French.'

'I can read that upside down too. What does the TYN stand for?'

Bingham smiled as he wrote.

'My amateur attempt at linking your name with your face; you are Jessica Hartnell, The Young Nurse.'

Bingham took a small stainless steel penknife from his pocket and sharpened the pencil. Jessica asked why he didn't use a pen and he chuckled at the notion.

'Sometimes I have to rub things out. What do you use when you write on a patient's record?'

'Ink. If anything is wrong we have to write it again and cross-reference back.'

'You leave a trail?'

'Yes.'

'That doesn't work in our business.'

Bingham closed the penknife and put it back into his pocket. He looked over at Jessica.

'Are you in any relationship ...' Bingham searched for a word, '... inseparable, marriage likely, if you know what I mean?'

'Probably not.'

'Because?'

'His politics come before everything.'

'What's *his* name?'

Jessica hesitated.

'I'll need an answer for every question, Jessica, or this interview will not be successful.'

'John Millar. He's very outspoken about the war and … communism.'

'He's being followed?'

'All the time, he says.'

'Do you think he's being watched while he's with you?'

'I suppose so, they're everywhere.'

'Does your Mr Millar know you're here today?'

'No.' Jessica sat back and stared at Bingham, a frown appearing on her forehead. 'Why?'

'Competing intelligence agencies have the nature of a

harem of sisters; they each covet what the others have.'

'But …'

'There is no but. You cannot work for us and continue your relationship with Millar. He illuminates everyone around him.'

'I'll make him understand.'

'No.'

Bingham excused himself and went to his desk to phone for tea and biscuits. His office was on the fifth floor, a vast, high-ceilinged room with two tall corner windows overlooking the city and harbour. The walls propped up empty bookshelves and were chequered with pale squares and rectangles where pictures had once hung.

Jessica got up and moved over to the windows, standing with her arms folded to gaze out over the city.

'I would stand here for hours if this was my office; you can see nearly all the harbour.'

Jessica turned from the window and looked around the office.

'What happened to the pictures?'

Bingham was back at the table, writing. He spoke

without looking up.

'The fellow who owned them took them home, apparently.'

'Do you know who he is?'

'One of the Grace boys, quite the lad in the RAAF, I hear.'

Jessica resumed gazing out of the window.

'There's a big sea today.'

'How do you know?'

'North Head, there's whitewater at its base.'

Bingham left his chair, walked to the nearest window and looked over the city rooftops to the distant headland.

'You have good eyes.'

Tea and biscuits arrived courtesy of the officially name-tagged Mrs Ginger, who examined Jessica in minute detail as she poured tea. Bingham closed the door behind her and came back to the table.

'Did you know anyone on the *Centaur*?'

'A flatmate died, and two nurses from the hospital.'

'I'm sorry to hear that.'

'I packed up her clothes and took them home to her mother.'

'There was one who survived?'

'Yes, a nurse from Quirindi.'

'Quirindi, that's a beautiful name for a town, as is Deniliquin. We have a station in a town called Gawler, named after some old warrior, no doubt.'

'Is that what you are? An old warrior?'

Bingham laughed.

'Yes, if that's what you call growing old too quickly.'

Bingham ferried the cups and saucers to an empty shelf by the door, came back to the table and re-opened Jessica's file. He looked at her and raised his eyebrows.

'What made you want to contact me?'

He waited a long fifteen seconds.

'It was a marked hospital ship. Two hundred and sixty-eight died including eleven nurses.'

'You won't save any lives working for me.'

'Then why do you do it?'

'It's expected.'

Bingham squared up his file and sat back.

'I think we're just about done.'

Jessica reached for her handbag, ready to get up. Bingham motioned her to stay, took a sheaf of documents from the file and slid them over.

'Read these before we go on any further.'

Jessica looked at Bingham, frowned, then took up the documents and read through them quickly, turning over the final page to see if there were more.

'Allegiance to the king? He's a George, isn't he?'

'The sixth. That's who we work for.'

Bingham tapped the document with his pencil.

'It's a permanent decision. Nothing must ever be said.'

An Invitation

Lorrimer left a copy of one of the bedroom photographs in Rostov's mailbox and waited four days, watching the buses the correspondent caught to the city and the trains he used to travel to Chatswood.

Nick Bellantoni drove Lorrimer over to the legation on two mornings and parked close enough to the entrance for Lorrimer to see Rostov entering the building. On the third morning, Lorrimer caught the same train as Rostov, sat behind him reading a newspaper then followed him as he left the station. Rostov stopped twice: once to crouch, tie a shoelace and look over his shoulder, and again at the mouth of an arcade, where he stopped and looked into a shop window for a moment, watching the reflected street behind him.

Lorrimer followed on the other side of the road keeping one half-block distant. When Rostov continued walking he took off his hat and crossed the road.

On the fourth day, Oskar took the 10.10am train from Town Hall to Hornsby and found a window seat; he looked up when a man sat beside him.

Nick Bellantoni opened his newspaper and flicked the pages over to the race results.

Milson's Point Station.

Nick folded his newspaper and left the carriage to be replaced by Lorrimer, who didn't take the vacant seat but took one step in and leant over the Russian.

Rostov looked up to see a face close enough to startle him; Lorrimer's open coat revealed the holstered pistol on his belt.

Lorrimer sat beside him and waited for the train to leave the station; he turned to the Russian, put a hand onto his lap, found the bulge of his testicles and crushed them. Rostov stiffened as Lorrimer counted softly from one to ten. When he released the correspondent he leant in close as if to share a whispered aside.

'Look at me.'

Rostov turned his head blinking away tears.

'We get off when I say. Okay?'

Rostov nodded and looked away.

Artarmon Station.

Lorrimer escorted Rostov from the train station and propelled him towards the footpath and Bellantoni's parked car, his hand under the Russian's arm. Nick opened the kerb-side back door and both men piled in.

It was a fine day for a cruise.

The Dark Tasman Sea

The Tasman Sea has dark and emerald depths and among the reefs and kelp-feathered water gullies is a graveyard of boats and bodies. An aquarium Lorrimer thought, compared to the black-mud dumping grounds of Lake Michigan.

They called for him in a dark Buick and took him away. Nobody saw anything.

He was fully dressed, bound from shoulders to shins in war issue duct tape, roped to a kitchen chair with clothesline and gagged with both his socks. His feet were submerged in a bucket of cement and both his knees had been shattered with a hammer so he could not move and disturb the hardening. His screaming went unheard.

They threw his hat overboard and used it as target practice. Everyone had guns.

When his feet were set in stone two men came for him, lifted him to the top of the boat's rail and tipped him over the side as everyone crowded to watch. The last thing he heard was a woman's shrieking laugh.

Others were folded into padlocked refrigerator caskets and dropped overboard, or bound alive in wire, weighted with anchor chain and slipped into the water at night.

Bellantoni had guided his uncle's trawler through the submarine barrier and a further two miles offshore before he cut the engine and called down the companionway for Lorrimer to bring Rostov topside.

He had been stripped of his clothes and there was a livid bruise on the upper ribs of his left side from a blow delivered by Lorrimer when Rostov had become agitated and started to resist. Lorrimer pointed to a hatch cover and Rostov sat head down with his hands clenched between his legs, twitching as if a series of electric shocks were travelling through his body. Bellantoni and Lorrimer watched, waiting for him to lift his head and take stock.

When Rostov finally looked up, Bellantoni picked up a rope from the deck, walked over to him and knotted it around his ankle.

Rostov's eyes followed the length of the rope to the stern where it was tied to an iron mangle secured against the boat's side.

He looked at Bellantoni in wide-eyed disbelief.

Bellantoni glanced at Lorrimer; Lorrimer nodded.

In one swift movement, Bellantoni picked up the correspondent and heaved him over the side, laughing as the tethered man splashed untidily into the water.

Rostov thrashed his way to the surface and clawed wildly for the side of the boat.

Lorrimer lifted a gaff over the side, let him take a grip, then pushed him a few feet away from the boat's side. Rostov found his voice.

'Please! I cannot swim!'

Lorrimer lifted the gaff away and watched as Rostov tried to keep afloat, thrashing about before disappearing in a flurry of splashing.

'He'd drown in the bath.'

They both watched as Rostov's head and arms broke the surface, his mouth open wide, before he went under again after more flailing.

Lorrimer gaffed him under the arm and raised him to the surface.

'Please,' Rostov gasped, 'you don't have to do this.'

He had grasped the wooden gaff with both hands and was trying to draw himself closer to the boat. Lorrimer leant over the side.

'I want to know about the courier network that runs between Hong Kong and Australia.'

'I am a correspondent. I know nothing of couriers.'

Lorrimer laughed.

'Well, fuck you too, Oskar.'

He lifted the gaff away and watched as Rostov fought wildly to stay on the surface before being pulled down again. He was tiring and the fight was leaving him.

Lorrimer gaffed him up sharp, the pike embedded into his armpit.

'That means company,' said Bellantoni, as a dark, stringy stain eddied away from the Russian.

'Sharks will be onto that in five minutes.'

Bellantoni took a pair of canvas gloves from his back pocket, put them on, untied the mangle, lifted it onto the rail-top and held it steady against the swell with one hand. He looked over at Lorrimer, got the nod and tipped it into the water, letting the rope run out through his hands.

Lorrimer shoved Rostov away with the gaff and watched as the rope trailed over the side and into the water.

Rostov flailed at the surface; he tried to shout but the sea rushed in and filled his throat, submerging his scream into a gurgle of seawater. He waved at them from beneath a rolling swell, eyes wide, mouth open, breathing water.

Bellantoni cut the mangle free and hauled Rostov back to the side of the boat, raised his body onboard, laid it on the deck and rolled him on his side, leaving him to throw up all he had swallowed as he hacked and gasped for air. Both men lifted him onto the hatch cover and Lorrimer steadied him while Bellantoni returned to the wheel, kicked the engine up and turned the boat for Sydney Heads.

Lorrimer waited for Rostov to lift his head.

'There is a courier network running between Hong Kong and Australia; it has been in place since the outbreak of war and I want you to tell me all about it.'

Rostov was shivering, his hands tucked between his thighs.

'I am a correspondent, nothing more. I will report you for this … this assault!'

Rostov burst into another spasm of coughing and belched out more sea water. Lorrimer took hold of the rope attached to his ankle, jerked him down onto the deck and stood over him with his hands on his hips.

'Assault? You mean this?'

Before Rostov could protect himself Lorrimer lifted his foot and gave his testicles a sharp poke with the toe of his shoe, then two vicious jabs. Rostov's hands fluttered down to his groin and he drew his knees up; his testicles had almost disappeared.

Lorrimer bent over Rostov and looked into his distorted face.

'Not what you're used to?' What boat does your courier use? ... Boat!'

Jab.

'The *Cycle*.'

Lorrimer propped him against the side of the boat; Rostov's shivering now looked like epilepsy and he was bleeding freely from the two-inch tear inflicted by the gaff.

'What's the courier's name?'

'NAME!'

Rostov flinched.

'Balanchine.'

'Russian?'

'No.'

Rostov was shuddering and his eyes were beginning to roll. Lorrimer pulled him upright, draped one of Rostov's arms over his shoulders then half-carried him to the wheelhouse and down the companionway to the only cabin.

When Bingham came aboard at Artarmon an hour later and stepped down into the cabin, Rostov was sitting on a bunk clutching a blanket around himself, trying to control his shaking. Lorrimer was seated at a small table and looked up with a tight smile.

'Welcome aboard the USS Interrogator.'

'How is our man?'

Lorrimer looked at his prisoner.

'He just needed a bath.'

'All the beans spilled?'

'Not yet.'

'What don't we know?'

'More than one name.'

Lorrimer leaned forward, took Rostov's hand away from the blanket, grasped the thumb and twisted it back and around until the joint popped. Bingham heard the snap and flinched as Rostov screamed and tried to pull his hand free.

Lorrimer leant into Rostov's face, close enough to breathe over it

'I hope I didn't break a nail there, Oskar. Are you listening?'

A mute nod.

'Who picks up the package from Balanchine?'

'Keyannik, Russian.'

'That's good, two for one. How does he know?'

'A message.'

'From?'

'Me.'

'To where?'

'His landlady.'

'What's her phone number?'

'My wallet.'

'Where does he live?'

'Harris Street, a boarding house.'

'Where does he take it?'

'My mailbox, he has a key.'

'Where is your key?'

'My watch pocket.'

Bingham stepped over to the bunk, picked up Rostov's trousers and fished it out of his fob pocket.

'Keyannik is now out of the courier business, and please don't break any more of his fingers, George, I'm not inclined to help him on with his trousers.'

Rostov was no longer focusing on Lorrimer; his eyes were closing.

Sleep.

An unbearable flash of pain travelled from his thumb to his shoulder. He gasped awake and tried to jerk his hand away from Lorrimer's grasp.

'Are you still on the planet, Oskar?'

Lorrimer leant into Rostov again.

'Listen carefully: the day after the *Cycle* gets into port Balanchine takes his package to the Gore Hill Cemetery and puts it behind grave 4A before 10am. He reads the plan at the station end of the road that cuts through the cemetery. When he's done, he leaves flowers on the grave.'

Lorrimer looked down at Rostov's mutilated thumb; it had ballooned to twice its size, was the colour of a cocktail sausage and looked to be radiating substantial heat.

'You should report in sick with that.'

He squeezed it.

'Who is your contact on the *Cycle*?'

Bellantoni drove Rostov back to the station and watched as he shuffled through the entrance like an old man.

Bingham and Lorrimer went back to the office with three new names, including Val Johanssen, skipper of the SS *Cycle*.

The Bird of Paradise

Sydney, 1945

The clatter of hooves ceased as the coach driver slowly guided his two horses off the cobbled road that bisected Gore Hill Cemetery and into a side passage where he parked under the shade of a line of Cypress Oaks. A dozen mourners waited for the coffin on the other side of a hedge of blue hydrangea, among them a priest with his arm around the shoulders of an elderly man.

A knot of gravediggers stood some way off, their long-handled shovels resting against each other like a picket of rifles. They were mostly older men, trench diggers from another war. They smoked and watched, waiting for their time.

Lorrimer had arrived an hour earlier and played the tourist, taking photos of headstones and mausoleums in a large section of graves that bordered the children's enclosure. He looked for a place where he could see the train station entrance but not be observed.

Lorrimer watched a man enter the cemetery gates and walk towards him. He was smoking, holding a small bunch of yellow flowers in his left hand and looking to his left and right as he approached the entrance to the children's enclosure. Lorrimer kept his camera down, not risking a flash of sunlight from the lens.

The man entered the enclosure and walked among the small plots. He stopped at one and squatted a moment before standing up and walking to the next. Grave 4A was at the top of the row and Lorrimer had only glanced at the headstone earlier, not needing to read the child's name.

The courier reached 4A, squatted, placed his flowers by the headstone then stood and stepped around to the back of the grave where he tidied up a few untended weeds. That done, he took a pack of cigarettes out of his pocket, lit up a smoke and walked away.

He reached the cobbled road and turned towards the hospital, walked through the cemetery gates, crossed Westbourne Street and strolled up to an empty bus shelter.

Lorrimer followed him out and watched him take a seat in the bus shelter before turning in the opposite direction.

Five minutes passed before a Crows Nest bus stopped to discharge half a dozen passengers. When it pulled away, the courier was still there taking another cigarette from his pack.

Lorrimer looked at his watch and waited for Jessica to appear. Bingham's choice. Lorrimer had kept his reservations to himself.

She walked through the hospital gates at 10:30am.

The courier sat up and watched Jessica pass by on the other side of the road, then stood and gazed at her until she entered the cemetery gates and disappeared from view. He walked a few paces from the bus shelter before turning and resuming his seat.

Jessica's shift had started early that morning in the casualty ward. An ambulance had brought in a frail and distraught old woman who had been found in her bath with a fractured wrist. The couple who lived in the neighbouring flat had been woken by her cries early in the morning and broken through the front door.

Mrs Franklin was later put into a ward across the aisle from the toothless and talkative Percy who was hankering for her to wake up and hear his stories about his old artillery battalion.

Percy sometimes gave Jess a low, speculative whistle when she passed by his bed; he had gangrene in both feet and spat out a bucket-load of sputum every day but there was hair on his head and lust in his heart. She flirted with him.

'I'll bring in me Military Cross and knock your socks off,' he promised.

Jessica walked down the cobbled road quickly, willing herself not to look around until she reached the enclosure. Three graves had flowers. One a faded blue hydrangea, another a glass tumbler of wildflowers on its side and the third a small bunch of fresh-cut yellow daisies placed against the headstone.

'If the flowers are there, so is the pickup,' Bingham had told her.

Jessica went to the daisies, and after a quick glance over her shoulder stepped behind the headstone and bent down to retrieve the envelope. She tucked it into a pocket in her uniform and walked out of the enclosure.

'Could I ask a favour?'

Jessica turned to see a solidly built man standing about five feet away. He had a camera strung around his neck, a snappy straw hat on his head and was looking at her with a hopeful smile. He pointed to a nearby headstone.

'I'd like to write down a name for the folks back home. Do you have a scrap of paper I could have?'

American.

Jessica walked over and took the envelope from her pocket.

'Here, use this.'

'Woolloomooloo,' Lorrimer murmured as he wrote, 'this place has some crazy spellings.'

He pocketed the envelope, tipped his hat and turned on his heel.

Relieved and slightly dislocated, Jessica reached the cemetery gates before stopping to look back. The American had gone.

A hundred feet from the hospital a man crossed the road, reached the footpath and walked towards her. Jessica smiled distractedly when he doffed his hat and met his eye for the instant it took them to pass each other.

'Excuse me? … Excuse me? *Hello.*'

Jessica stopped, half-turned and looked back.

'Are you following me?

'No, well … yes.'

The man spread his hands, palms up.

'Ed Baxter,' he said, 'I'm hoping he's a mutual friend.'

Now she had to hurry away.

'No, wait. Please.'

'Please leave me alone.'

'You came up in a conversation.'

Jessica felt a knot of tension forming in her stomach as she walked.

'I was with him two weeks ago in Rabaul.'

Jessica halted mid-stride, turned and looked into his eyes to see if she could read a lie.

'He told you my name?'

'Mata Hari.'

They stood on the footpath facing each other and Lorrimer got both their profiles in one shot.

'I must get to work.'

'Can I buy you a cup of tea when you finish? A drink?'

The Bookmaker

He was sitting at a table next to the servery and stood as Jessica approached, waiting until she was seated before asking if she would like a drink.

'Please, a vodka with soda and ice.'

He ordered through the hatch.

'I'm sorry for startling you earlier. I'm Tom.'

'Jessica. Jess is fine.'

He smiled, as if about to give her some good news; his eyes were clear and without guile.

As he waited for the drinks Jessica examined him in minute and scattered increments, his hair colour, the lines about his eyes, how he rested both his palms on the servery top, the broadness of his cheekbones, the way he set his mouth.

There was his scent; a faint lemon essence that gave relief from the smell of tobacco smoke that came from his clothes and hands. Tom brought the drinks to the table, sat down and lifted his glass.

'Cheers.'

They each took a sip. Jessica sat back in her chair and Tom took out his cigarettes and lighter.

Jessica shook her head.

'How do you know Ed?'

Tom took a long pull at his smoke and laid it in the ashtray.

'In Rabaul, when Ed was on the *Crusader*. We met at the airstrip. I was running a betting stand when the Yanks were having a racing meet, the last one before they all went home. Ed was looking for an Australian to talk to.'

Tom gave her a grin.

'Reckoned he knew a little bit about Harley Davidsons.'

Jessica smiled.

'Of course, with Ed it's only bikes.'

'He wrote the book. Ed had been watching the Yanks racing for a while and had an idea how we could take some money off them.

'I must have looked stupid because the next time they came around he had to show me how the Yanks took the curve wide because the Harley footplates stopped them laying their bikes over and getting tight on the turns, you know, closer to the ground. Ed told me he'd won a few races by sawing off the pedals and riding on the struts.

'It all sounded good enough to me so while he went off hunting for a bike and a hacksaw I rounded up a few blokes I knew and told them a fiddle was on.

'There were dozens of Harleys parked around the place, all of them US army; Ed's got a head like a coconut so nobody bothered him when he wheeled one away.

'We got him into the last three races; the Yanks put him on outside odds of twenty to one for the first race and we took them on. I had a fiver on him myself.

'He won that easy, burned them all off the track when he came around the last curve, rocks and dust everywhere. The Yanks dropped him to six to one for the second and he won that by a half-mile. I put a tenner on him that time.'

'As per plan?'

'Better than Pearl Harbor. The third fiddle kicked in on the last race when I put him on at four to one. I needed more than one bag for the money the Yanks were throwing at me; their bookies were only offering even money.'

Tom laughed.

'They never saw it coming.'

He drained his glass.

'Jess?'

'You go ahead.'

Tom left for the public bar to get a drink and Jess smiled at his idiosyncrasy, as if using the servery hatch was only appropriate if you were ordering for a woman. She watched him walk away and when he returned with a small beer and sat down they smiled at each other across the table.

'I think I know what's coming,' said Jess. 'We've had a bookmaker or two come through the wards with their racing stories.'

'It was the first time the Yanks ever saw someone nobble a motorbike. Ed was dead keen for taking it on, the flinty old coot. Halfway through the last race he dropped the bike onto the dirt and came up lame, claimed he'd broken a bone in his foot so one of the crew doubled him up and they both skedaddled back to the ship, left me and a few mates to deal with the Yanks who wanted a refund. What they didn't know was the bloke ferrying Ed back to the boat had all the money in his knapsack.'

'That doesn't sound fair.'

'You don't give a bloke his money back when his racehorse falls over, besides, these blokes were Americans, they were knocking us off with shotguns up in Brisbane. I got out minus a tooth and some bark off my knuckles before the MPs broke it up, met Ed back at the boat and we had a drink or five. We did okay.'

Tom smiled.

'It's the Wild West up there. Anyway, that's when he told me about the Major and his Mata Hari, and some other bloke, an American.

'He said the Major had a vulture on one shoulder and a bird of paradise on the other. We were both mildly affected by the hooch at the time.'

Two women came into the room and looked at Tom with disapproval, elderly ladies who thought that parlours weren't for men. Tom smiled up at them.

'A last drink, Jess, to go?'

She shook her head.

'Tom?'

'Yes?'

Jess leant forward and whispered across the table, knowing the dowagers were listening.

'Do you know what's in the envelope?'

'Wouldn't have a clue,' Tom said quietly. 'I know it's skullduggery of some type: currency, identification papers. Johanssen has a hand in most of it, everybody does up there.'

Jessica sat back.

'Johanssen?'

'The skipper. He's a smoky old bastard, excuse the French, gets some strange passengers now and then.

'He introduced me to one who got on the boat in Hong Kong a couple of years ago and I've been doing work for him ever since. Sometimes I'll pick up a pouch in Sydney to take back to Hong Kong as well. I tickled open the lock on one once and had a look inside, pinched a roll of film.'

'Did you get it developed?'

'Maybe.'

'What was on it?'

'Blocks of numbers, pages of them.'

'Won't they notice if the film is gone?'

Tom shrugged.

'I'm not the only one handling it.'

They both looked up as an elderly couple entered the parlour. Jess watched them walk to a vacant table and sit down as Tom finished his beer. He put his glass down and Jess turned to him.

'Why did you wait for me?'

Tom sat forward and clasped his hands together on top of the table.

'The routine changed to a place near a hospital so I thought I'd wait and see who showed up.'

'And if it's all right with you, Jess, I'll do it again next time.'

They both stood. Jessica gathered up her coat from the back of her chair and they looked at each other in silence, quite still, aware of the straining ears of the two older women sitting a table away.

Jessica put on her coat and fastened three of the five buttons before looking up.

'We can't meet here again.'

She left first. Tom bought the two dowagers a sweet sherry before strolling back to the station whistling like a boy.

A Snake's Nest of Doubts

Sydney, 1946

'Show me what you saw.'

Lorrimer placed a sheaf of photographs on the table and sorted them from first to last, seven in all.

'This was after she'd given you the package?'

'Straight after.'

'Why didn't he go back to the station the way he came in? Why come out that way? It's twice as far.'

Bingham took the photos, looked through them and dropped them onto the table in turn, then walked to his office window and looked down at the evening traffic.

'What do you make of it, George? … George, what do you make of it?'

'He knows her.'

Bingham remained at his window.

'How was she with the handover?'

'She didn't drop anything.'

'How did she look?'

'Fine, no nerves.'

Bingham came back to the table and sorted through the photos until he found the one of Jessica turning around to look at the courier.

'Nobody is that careless.'

'Who? Him or her?'

Lorrimer picked through the photos before coming up with Jessica walking towards the hospital and the courier crossing the road from the opposite side. He pushed it over the table to Bingham.

'You hired her, JB, you did the homework.'

'And you saw them enter the hotel?'

'Him first, her an hour later.'

Bingham reached for his phone.

Called In

Jessica and Bingham were sitting at the table opposite each other as Lorrimer haunted the now darkened window.

She slowly looked through the photos before putting them down and sitting back in her chair.

'You didn't say I would be watched.'

'No, I didn't.'

'And followed.'

'It's not a sign of distrust, Jess.'

'It is when it happens to John. Am I to be watched every time?'

Lorrimer stirred. Bingham answered.

'No.'

Lorrimer turned and gestured at the photos.

'Anything there you'd like to tell us about?'

'You seem to know enough already.'

Bingham picked up the photos and leafed through them. He chose one and showed it to Jessica. Tom sitting in the bus shelter, smoking.

'Did you know he was waiting for you?'

Jessica shook her head.

'No.'

He picked out another.

'You spoke to him.'

Jessica gazed at the bare wall behind Bingham, slowly clasping and unclasping her fingers.

'Then you met for a drink.'

He sat forward.

'Do you know him?'

Jessica looked past Bingham.

Lorrimer walked up to the table and sorted through the photographs, picked one of the street shots and pushed it over to Jessica.

'You two look like you know each other pretty well, Jess. What was the good news?'

Jessica didn't hesitate.

'He's my bookmaker. I won some money.'

A loud snort from Lorrimer.

'How does he pay you, Jess, in kopeks?'

Now she detested him.

Bingham gathered the photos into a bundle, pushed his chair back, stood and walked over to his desk.

'I think we're done here, George, I'll see Jess home.'

Lorrimer took his jacket and left the office quietly, closing the door behind him. Bingham put the photos into a desk drawer then came back to the table and sat down, put his hands on the glass and waited for Jess to do something other than stare at the empty walls.

She met his eyes.

'You didn't know him, did you? You walked right past him.'

Bingham surprised her by getting up and fetching a bottle of vodka from his desk drawer together with two small glasses. He showed her the bottle.

'Polish.'

He sat down and poured, pushed a glass over to Jessica

and raised his.

'It's a devil of a game, isn't it?'

They sat silently for half a minute; Jessica fiddled with her glass, revolving it on its base.

'You'll meet him again? Next time he's in port?'

'Yes.'

'Does he know what's in the envelope?'

'We didn't talk about that.'

Bingham waited.

'What did you talk about?'

Jessica's mouth softened a little.

'How to steal money from Americans.'

Mr Johnson and Mrs Stelson

Sydney, 1946

Lorrimer flipped the pictures over one by one until Bingham looked up.

'Where are they now?'

Jessica saw him from the top of an avenue that led down to the swimming baths. He was sitting below her on a grassy slope with his back to one of the great Norfolk pines that studded the hill, his arms around his knees, watching the great lines of whitewater sweeping into the cove. The sea was boisterous inshore and corrugated to the horizon with approaching swells.

Jessica followed Tom's line of sight to see a surfboat poised on the crest of an immense wave sweeping into the bay. The crew had gathered in the stern in an attempt to stabilise the boat's descent and were grasping at the sweep's oar to assist him as they fought to keep the boat from broaching. She watched it slowly dip to vertical then spear into the base of the wave, raising a twin cascade of water from its flared bows before being thrown over by the whitewater, catapulting the crew and oars into the surf.

Tom stood and turned to the road, spotted Jess and waved her down the avenue where they met at the top of a set of steps overlooking the southern end of the beach. The surfboat had been dragged up onto dry sand and a couple of the crew were jogging along the beach, looking for the oars Tom could see being tumbled against the rocks below him.

In the midst of the turmoil, a handful of brown-backed youths grasped a hawser strung across an open rock shelf, daring the thundering seas to sweep them away. Walls of hissing whitewater swept over them and they disappeared for long seconds at a time, only to be caught again by the back surge as the wave rebounded from the cliff base. Tom could hear their laughter as they emerged from the surges and felt an urge to join them.

Hundreds of people were gathered on the beach, sunbathing and sitting around scatterings of rugs and blankets. Boys raced through them, swerving around the family gatherings, leaping over solitary sunbathers and showering them with fine sand before sprinting the last few yards towards the ocean and somersaulting into the shorebreak to be borne back by the strength of the sea and left sprawling on the wet sand as the wave receded.

Two veteran beach inspectors patrolled the shoreline; both wearing white shorts and white broad-brimmed canvas hats, stopping every few yards to watch the sea and those swimming in it. They glared at the fools who dared to attempt the waves further out and signalled them ashore with long-winded shrieks from the metal whistles they wore around their necks.

Among the crowds, one fat little man the colour of dark umber was spraying a young woman with tanning oil. He had an area set aside in the middle of the beach and a line of men and women of all ages were waiting their turn. The young woman was turning this way and that under the fragrant mist as he smoothed his home-made emulsification onto her arms and shoulders.

A line of appreciative young men in uniform stood watching at the rail above the beach, American sailors among them in their dixie cup hats. As Jessica and Tom walked past they heard a low, fugitive whistle.

'Don't look back,' Jessica said, 'one of them might recognise you.'

They walked from the beach to the pavilion, past alcoves that housed a dozen chess players, older men waging peaceful wars against each other, their games ending in laughter as they arrayed their pieces into battle lines once more.

Tom steered Jessica into a café on Campbell Parade, the Gelato Bar, where they found a booth and sat facing each other over the table.

'Are you married, Tom?'

Tom shook his head.

'No?'

'Never.'

A dark shape appeared at their table. George, the proprietor.

'Madam, sir?'

Tom looked up with a smile. George inclined his head, just so.

'You are well, sir?'

'Yes, George, I am, and you?'

'Excellent. The city must be empty today, they are all here.'

He gestured at the people walking past his door.

Tom introduced Jessica to the old Hungarian who overdid everything and leant in to take her hand.

'Coffee, Jess?' George can do a Viennese with real cream.'

George raised an eyebrow in gracious acceptance of Tom's request, moved away to the counter and returned with two small strudels on an intricately engraved brass dish, both dusted with fine sugar and just off warm to the touch.

He placed the dish on the table and returned to the counter to rattle his cups and spoons as a strong aroma of coffee spread through the café. A couple on their way out blocked a middle-aged man at the door who stepped back to let them pass.

The coffee arrived with a small bowl of brown sugar crystals and a ceramic jar of thickened cream.

'Dollops, please,' said Tom. 'Leave no waste.'

'I didn't think you could get good coffee anywhere.'

Tom lifted his cup and took an appreciative sip.

'I know who he gets his beans from.'

George came by a minute or two later and with a courtly flourish positioned two more sweetmeats on the brass dish before taking their empty cups away.

Later that evening as he lay in bed with his wife of fifty years, George mentioned that his friend had visited again.

'Alone?'

'No, with a much younger woman.'

'Pretty?'

'Something more than that.'

'He is a lucky devil then, isn't he, Georgie?'

George leant over and breathed into his wife's ear.

'My strudels are all a man needs when he is in the company of a beautiful woman. Luck and the devil play no part, my little szirom.'

A soft laugh from the pillow beside him.

Tom had booked two rooms in a harbourside hotel earlier in the day, asking if dinner could be served on the balcony. The receptionist dithered on the phone, not ready to accommodate the request, suggesting that a meal in the dining room might be best.

'The balcony is not suitable for dinner, sir,' he said, 'the kitchen is too far from the rooms.'

'How about something cold?'

The receptionist sighed, and Tom heard him walk away, open a door then close it. Seconds later he heard him return and pick up the phone.

'Sir?'

'Yes? Any luck?'

'It is not outside our capabilities to provide you with a selection of cold cheeses and meats.'

'Wine?'

'A Penfold's table wine is recommended.'

'Oysters, will you have any, fresh?'

A pause.

'Yes, sir, I believe so.'

'A dozen, please.'

Tom heard the scratch of pen on paper.

'This will be for Mr Johnson and *Mrs* Stelson?'

'Yes.'

'And you will be paying for both the rooms and dinner?'

'Yes.'

'Is there anything else you would like us to do for you, and *Mrs* Stelson?'

'Flowers?'

'Flowers. Which room? ... Sir?'

'Both.'

Another scratch.

'Will that be all, sir?'

'Anything in the way of Champagne?'

'Only if the King of England were visiting, Mr Johnson.'

They travelled from Bondi to the city by bus then onto Milson's Point by train, walking the last few hundred yards from the station to the hotel in a softening light, past a group of boys playing cricket on the road.

The receptionist was Mr Towars, who signed them in and handed Tom the room keys. Towars was an extremely tall, thin man who looked as if he had received a blow on the side of his chin so severe it had dislocated the bottom half of his jaw from the top.

'Left at the top of the stairs, rooms five and six, bathroom at the end of the hall.'

He smiled, all teeth. 'There is an adjoining door to the rooms but it's locked.'

Tom gave one of the room keys to Jessica and lifted their bags.

'We'll be right, thanks.'

The adjoining rooms shared a balcony overlooking a small inner-harbour cove with a collection of upturned dories lying along the sand at the high-water mark. A half-cabin cruiser was moored offshore, two men fishing from the stern.

Jessica found Tom on the balcony, sitting on a chair with his feet on the wooden rail, watching the harbour traffic.

The northern span of Harbour Bridge filled the sky to their right and sailing skiffs flew on its inkblack shadow, their spinnakers ballooned tight by the hard northwesterly.

'Drink before dinner?'

'Please.'

Tom went downstairs to find the bar crowded and loud with the conversation and laughter of more than a dozen men. The lone barman was a man of about sixty working double-handed, filling an order for six glasses from a single beer tap. He glanced up at Tom as he switched a full glass for an empty one.

'Yeah, mate?'

'Vodka, soda …'

'Hang on.'

Tom watched him draw the last glass, place it on the bar with the others, take some money from a florid-faced man, register the sale, sort the change and hand it back. He looked at Tom.

'… and?'

'Ice, plus a schooner of your best beer. I've already ordered a bottle of wine.'

'You got a room?'

'Yep.'

'Number?'

'Six.'

'I'll get Sticks to bring it up from the cellar.'

'Sticks?'

'The bloke on the desk, legs like tomato stakes.'

An old man sitting nearby cackled, and squinted over at Tom.

'Not local, are ya mate?'

'No.'

'Where ya from then?'

'All over, how about you?'

'Born down the road.'

'Born on the road, I heard,' said the barman to Tom as he put the drinks on the bar. 'Mum was caught short getting into the taxi on her way to the hospital and he landed head first on the bitumen.'

'Beats being raised in Queensland, Ted, you blokes need ten fingers to count to five.'

Jessica was sitting on the balcony reading when Tom returned. He put the drinks on the table and arranged his chair for a better view of the harbour before sitting down. Jessica put her book aside and they lifted their glasses, softly clinking them together.

A green-hulled ferry motored through the skiffs, giving a few short blasts of its whistle to clear a passage. A pool of lamplight flickered from a headland about a hundred yards away, and from time to time cheers and loud yahooing reached them through the warm evening air.

Tom got up to answer the door and admit a waiter pushing a cloth-covered trolley.

'We're outside.'

The waiter, a tall youth with an insolent flop of dark hair shadowing his forehead, pushed his trolley through to the balcony and produced a large plate of mixed cheeses and sliced meats, one small jar of chutney, another of pickled herring, two sets of napkin-wrapped cutlery, a plate of water biscuits, two white bread dishes, a large metal dish of shelled oysters with wedges of lemon and ice slivers decorating the edges and finally, from the bottom shelf of his trolley, the bottle of wine, ice bucket and two glasses. Tom slipped a few coins into his hand at the door.

Jessica declined the oysters with a small shudder.

'You don't like them?'

'Hate them, the thought of swallowing one …'

Jessica watched as Tom emptied an oyster into his mouth before reaching for another. She slowly unwrapped her cutlery, spread the napkin across her lap, took a biscuit and wedge of cheese from the plate and dipped her knife into the chutney jar.

'My father liked them with Worcestershire sauce and bacon.'

Tom reached for his third.

'Heresy. Men have been shot for less.'

Jessica bit into the biscuit carefully. Tom took another oyster from the dish as a kookaburra sounded from a nearby tree.

'I've seen Joy put one in her vodka.'

'A friend of yours? Good for her.'

Jessica laughed.

Dinner took another hour before Tom went into the

bedroom to ring for someone to clear away the dishes. He came back, stood by the rail and lit up a cigarette.

The lightless void of a blacked-out warship slid past the cove entrance, extinguishing all the lights across the harbour and making the darkness complete.

'How much longer are you going to be at sea, Tom?'

Tom flicked the cigarette away and sat down. He reached over the table, touched the back of her hand with his fingers and let them rest there.

'Until I find something better to do.'

A knock on the door.

The dark-haired waiter cleared the table onto his tray, bundled the napkins, gave the table a wipe and resettled the half-empty bottle and glasses. As he worked they could hear the hoots and whistles from down in the headland scrub.

'What's all the noise?' Tom asked.

The waiter set the edge of his tray on the table and looked at his watch.

'Local Saturday night two-up, I'll be down there in fifteen minutes.'

He let himself out as more cheers rose from the headland.

Jessica reached across the table to touch Tom's hand.

'We're not going to be tempted, are we?'

They looked at each other as a lone victory cry floated up from the scrub.

'No,' said Tom.

A Change of Plan

Sydney, 1946

Bingham was preoccupied when Jessica called his office and although courteous as always he whittled the conversation down to two minutes before attempting to break it off. She had interrupted him.

Afterwards, she rang Maroubra.

'Mrs Baxter? My name is Jessica Hartnell. Ed gave me this number. I hope you don't mind me calling?'

'You're Jess? The nurse? He's not home, I'm afraid, he's away most of the time now.'

'Can I leave a number with you? I'm going down to Melbourne.'

Jessica's suitcase was too heavy for her to lift into the boot of the taxi without the driver's help. Before climbing into the car she looked up to wave at the blurred face watching her from an upper window.

She gave the driver instructions to take her to Central Station and gazed out of the taxi window at the harbour as they travelled over the bridge, its coves and islands, the guardian headlands that allowed passage to the ocean.

Tom out there somewhere.

The Lad from Beaumaris

Melbourne, 1947

When the air lost its heat in the afternoons and a breeze swept in from the sea, Jessica sometimes walked down to the beach from her parents' home to stand in the cool billows of air. Later, she would slowly pick her way through the beached sea wrack in bare feet, pushing the smaller pieces of timber away, exposing what might lie beneath.

Rodney Beecham stopped by the Sandringham Hotel after spending an hour with a client who couldn't pay the next instalment on a second hand Hillman Minx Beecham had sold him three months previously. The tedious negotiation had wearied him; he didn't want the car back and the oaf he was dealing with knew it. Beecham accepted the inevitable and settled for less. No slow talker himself he was disappointed at being out of pocket.

He took his drink from the crowded public bar to the quieter lobby lounge where he could sit by the tall arched windows looking over the promenade to the calm sea of Port Phillip.

A young woman was sitting alone reading the newspaper, and glanced up as Beecham walked past her chair. He smiled but she had already turned back to her paper.

She was reading the classified section of the Melbourne Herald: second hand car sales. Beecham's Superior Used Vehicles had three cars advertised today. Low mileage, six-month guarantee, special terms.

He left his business card with Erica, the receptionist, and asked if she could pass it over to the young lady before she left. A subtler approach sometimes bore him custom.

Two days later a woman rang his office, gave her name as Jessica Hartnell and asked to speak to Mr Rodney Beecham.

'You've got him, Miss Hartnell, can I call you that?'

'Jessica is fine.'

'Jessica it is. Call me Rod. You're interested in a car?'

'Yes.'

Why don't you call by today and I can show you what's in the yard. Do you have a trade?'

'No, I've come down from Sydney by train.'

Rod Beecham never hesitated when presented with an

opportunity and quickly glanced at his desk calendar.

'Why don't I pick you up tomorrow morning, bring you out and show you what's for sale? I have a few used American models, not nearly as expensive as you'd buy closer to town.'

Jessica hesitated.

'Where are you?'

'Moorabbin.'

'Can I get a bus from Mentone?'

'Sure, it takes half an hour each way, I'm about two hundred yards from the bus stop.'

'Then I'll come by bus.'

'Only one problem,' said Beecham inventively, 'that particular bus only runs early in the morning and late in the afternoon.'

He showed up at 9am in a loudly muttering convertible roadster, top down, and waited for Jessica to come out of the front gate before lifting himself from his seat, vaulting his legs over the side and jogging around the car to open the door for her. Jessica had never travelled in a car so low to the ground, and after carefully negotiating herself into the figure-hugging seat they travelled to Beecham's Superior Used Vehicles: a half-acre lot in a featureless street of like car yards and tin-fronted panel beating shops. A large truck following them bleated as Beecham slowed before turning into the car yard.

Beecham's office was a caravan installed behind five rows of second hand vehicles, and after helping Jessica out he drove the roadster onto a small display ramp at the front of the yard, giving the bonnet a couple of buffs with a soft chamois he kept in his coat pocket before stepping back down.

Beecham was a sparsely built man with little difference between the width of his shoulders and the narrowness of his waist. He wore a small black moustache and a good crest of black hair on his forehead with just a little too much oil; his suit was a month late for dry-cleaning but his shoes gleamed as highly as the roadster's paintwork.

He unlocked his office door and held the door open for Jessica.

At first glance everything dismayed her. The dusty table and two kitchen chairs squeezed between his desk and a refrigerator, old advertising hoardings stacked against the walls, the floor not swept for weeks and peppered with mice droppings.

Beecham brushed his hand over the table and pulled out a chair for Jessica, then broke into a spasm of hard coughing. He gestured at Jessica to sit down as he turned away, dug into his trouser pocket and pulled out a folded handkerchief.

When his coughing didn't cease Jessica stepped across to the small sink in the corner of the van, found a stained teacup and half-filled it with water. Beecham accepted it, gasping, and took a long swallow. He waited a moment to catch his breath.

'Sorry about that, lifelong condition I'm afraid.'

The harshness in his breathing continued to break out into small, wet coughs and Jessica waited quietly until he recovered.

Beecham refolded the handkerchief and put it back into his pocket, but not before Jessica saw the red leavings of his prolonged coughing.

He took a small bottle from his trouser pocket, unscrewed the lid and took a nip.

'The quack reckons a quarter of a teaspoon only,' he grinned as he screwed it shut, 'any more and I'll be arrested for me own murder.'

Beecham peered through the caravan door as a man walked into the yard and headed straight for a Vauxhall in the front row, stooping at the driver's window.

'Excellent,' Beecham said, lively again, 'he's back.'

He looked at Jess.

'Want to help sell a car?'

'How?'

'Come to the door in five minutes and look at your watch. I'm going to tell him that's the car you want too.'

Jessica stepped over to the van window.

'I wasn't thinking of a *black* car.'

'I'll tell him you're shipping it to Sydney, black's the fashion up there.'

He took the steps down two at a time.

Beecham sold her a Ford Prefect two days later, fully discounted, and talked about moving west, to Adelaide.

'They all want American cars. I'll make a fortune!'

The Fifth Floor

Moscow, 1945

The entire length of the examining room on floor five was taken up with six oak tables, one for every inhabited continent: Asia, Africa, North America, South America, Europe and Australia, and at the end of each table an NKGB officer manned his supervisor's pulpit.

Diplomatic mail was delivered throughout the day in canvas sacks which were emptied onto the tables, turned inside out and shaken empty to the supervisor's satisfaction before being folded and taken away. Nobody spoke; the only noise was the heavy percussion of the soldiers' boots as they moved about the room. The examiners, all women, stood back and watched their work accumulate.

When the delivery was complete and the soldiers had left the room, the door was locked from the outside. The supervisors then instructed their examiners to open the unloaded material, the envelopes, pouches and packages. Tobacco tins with their lids soldered down, sealed cigarette packets. The security flotsam of a foreign office abandoned or suspected. Courier parcels dropped into safe mailboxes and sent on to

Russia. A greasy piece of paper among them, densely writ, roughly folded, poked into an envelope and hidden in a pocket until a trusted courier arrived. Information subtly gained a hundred times a day in a hundred cities, some carried to Russia in diplomatic suitcases, one for the diplomat and one for his wife. This being the slowest and least favoured route used by embassies to transfer information, but one made necessary by the NKGB's overriding suspicion that their incoming cables were being intercepted.

Marta Shubin raised her hand.

She had used pinch pliers to cut open the chain on a secured leather pouch before emptying its contents onto her table. Film canisters had rattled out and rolled away in all directions. Marta gathered them in and counted fourteen. The tally slip folded inside the pouch listed fifteen.

The supervisor leaned over his pulpit, disapproval on his face.

'Speak.'

'I have a discrepancy.'

'Keep your hands on the table.'

The NKGB officer was a barnyard pig of a man, a bumpkin who chewed peppermints throughout the day and stared at the women. Marta stood facing her table and waited for him to leave his perch. She could smell his breath as he moved closer, then the insistent pressure of his body as he looked over her shoulder, aroused by a widow of forty-eight who wore a stained smock and blunt work boots, her grey hair tied into a bun.

He moved to her side and counted through the canisters with his thick fingers, then picked up the tally slip and peered at it closely. He spoke to Marta without looking at her.

'A discrepancy of one?'

'Yes.'

He took the pencil stub from his jacket pocket, made a note on the tally slip then gave it to Marta, who put everything back into the pouch and placed it into a bin with other material that needed further processing.

Weeks passed before the pouch was re-opened, the fourteen films developed and the sheaf of coded messages taken to the cryptographers' rooms where they were tagged and placed on a shelf to be dealt with in turn.

The exposed films and tally slip were archived, the bumpkin's note unread.

Months passed, nothing was done because there was too much to be done; the material that needed deciphering in Moscow was now being measured in bales and weighed in hundredweights.

A follow-up cable sent from the Russian Embassy in Canberra asked Moscow, again, if it could confirm receipt of a high-grade message sent via Hong Kong. This second request unloosed a large and un-coordinated number of demands and follow-ups from several Moscow departments. They wanted courier shipment dates, routes used and the names of all those who had either handled the message pouch or assisted in its passage. They demanded copies of everything.

Canberra replied immediately: impossible, some of the original documents had been kept, others burned; they asked Moscow to confirm that the number of items received was the same as on the tally slip.

There was a further delay while Moscow searched their card indexes and another month before two women working in the sombre quiet of an archive tunnel found a cardboard box containing the pouch.

When all the material had been collected, Marta Shubin was found and arrested, her two-room apartment in Moscow dismantled and searched before she was taken away and interrogated in Lubyanka Prison. During the weeks she was imprisoned Marta wondered whether the whimpering she could hear at night, the soft, beseeching calls for help that seeped from somewhere along the stone corridor, came from a woman she knew who had worked at another table.

The Russian Embassy in Australia confirmed that the missing film contained a message that John Bingham's Gawler Station was intercepting the embassy's cables and feeding them to Meredith Gardner's rooms in Virginia where they were being decrypted. The information had been provided by the agent, Otto.

The pouch had been carried to Hong Kong on the merchant ship SS *Cycle*; the courier who brought it onboard in Sydney was code-named Balanchine.

Catastrophe

Kowloon, 1947

Val Johanssen plundered Kowloon for its street food and was known for his generosity as he tramped and snuffled a vast passage through the nighttime stalls. The women pressed hot morsels on him as he waded through the crowds, stopping to peer into their saucepans and inhale the aromas. They could not feed him enough for his coins. The children trailing him laughed at his great white strangeness and the way his massive rump wobbled and swayed in his clothes. The spiced air of Kowloon's food markets always aroused his hunger; every cooking pan he bent over speckled his face with fine spats of cooking oil and bathed him in a fog of spices.

Johanssen took a rear table at their usual place, an open-fronted restaurant where they could take an hour to eat as they watched Hong Kong pass by. He ordered a cold beer and waited for Rostov to appear out of the crowds. This was their table when the *Cycle* was in port, but the Russian appeared neither hungry nor thirsty when he arrived. Johanssen thought he looked hunted, and weary.

Rostov walked through the tables quickly, pulled his

chair out with a harsh scrape and sat down, breathing deeply, glancing back at the way he had come.

Johanssen sat forward.

'Oskar.'

Rostov turned his head.

'Good evening to you.'

Rostov shook his head and looked away.

'There has been a catastrophe.'

Johanssen looked around the restaurant, then to the street outside. He shrugged.

'This is Hong Kong, everything is exaggerated.'

A waiter walked through the tables carrying a large dish of deep-fried shrimp and Johanssen eyed its progress to a nearby table. He turned back to see Rostov looking at him.

'Film was found to be missing from one of your pouches, several pages of coded documents.'

Johanssen sat back.

'When?'

'Six months ago, a year.'

'And I'm told now?

Rostov stared at him.

'The courier responsible is still on your boat, Johanssen, he is still *engaged*.'

Johanssen raised both his hands, palms up.

'Nothing of that nature goes missing from my boat. Impossible! You have seen the safe, you bought it and had it installed yourself.'

'He picked the lock.'

Johanssen laughed.

'The safe is in my cabin behind the bridge. They must be wrong, Oskar, it was lost elsewhere, surely.'

'He picked the lock on the pouch, you fool, before he brought it onboard.'

Rostov had a brittle look about him, as though the night air was making him ill. He looked around, distracted by a sudden uproar outside the restaurant and the shrill voices of two women. He leaned across the table, closer to Johanssen.

'He is finished.'

A boy sidled over to the table, the owner's son, Terrence.

'Food now? You eat now?'

Johanssen waved him away.

'Do you see his mail?'

'Yes.'

'Who does he write to?'

'A woman.'

'Write down what you know.'

Johanssen beckoned the boy back.

'Pencil ... pencil and paper,' he raised a palm and wrote on it with his finger.

'You want to pay for food now?'

'Later, pencil and paper now. Kuai! Quick, Terrence, quickly.'

The boy came over with a pencil and paper and two glasses of water.

'You eat now?'

Johanssen looked at him and smiled.

'Soon, come back soon.'

He wrote a few lines and handed the scrap of paper to Rostov.

'A nurse?'

'The hospital is visible from the harbour, no doubt he waves at her every time he sails past.'

Rostov took his glass and drained it, then sat for a moment breathing unevenly. Johanssen saw the skin around his eyes was dark from bruising, and the man looked tired beyond sleep.

'How long has he been writing to her?'

Johanssen spread his hands.

'You expect me to know too much, Oskar. I don't know.

Rostov persisted.

'A year?'

'Possibly more.'

'Packages, did he ever send her one?'

'The ship's mail is only for letters.'

'Where is he now?'

'On watch till midnight.'

The Russian took a handkerchief from his pocket and swabbed at his face and chin.

'Put him off the boat; if he objects use what men you need, but get him off.'

'Tonight?'

'Give him time to pack; don't walk to the dockyard gate with him.'

'This business between us … what happens to that?'

'It is finished.'

Johanssen sat back, all thought of food forgotten.

'What did the documents say, for God's sake, Oskar?'

Rostov watched a youth moving past with the crowds; he was barking at the people who parted around him and grasping at himself obscenely.

'How am I to know? Approvals for promotion, pay rise requests for the cipher clerks, everything is sent.'

He looked steadily at Johanssen: 'Everything.'

'Am I implicated, Oskar? Is that why you're here?'

Rostov looked at Johanssen with more exhaustion than anger and rose to his feet. He put a hand on Johanssen's forearm.

'Be thankful you are at sea more than you are on land, Val. Put him off the boat, tonight.'

Johanssen always had trouble finding a rickshaw driver willing to transport his weight for even small distances and tonight he tramped a desperate mile through Kowloon's more wretched streets before one stopped to pick him up, a brown whippet of a man with no teeth and a long oiled rope of knotted hair hanging down his back. He pulled the fat man to his boat before disappearing into the darkness outside the dock gates. Johanssen slowly laboured up the ship's gangway, resting every second step; all of this, no dinner, and now he was to lose another friend.

Kowloon Town

Tom's watch had changed an hour earlier. Johanssen sent one of the crew down to wake him and get him up to the bridge with all his gear. Tom was a capable seaman and popular among the crew; his absence the next morning would take some explaining.

Tom walked onto the bridge dishevelled, fully awake and fired up. He dumped his seabag on the floor and ignored the mug of tea Johanssen had waiting for him.

'Why am I out of a job, Val? Why the bum's rush in the middle of the night?'

'I'm sorry, Tom, the decision was made for me. You must leave the ship.'

'Must I, Val? And why tonight? What's the time, one o'clock? Why the hurry to get me off?'

'I ... was instructed.'

'Well it wasn't a message over the ship's fucking phone: I've been on duty all night. Someone has had a word in your ear ashore, haven't they?'

Tom wanted to punch his skipper, hard, right into that suet bag of a stomach. Rupture something. He took out a cigarette and lit it, blew smoke over the rail and swore.

'This is very inconvenient, Skipper. I'll let you know that much. What about my pay?'

Johanssen handed him an envelope and Tom grabbed up his bag before abruptly turning his back and making for the gangway. Nobody was about and Kowloon Town lay dark and silent under its customary haze of woodsmoke and wet fog. He clattered down the gangplank before Johanssen, labouring after him, could catch up and was soon lost in the shadows beyond the dockyard gates. Johanssen, apprehensive, waited for five minutes, squinting into the darkness, listening for any commotion.

Tom walked along the deserted waterfront road until he rounded a corner and came upon a sampan fleet moored in the middle of a small cove, a couple with their braziers lit. He put his seabag in the shadow of a wall and took out a cigarette.

Keyannik came for Tom as he was standing on the edge of the sea wall, smoking and looking out across the harbour.

Tom heard the soft step and turned as Keyannik aimed the knife at his right kidney with one hand and reached for his coat collar with the other. Tom took an instinctive step backwards into the void, grabbing at

Keyannik's sleeve. They both fell into the black water, a fetid brew of sewage and engine oil almost too thick to make a sound as it received them.

Keyannik broke the surface with a gasp and scrabbled at the sea wall to find a grip, his eyes burning from the oil. He gagged on some of the scum he had swallowed and peered around in the dark.

Tom had gone, and the only way out was a landing under a distant lamplight. Keyannik began to inch along the slimy rampart of stones hand over hand, gaining occasional purchase with his feet.

Shuǐ Guǐ

Chen climbed from his hammock and walked out onto the deck after being roused from sleep by the boat's unusual motion. The sea was calm and there were murmurs of conversation and slow laughter from the gamblers nearby; a freighter's wash in this sheltered cove would have everybody cursing. Chen walked up to the bow to check his mooring line and saw the head of an octopus, a tentacle grasping the rope.

Chen's instinct was to yell at the shuǐ guǐ and frighten it back underwater.

'US dollars,' Tom called from the water, and gave the rope another sharp tug.

Chen appraised what little he could see of the man, then picked up a small bamboo ladder and slid it over the side. Once on deck, Tom negotiated a ride back to the quayside where he slipped ashore to search among the shadows for his seabag. There was no sign of Keyannik, no dropped knife. His bag was where he had left it.

The trip across the harbour to Hong Kong Island took half an hour in a sea made choppy by a damp easterly breeze and Tom shivered his way through the crossing perched up on the sampan's bow like an oversized cormorant.

The few people about early that morning took only a passing interest in the bedraggled seaman as he walked along the Wanchai waterfront, eager to be off the street and into the mission.

The Wanchai Seaman's Mission stood as white and grand as any colonial hotel in Hong Kong, an elegant five storied wedding cake of stonemasonry with deep upper-storey verandahs overlooking Gloucester Road and the harbour towards Kowloon. Tom entered by the front door only to be stopped by an elderly Chinese woman cleaning the floor; she looked at his footprints and general appearance with great dismay, pointed back outside and gestured that he should go around the building.

'Other door,' she said, 'round there.'

Tom made his way to a white-painted wooden door where a pair of unsmiling Chinese eyes looked at him through a peephole before sliding it shut with a snap. Tom knocked on the door and waited, the slot opened again and the same two eyes looked at him with the same indifference. Tom raised a hand up to slot level and waved an American dollar.

After signing a register, he was led to the showers and changing room. 'Fi' minutes,' he was told by an attendant, 'then you go.' About a dozen men stood around the walls, older men, some taking their clothes off, others dressing. Nobody spoke.

His clothes were ruined by the oil and sewage, only the boots were wearable.

Tom stripped, threw the clothes into a waste bin and walked into the shower room where he was given a clean towel and dry soap. The showers were short and hot.

He breakfasted in a large lower-floor room filled with benches and tables and the comings and goings of dozens of men.

The women serving the food were efficient, and watchful of the vagrant seamen who filed past them with their plates lifted, men whose gaze was only for the size of the portions being dealt.

Tom's interview followed breakfast; a melancholy ten minutes with Superintendent William Haller, who told him he had lost his Hong Kong family in the first days of the Japanese invasion. Tom's name was added to the available seamen list posted onto the hallway noticeboard and he came by before dinner to look for any familiar names without success.

Tom hadn't been on a ship hire queue for over five years. He had three hundred US dollars in his pocket and no papers from his years on the *Cycle*. He was down to his last change of clothing and his wet boots left imprints on the hallway floorboards as he walked outside to have a smoke and look at the harbour traffic.

Australia looked years away.

The Black Cat Nightclub

Ambon, 1947

A black man carrying two skin-topped native drums and wearing dungarees, boots and a stained white singlet stepped from the crowded floor onto a small stage in the corner of the room. He placed his drums on the boards before walking off the stage in the direction of the bar and returning with a three-legged stool and small shot glass.

The drummer tossed back his liquor, sat down behind the drums and began to beat a soft rhythmic pattern on the skins with his fingertips, shifting around on the stool to get comfortable. Somebody on the floor shouted for quiet, another whistled loudly and the drummer slowly filled the room with a deep and insistent primitive rhythm.

A nuggety little sailor climbed up to the stage, turned to the crowd and hoisted his beer mug. His crewmates in the booths cheered as he finished his pint and shouted more loudly still when he pulled a silver harmonica from his back trouser pocket.

The sailor turned to the perspiring drummer who flashed him a smile without interrupting the frenzied movements of his hands on the skins, looped two fingers through the mug handle, brought it up to the side of his mouth, placed the harmonica against his lips and blew a long, amplified blues note into the room before driving into the drummer's rhythm and matching his pace.

The uproar increased, beer flying in the booths as men stood and pounded their mugs on the tables, one or two throwing their heads back and howling like dogs. Two men danced up to the small stage, reeling this way and that, doubly drunk. One earned a roar of appreciation when he slipped on the floor and fell sprawling, another when someone threw a bottle at his head.

Malay women refilled beer mugs and liquor glasses as the crowd pressed up to the bar clamouring for more, demanding one drink for the trip back to their booth and another for when they regained their seat. They bumped and shoved their way past each other, rarely spilling a drop.

A couple of younger girls worked the room mopping up spilled liquor and collecting empty glasses; all wearing soiled cheongsams and at the mercy of the strong, drunken hands that occasionally grasped at them. Ernesto, the club owner, sat at the far end of the bar playing backgammon with a US petty officer whose face matched Abraham Lincoln's for its sourness of temperament.

Tom bought a drink, found a wall for his back and

settled in for another night in the wilderness that was Ambon; a trading settlement since the days of the Dutch East India Company now beset with deserters, gold miners, Allied seaman, looters and US marines on their way home from the Philippines. The room had an unlawful quality, the men lost to drunken revelry.

He watched as one of the girls was seized by her arm and drawn into a crowded booth. Her cries made no sound in the cacophony as she was dragged over the table, unsettling the drinks. She was on her back, pushing away the hands that squeezed her breasts, trying to kick away others that grasped her legs and thighs.

A heavily tattooed Islander took the girl by her hair and pulled her towards him, swatting at the other hands. He ripped the front of her cheongsam away and lowered his mouth to one of her nipples while kneading her other breast with his massive hand. His companions goaded him on, howling their approval.

Tom put his beer on the floor and pushed his way over to the booth. He leaned in through the men and in one quick movement took the Maori's shirt with his left hand and pulled his head upright, away from the girl, before jerking the man's head into a short sharp punch from his right hand. The Maori put a hand to his face, pulled it away and saw blood. Bellowing like a steer he came out of the booth arm over arm, pushing the others aside. The girl slid onto a seat and tried to cover herself as the Maori's companions followed the fight onto the floor.

A tight ring formed around the two men as they brawled, Tom spending most of the time on his back trying to deflect the heavier man's blows with his arms. He reached up after one swing, grasped the big man by his shirt collar and jerked his face down hard onto the bone of his own forehead. A couple of the onlookers groaned at the sound and the Maori rolled away as blood leapt from the cuts above his eyes. Ernesto sent over a thick-necked bouncer who waded through the mob, separated the two fighters and pushed Tom towards the door.

Tom, stunned and disorientated, walked out of the bar and onto the street through two military policemen who were using their truncheons to bang a couple of shouting heads into submission. Another fight had spilled from the bar and grown into a scattered free-for-all on the street outside. The police took one look at Tom as he passed between them, judged him fairly dealt with and carried on with their work.

Tom made his way towards the waterfront. The only lights visible were those of the *Crusader*'s gantries; the big ship would have an aid station. Halfway to the dock he stopped to lean against a warehouse wall and slid slowly to the ground.

Reunion

Captain Mick Spryce, Lieutenant Ed Baxter and Engineer Keith Role were standing in the stern of the *Crusader*, leaning over the rail and looking down at a length of rope that was slowly drifting with the current from beneath the hull.

'What miserable bastard,' muttered Role, 'would leave a hundred feet of loose fucken hawser in the drink?'

The outer harbour at Ambon was calm, the water reflecting occasional flashes of sunlight into the men's unguarded eyes.

'Who's going down?' Spryce asked. 'It can't be that hard.'

'Not me, the needlefish up here are worse than piranha.'

'Ed?'

Baxter leant over a little more and craned his head to get a clearer view.

'Someone's going to have to go around and see if there's any more on the other side.'

Spryce turned to Role.

'Away you go, Keith, it's only three-quarters of a mile there and back.'

Role departed a little sluggishly; he would have preferred staying in the sunshine to watch the proceedings rather than getting involved.

'Hope you can hold your breath, Ed, there's an acre of barnacles for that thing to be trapped around.'

Spryce had a man throw a cargo net over the side of the boat and Ed climbed down to the water naked with most of the crew hanging over the rail whistling and catcalling. Role joined them after finishing his tour and poked his head over the side waiting for Ed to reach the water.

'Hey, Ed!' he called in a booming voice that could be heard over everybody else's racket. 'Don't let one of those little needlefish slip up the eye of your old feller.'

'Or that big white arse,' shouted another.

Later that evening, long after the *Crusader* had docked and seen half its crew go ashore, Baxter was rostered on as the watch officer and stationed at the head of the gangway with crewman Jack Mayes, an old friend from Bondi. They were watching two men proceeding very slowly from the distant dock gates towards the gangway, both in some disorder, and as they drew closer to the boat, Ed could see that one man was supporting nearly all the weight of the other on his shoulder.

When they reached the top of the gangway, Ed stepped over and looked into Tom's semi-conscious face; he had a large, multi-coloured bruise on his forehead and blood was running out of his hair onto his shirt which had been torn open and smeared with beer and dirt from the barroom floor. There was more blood on his singlet and a couple of vivid welts on his neck.

The man carrying him had also been involved in some sport and could only look at Baxter out of one eye. He shifted Tom's unresponsive weight on his shoulder.

'Sorry, Skipper, bit of a mess.'

'Name?'

'Tommy Keane, able seaman.'

Keane straightened himself up under Baxter's glare and managed a crooked smile.

'Someone didn't like him.'

'What is he doing on my ship?' Baxter nodded at the semi-conscious man.

'He's not too well, Boss, might need to see the nurse.'

'Jack,' Baxter said as he stepped away from the two men, 'take this bloke below, will you? He's making a mess of the deck.'

Mayes helped Tom down to the sickbay as Ed slowly and judiciously examined Keane from head to foot.

'What are you doing coming back to the ship out of dress, Able Seaman Keane? Where's your cap?'

Keane shrugged.

'Lost ashore, sir, bit of a panic.'

'Out of uniform, under the influence of liquor, involved in an onshore fracas on foreign soil thereby disgracing the King's uniform and disrespect to an officer. That's five infringements Able Seaman Keane.'

'Hang on, Ed, when was I disrespectful?'

Ed stepped up into Keane's face and looked into his good eye.

'By being here, Seaman, and fouling my air with your black breath. Now go below, find a clean shirt and singlet and deliver them to the bloke in sickbay.'

'The laundry's shut, Boss, where am I going to find anything this time of night?'

'Get it out of your own kit, and while you're at it get him a tie. I want him to look better going ashore tomorrow than he did coming aboard tonight, and find a laundry bag to stow his dirty kit. Now move yourself below!'

Keane threw a salute like a man killing a fly on his forehead.

'Aye sir, right away, sir, at the bloody double, sir.'

Ed remained on deck for the last half hour of his shift listening to the sounds of the town. He'd given up going ashore at night; the old Dutch settlement had a hard luck story on every corner with bearded and stinking deserters trying to cadge a lift back home to America or Australia, or half a dollar for a drink. When his relief arrived he made his way down to the sick bay.

Keane had gone back to his quarters and Tom was sitting on the only bed holding an ice pack to his forehead. He'd taken off his shirt and singlet and Ed could see the bruising that covered his upper arms and forearms.

Tom tried a smile. Ed saw a glass with a submerged pair of dentures on the bedside table. He looked back at Tom, who was exploring the inside of his mouth with his tongue.

'What were you doing, fixing cockroach races?'

'I was getting to know the chief stoker on the *Lady Ruth*.'

'You're on *that?*

'Yeah, why?'

'The engine was almost through the hull when I worked on it. You're getting too old for this kind of bullshit, Tom.'

'I'm finding that out.'

'How does the other bloke look?'

Tom put the ice pack down and examined the abrasions on his knuckles.

'As ugly as a hatful of arseholes. I just hope I didn't get these from his teeth, I'll be squeezing pus out for a week.'

Tom leant over the bed and held up Keane's white tie.

'What am I going to do with this?'

'Stick it in your pocket and use it as a bandage next time. How long have you been here?'

'I was thinking about getting married to one of the bar girls, but living with a pack of wild kids like some of the deadbeats in the hills put me off. I've signed up on the *Ruth*, then it's home with enough money for a start.'

A man stuck his head into the doorway and looked over at Tom.

'You all right?'

Tom nodded and the head went away. He pushed at his forehead with a finger, feeling the depth of his bruising.

'What do I look like?'

Ed laughed

'Not pretty.'

Tom ceased his probing.

'I told her that story.'

'Who? What story?'

'Jess. I told her about that day at the races.'

'How did you two meet?'

Tom poked at his bruises again.

'Any idea where she is?'

'She packed it all in and went to Melbourne.'

'Melbourne?'

'Over a year ago.'

'What's down there?'

'Her mother.'

Tom looked up.

'Mother?'

'*And* father.'

'When was it you last spoke to her?'

'Not long, the last time I was in Sydney. She said she was about to move again.'

'Where?'

'Further away, Adelaide.'

'By herself?'

Ed shrugged.

'Don't know, Tom, didn't like to ask too much. The wife thinks she's had a baby and getting as far away from everyone as she can. I didn't know you knew each other.'

'Whereabouts in Adelaide?'

'Why? You thinking of seeing her again?'

Tom reached over for the glass containing his dentures, took them out with his thumb and forefinger and clicked them into his mouth, bottom one first. He stood and pulled on Keane's singlet and shirt. Ed looked him over; Keane's shirt was tight on his shoulders

'What do you reckon,' Ed said, 'find some fresh air?'

Tom found his boots and slipped his jacket off the back of the chair. The back was scuffed and stained with liquor; he brushed some of the loose dirt off.

'The last time I looked like this was at the end of the no-holds-barred all ships in port every man for himself South West Pacific toe wrestling competition we had over in Rabaul, the one where you and me ended up in the final. In the bloody dirt!'

'I remember you tore a few toes out of alignment.'

Tom laughed.

'Didn't last too long, did you?'

'Not with your feet, you bloody ape-man.'

Ed tossed him the laundry bag Keane had left hanging on the bedstead rail.

'Stick your kit in that.'

The two men went topside and leant over the ship's rail. A strong smell of sewage hung over the water and noises were still coming from the town, foolish yelling and manic laughter.

Tom looked down into the narrow slit of black water

that writhed between the boat's hull and the stone jetty.

'Tell me, Ed, how deep were you in that stuff? I don't want to know what went on, but did you see something … not right, dangerous?'

'For me?'

'No, for Jess.'

'What's she got to worry about? All she did was pick up and deliver.'

Tom patted his pockets, searching for his smokes, found a crushed pack in his jacket and poked out a cigarette.

'I was put ashore in Kowloon in the middle of the night a while ago, no explanation, then a bloke tried to kill me.'

'Someone you know?'

'No, and he wasn't a Chinaman with a hatchet; this bloke had round eyes and his knife was aimed at my right kidney. He got very close, Ed.'

Tom looked down at the water slopping against the hull.

'I pulled him into the drink, hoping he'd take a mouthful of the stew and choke to death.'

A couple of rats crept out of the long shadows beneath them, cautious and sly they scurried and stopped, rearing up on their hind legs then slipping away with their peculiar humping run.

Tom took an almighty pull on his cigarette and flicked it away, holding the smoke in for a long time before letting it go.

'Why would someone want to kill you?'

Tom shrugged.

'I knocked off a roll of film a while ago, been carrying it around ever since.'

'People are being killed in Hong Kong every night.'

'He was waiting for me.'

'How do you know that?'

'The skipper sent me straight to him. The bloke wasn't kidding. If he's not dead I'll be looking over my shoulder for the rest of my life.'

'And you told Jess about the film?'

Tom hunted up his cigarettes, then his lighter.

'Yeah.'

'Do you still have it?'

'You're starting to sound like a cop.'

'Get rid of it, mate, my advice for nothing.'

'That'd be right, then who do I tell that I don't have it anymore?'

Ed stood back from the rail and stretched, looked at his wristwatch and grunted. Tom folded his arms on the rail top. The loops and whirls of current in the black water beneath him looked like the trails of fast swimming fish.

'The Yank, trust him do you, Ed?'

'No reason not to.'

Ed looked over at his friend.

'It wouldn't be the Yanks, Tom; they'd just stick a gun in your ribs and put their hand out for it.'

'You're not helping.'

'I'm done is what I am. All of me wants to go and lie down.'

'Can I drop something off for Jess tomorrow?'

'We're off on the tide, about midday; if it's not too big I can get it in the ship's mailbag.'

'I'll get a dalang puppet, the kids here like them.'

MI5

Roger Hollis of the British Secret Service was handed a buff-coloured envelope when he arrived late in the evening at Bombay Airport, en route from London to Australia. The handover was accomplished when a small, portly Indian man wearing a good suit and well-brushed bowler hat met him as he entered the terminal.

He remained silent as Hollis took the envelope, flipped it over and saw there was nothing written on either side. He looked at the courier.

'Who sent you?'

The courier remained silent, his hands clasped in front of him.

Hollis stood aside to allow other passengers to pass into the building, among them several of his party.

In his smallness and dumpy quiet the courier reminded Hollis of the tailors' dummies he had seen on the sidewalks of Hong Kong.

He hefted the envelope in his hand.

'This is?'

'For you.'

The courier took Hollis's passport and guided him through customs before giving it back and leading him through the terminal hall and outside into the sweltering night. They walked towards an American Dodge parked behind a line of taxis. The courier unlocked the car and Hollis climbed into the front seat, flicked on the interior lights and opened the envelope. His escort remained outside, a step or two away from the car.

Hollis stopped reading after a minute, patted his breast pocket and looked up at the finger tapping his window. The courier was holding up a pencil. When Hollis wound down the window to take it, the courier told him a taxi was waiting to take him to the British Embassy.

Hollis rubbed the pencil over a line of indentations at the end of the message, exposing the signature.

I 7 18 31 45

Otto.

Eighteen hours later Percy Sillitoe, head of the British MI5 contingent, led Roger Hollis and their small party off a commercial flight and into the blustery weather at

Canberra Airport. The sky was unsettled with vast barriers of cloud approaching from the south; the cold and blustery wind hurried them off the tarmac and into the shelter of the airport buildings.

Hollis shared a taxi with Sillitoe, and they both gazed out at the dry fields and low ranges as they travelled the couple of miles into Canberra.

'Not Cambridgeshire, is it?'

Sillitoe snorted.

Hollis pointed.

'Over there, Percy, under those two trees.'

Half a dozen kangaroos were gathered under the shade of two massive eucalypts that had survived the clearers' axes and bushfires. One tree displayed a huge breach in its side, blackened with fire that had burnt its way to the centre.

'They'll probably be wandering the corridors of Parliament House.'

Sillitoe turned to his colleague.

'Who met you at Bombay?'

Hollis let a moment pass before answering.

'Someone with information.'

Sillitoe turned back to his window.

'I've met precious few Australians, let alone their PM and external minister; what do they like to talk about?'

'Cricket. Endlessly.'

The Australians were waiting in the prime minister's anteroom when the English arrived, and after the introductions were done Hollis asked if he could borrow a typist to make an amendment to the meeting's agenda.

PM Chifley, Defense Minister Dedman, External Affairs Minister Evatt and Percy Sillitoe moved into the PM's office where they helped themselves to tea and coffee while they waited for Hollis to join them. Sillitoe took his tea to a window that overlooked the parliamentary gardens, hoping to see some wildlife. Chifley joined him.

'I must advise you, Mr Prime Minister,' Sillitoe said, 'I know very little about cricket.'

Chifley laughed and pointed to a small table covered with the day's newspapers.

'Bradman's on the front page of all of them; I'm afraid you're getting a walloping.'

When Hollis returned, he waited until everybody was seated, received a nod from Sillitoe and opened the meeting. He was a slimly built man with little authority in his voice and less in his soft mouth and apologetic posture.

He looked around the table, then turned to Prime Minister Chifley.

'Prime Minister, we have reason to believe that there has been a serious breach ... a *leak* of secret intelligence from your External Affairs Ministry.'

'*My* department?' said Evatt, who was sitting on Chifley's left and sharing an ashtray with him.

Bert Evatt, a handsome silver-haired man, was not known for smiling, even when winning an argument. He caught Hollis's eye and held it.

'You have proof?'

'A defector,' replied Hollis, 'has given us some extremely helpful information.'

'How did he learn of it?'

'In the course of his profession.'

'Profession?'

'Yes.'

Evatt ground his cigarette out in the ashtray.

'And that was good enough for MI5?'

Hollis glanced at Chifley, who seemed only marginally interested, before looking back to Evatt.

'I don't know what you're alluding to, Minister.'

Evatt opened his folder and picked through the papers. He took one sheet out, closed the folder and looked up at Hollis.

'The leaked information: your notes say it was a report of several dozen pages?'

Hollis nodded. 'It was supposed to be distributed under strictest secrecy protocols.'

Evatt put the sheet down, picked up his pen and passed it from one hand to the other. He spoke without looking up.

'Your defector, did he manage to get his hands on a copy?'

When Hollis didn't reply, Evatt glanced up at Sillitoe. Sillitoe shrugged.

'There is nothing more to tell, I'm sorry, Minister.'

Evatt put his pen down and sat back in his chair, patted his coat for his cigarettes then thought better of it.

'Mr Hollis, did you make up this fairy story in the taxi on the way here from the airport?'

Hollis smiled, just a small movement of both corners of his mouth.

'Your department is leaking, Minister, and the Crown wishes you to do something about it.'

When the anteroom doors had closed on the Englishmen's backs and the table had been cleared, Chifley stoked up his pipe and took a quick look at the newspapers.

'I don't think the English will win a test this year, we've got them bamboozled.'

'Sillitoe,' said Evatt, 'what did you make of him?'

Chifley sucked his pipe then blew a cloud of grey smoke into the room.

'Bloody silly name.'

Sillitoe waited until their taxi was halfway to the airport before turning to Hollis.

'You knew he wouldn't believe that defector business, didn't you?'

'I had no doubt.'

'Then what was the point?'

They passed the same pair of giant eucalypts, empty of life.

'Somebody has something they shouldn't.'

'Do you know who?'

'No.'

'But you have an idea?'

'Perhaps.'

Later that evening, Chifley called Eric Lloyd, director of the Commonwealth Investigation Service and told him that MI5 had the keys to John Bingham's office.

When Hollis met Lloyd in Sydney the next day he formally requested copies of all John Bingham's intercept files, case files, security clearances, personnel files, authorities to enter, legal obligations, photographs, specific watchers' notes, official diaries, letters. Contacts. Couriers. Operation overviews.

'A long list, probably a day's work for two men.'

'Mine?' asked Lloyd.

'No.'

Lloyd agreed to Hollis's request and the two men took lunch together later in the day at Tattersall's Club in Elizabeth Street, a short walk through the city to an elegant building with windows overlooking Hyde Park and a large Gothic cathedral awaiting its spires.

Lloyd surprised Hollis by challenging him to a two-lap sprint in the club's pool before lunch; an invitation diplomacy could not refuse. The club supplied them with swimming trunks so ill-fitting Hollis thought he might lose his if he let the waistband go, an over-laundered white towel and an official timekeeper who invited them onto the blocks and asked them to stand ready while he set a large clock. Three seconds later and without prior warning he blew the start whistle.

Hollis floundered home after being well-beaten by Lloyd who glided past him early in the first lap using a practised overarm and rarely breathing between strokes.

Lloyd was a regular lunchtime swimmer, and Hollis's lap times were the source of some humour in the changing room where he had to persevere with the droll mockery of a quartet of Australians changing back into their RAAF uniforms.

Their lunch table had been set up by the side of the pool beneath one of the large-paned windows looking over the canopy of Hyde Park. Lloyd smoked his way through his salmon. Hollis ate a salad and talked about golf and an older, quieter Orient.

Bingham's Office

Sydney, 1948

'Photograph all the files. Don't take anything away,' Hollis instructed his two colleagues the next morning.

'When he asks, you are to tell him that you have access to his office and files under the explicit instruction of the prime minister. If he needs more than your identification you can give him this.'

Hollis handed the senior man a sealed, crown-embossed envelope.

'But don't volunteer it.'

John Bingham had just arrived at his office and was drinking tea and reading the Sydney Morning Herald at his desk when a secretary rang to tell him there were two visitors in the outer office who had given their names but had yet to officially identify themselves. Bingham asked her to send them in.

His visitors introduced themselves as Mr Ashton and Mr Farrell, showed their identification and requested the use of his office and access to all his files.

'Do you have a safe, sir?' said Farrell. 'And these are the keys to everything? We'll be here all day I'm afraid.'

With impeccable manners, Farrell and Ashton took possession of Bingham's office for nine hours, emptied all the drawers and cabinets of their files and placed them in stacks by the table. The two agents alternated between arranging documents to be photographed and operating the camera.

Bingham retired to the outer office with his newspaper, found a vacant desk and waited for the day's usual phone calls. After an hour and a half of silence, he took his hat, left the office and rode a lift down to the ground floor where he hesitated for a moment, deciding whether to walk north to Circular Quay or east to Hyde Park.

He did neither, and after taking an aimless stroll around the lobby, took the lift back up to his temporary desk, tried Lorrimer's number without success then spent the day gazing out of the windows and reading any visitors' magazines he could find.

Home

Baxter's demobilisation papers were waiting for him when the *Crusader* arrived at Port Moresby, together with an army travel voucher that would get him home three weeks before the boat reached Sydney. His farewells were hurried and as Baxter made his way down the gangway he heard a whistle. He stopped and looked up. Keith Role was leaning over the bridge smiling down at him. Baxter waved once then hefted his seabag onto his shoulder, stepped off the gangway and walked towards the dockyard entrance, passing a line of large trucks waiting their turn at the boom gates. Baxter stopped at one and called up to the driver.

'Which way's the airport?'

'You just jumped ship?'

Baxter shook his head.

'Demobbed, going home.'

'Lucky bastard. Hop in, that's where this load's going.'

Baxter spent three hours flying to Rabaul strapped into the fuselage of an RAAF Lockheed Transport sitting alongside two Catholic missionary sisters on their way home after recuperating from three years' imprisonment in Manila. He managed a short conversation with them before the engines started, making it too noisy inside the aircraft to continue. They smiled at him with some embarrassment before looking away; many of their teeth were missing. He couldn't guess their ages.

A nun in a Redemptorist habit was waiting at Rabaul Airport to meet the returning sisters, and Baxter joined them and the other passengers as they boarded a small airport bus to town. He had half a day to spare before his connecting flight to Townsville.

Baxter sat next to the Redemptorist. She turned and smiled.

'Did you have a good flight?'

'Not too bad.' Ed nodded in the direction of the two missionaries. 'They look happy to be back on the ground.'

The nuns were craning their heads from one side of the bus to the other, trying to look out of all of the windows.

'They're looking for the children. We've planned a surprise.'

Baxter turned and looked down into her round face.

'Would you like to join us?'

'It'll be my pleasure. I'm Ed Baxter.'

'Sister Theresa. Call me Theresa.'

The bus stopped at Blanche Bay's main beach after a twenty-minute ride past the outlying villages and through the ruined town centre of Rabaul, where what remained of the Dutch colonial buildings was disappearing beneath rampant vine growth and flowering bougainvillea.

When the homecoming sisters stepped off the bus they were met with cries of joy then unrestrained weeping as the older women came up to touch and embrace them. One elderly Tualinbari woman took a sister's hand and placed it on her own lined cheek, wet with tears. The missionary bent down to listen to the old one as she spoke.

Baxter followed the sisters as they walked from the road to the beach, where a larger group of women and children were gathered around a long table spread from end to end with fruit, fish and bread. Two army deckchairs, both garlanded with flowers, had been placed in the shade of some palm trees.

Theresa reached the table, turned, looked for Baxter then pointed to a small and noisy group of children who were throwing themselves around in the shore break, tumbling in and out of the waves.

'Today is their sports day, the babies who survived. They are to have relays and three-legged races as soon as someone can get them out of the surf.'

Baxter spent half an hour watching the races and eating fruit, distracted by the sight of white water on one of the reefs that protected Rabaul Harbour. Maroubra beckoned from two thousand miles away. He hadn't caught a wave in over three years.

Baxter left the party and stretched out under a palm tree a little further along the beach; he still had his sketching pad and pencils, almost unused from the day Ellse had packed them.

'Draw some palm trees and beaches for me,' she had said, 'and none of those girlies in grass skirts.'

He heard women singing, children laughing and the breeze passing through the palms above him before falling asleep to dreams of storms and vivid flashes of light.

Baxter woke to a circle of wide-eyed brown faces peering at him. The little girls grinning from behind their hands and glancing fleetingly into his eyes, the boys jostling each other for a closer look at his drawing.

Theresa walked up and apologised for the children's behaviour.

'I'm taking them around the corner, you might find something to sketch there.'

Baxter picked up his book and pencils from the sand, got to his feet and walked down to the shoreline with Theresa and the children. To the youngsters' delight he dashed off drawings until they all had one.

'Can I sketch you?' he asked Theresa.

Theresa reached up and touched her veil.

'You wouldn't have to bother about hair or ears.'

'Where are you from, if you don't mind me asking?'

'Tumbulgum.'

'Where's that?'

'Near Uki.'

'Uki?'

'That's a town not far from Mullumbimby, but nearer to Murwillumbah.'

'We had a fellow in the Nackeroos used to be called Tumblebum, do you think he might have come from up there?'

Theresa laughed.

'That's what dad calls my brother, he was always tripping over things when he was little.'

The group walked to the end of the beach and rounded a low headland of dunes leading to a long, narrow stretch of sand littered with abandoned war machinery. A landing barge gaped at them from the shallows, its belly filled with the rusted chassis of a dozen jeeps.

They watched a couple of the children climb onto the wing of a half-submerged aircraft and wait excitedly for a good-sized wave to surge up from seaward. When the wave arrived, and a second before they were all to be swept off their feet, they jumped into the shallows, shouting with laughter.

'Most of these little ones are from fishing families who were lucky enough to have a canoe – they could escape from Rabaul to another island when the Japanese came. The others were left with their grandparents when their mothers were taken away and their fathers used as slaves, forced to clear runways and drag the artillery into the hills. Many of them died when the Japanese took all the food from their gardens.'

After telling the children to stay on the beach, Theresa led Ed into the mangroves where small collections of bones were scattered among the roots, deposited beneath the trees by a thousand tides and partly covered by a fine silt.

Theresa told Ed of the wild dogs that roamed the desolate stretches of coast, a piebald and mongrel breed of small, savage beasts that shadowed along the beaches, loping silently between sun and shade, watching for small reef sharks swimming close to the shore.

'Once a dog has bitten into the shark's tail and can hang on all the others rush in and drag it up onto the beach. They sound like hyenas when they feed.'

Ed and Theresa left the mangroves and returned to the beach. Theresa put a finger to her lips, whistled to get the children's attention and waved them back. She and Ed slowly followed, watching as the little ones ran around the headland.

Theresa pointed up into the interior where jagged mountains rose from the thick forests, capped in a tropical levanter.

'They're still up there, the wretched souls. A couple of army doctors tried to go up and help them last year but the Japanese fired at them from the crags. One of the doctors crept up close one night, just to see how many there might be. He said that in the light of the campfires they looked like Buddhist hermits, but for their rifles.

'They've been left to starve in their caves; it's too dangerous for anyone to try and help them.'

Baxter's papers got him a seat on a Lockheed Lodestar flying the six hours and five hundred miles to Townsville. Among the passengers were two brothers on their way home from Wewak. They had a plan. Mick, the youngest, did all the shouting. They'd heard about gold hidden in the hill plantations above Wewak.

'A Dutchman,' Mick yelled over the noise of the engines, 'hid his gold dust up there before he got out, and according to the bloke I bought the map from, he buried it in the local graveyard.'

Mick dug out a sheet of paper from his shirt pocket, unfolded it and traced his finger down some wayward track before jabbing the spot. He looked over at Baxter and shouted over the roar of engines.

'Right here. He's poured oil over the ground so nothin's going to grow. We'll be in and out in a week with enough gold to buy Tasmania.'

Baxter gave him a thumbs up. Mick folded the map and slid it back into his jacket pocket, giving it an optimistic pat. He looked up at Ed and winked.

Baxter flew to Rose Bay in a Sutherland Flying Boat with air conditioning, soft leather seats and a young WAAF hostess. He was one of four returning servicemen on the aircraft, the other three were infantrymen, all dirty and tired. They had carried their weapons aboard and stowed them under their seats; when the hostess asked if they could be put with the baggage in the plane's hold, one of the soldiers looked up at her with bloodshot eyes and shook his head.

'She's my second wife, we always travel together.'

'Does the first one know you're coming home?'

The soldier smiled.

'Townsville has telephones.'

The Sutherland moored after a wild harbour landing. A roaring southerly was buffeting Sydney and the harbour was alive with whitecaps and small sailing skiffs; one streaked across the plane's landing path only moments before the float on Ed's wing touched water.

Ed followed the soldiers as they walked from the plane across a mooring pontoon to a short gangway, then up onto a small wooden jetty. One wore his Thompson sub-machine gun strapped across his chest; the others had scarred Lee Enfield rifles over their shoulders. They all carried stained kitbags and their slouch hats were faded and holed beyond ruin. Ed had tried to read their unit patches during the flight without success.

The welcoming committee was a couple of jetty fishermen who both stood up from their canvas deckchairs as the soldiers walked by. One offered a word to the machine gun carrier and was rewarded with a smile and a handshake.

The soldiers took different paths when they reached the road; two walked to a nearby tram stop, the other in the direction of a white-haired man standing by the far side of New South Head Road. They looked at each other as the soldier waited for a break in the traffic.

Once he was across the road, they shook hands for a long time. The older man reached out to take the soldier's kitbag, tested it for weight and swung it up easily onto his shoulder. Ed heard a yell from further up the street and saw two small boys running towards the men, both flat out, behind them two women, one with a white handkerchief to her face.

Baxter walked through the avenue of giant Moreton Bay figs that led to Rose Bay and waited for a tram to take him to North Bondi. From there, he caught a bus to Bondi Junction then another tram through the coastal suburbs until the Pacific came into full view on the run down to Coogee Beach. The sea was throwing up tumultuous white water against the cliffs to the south and the small rock island that lay a mile offshore looked overcome. Baxter peered hard through his window, hoping to see someone out there riding the heavy seas.

He entered his house twenty minutes later, dropped his kitbag on the floor, hung his hat on the peg and emptied the currency of five nations from his pocket into a bronze change dish on the side table, an old pre-war habit. He stood quietly and waited a moment for any reaction from inside the house, then took a deep breath and filled his lungs with the air of home.

Ed walked along the hallway, through the kitchen and towards the door that led to their backyard. The kettle on the stove was seeping steam from its cap and a single teacup and saucer had been placed on the kitchen table. His hunger betrayed him and Ed couldn't resist peeking into the refrigerator on his way past.

He reached the screen door and opened it to see Ellse in the yard trussing up tomato vines in a small vegetable plot that wasn't there a year ago. He called from the top step.

'Special delivery for Mrs Baxter.'

Death of a Bomb Thrower

Sydney, 1948

The balcony of John Bingham's Point Piper apartment overlooked Lady Martins Beach, a narrow strand of golden shoreline divided by a long wooden pier. A dozen people were on the beach sunbaking or swimming, others were fishing from the pier and a few diving among the piles.

In the distance, a red speedboat roared its way towards Clark Island, throwing cascades of water off its bows as it sliced through the harbour chop. The air was calm, the sky an unblemished blue and Lorrimer could hear conversation from the balcony above him; two women planning what to wear for dinner at the Royal Sydney Golf Club.

Bingham's balcony was warm in the mid-morning sunshine, the air fresher than inside the apartment. Lorrimer leaned over the railing and watched a small boy fossicking about on the shoreline beneath him, picking up small items and putting them into his trouser pockets.

A gardener of sorts, Bingham had erected two roughly cut wooden shelves on house bricks to accommodate a set of matching ceramic pots planted with miniature trees. Lorrimer bent over and examined their gnarled limbs; they appeared to have withstood a life of torture under the binding wires. He took a few deep breaths before going back inside and closing the door.

Bingham had been dead for days.

Earlier that morning, Lorrimer had arrived at Bingham's office for a scheduled meeting and found it empty with his files stacked on the table and against the walls. Neither of the two secretaries in the outer office could help him. Bingham hadn't called in.

He rang the Gawler station and was told that two Englishmen had come to Adelaide from Sydney with the authority to examine their intercept records and question everybody, including staff on leave. They too had been unable to contact Bingham.

Lorrimer drove from the city and was parked outside Bingham's apartment block within twenty minutes. He knew there was a dead body inside the apartment before picking the lock.

Lorrimer found the old man in his bedroom.

Both Bingham's shoes were on the floor; he'd managed to untie the laces and remove them before falling back onto the bed and dying.

Bingham's arms were outflung and his mouth open in a grinning rictus, his bowels had opened and the stench in the enclosed room was overpowering.

Lorrimer walked back through the bedroom, closed the door and returned to the kitchen.

Bingham's pencil, telephone and tipsters' sheets were on the kitchen table in front of his chair, arranged on a sheet of butcher's paper. He had been listening to the races and had decorated the borders of the butcher's paper with an intricate maze of pencilled doodles. Lorrimer pictured him, pencil in one hand, the race-caller's voice insistent as the horses neared the finish and the phone at his elbow, ready for another call to his bookmaker.

Bingham had drawn a ship: a double-stack steamer under belching smoke, pennants streaming to the wind, her name etched onto the hull.

Lorrimer returned to his car, unlocked the boot and took out his camera case. He had replaced his old flash-camera with a new Leica but kept the older case with its collection of travel labels.

His pistol lay inside, wrapped in a soft chamois cloth. Lorrimer checked the remaining exposures, closed the case and walked back into the apartment block.

Someone was waiting for him.

An elderly woman; her apartment next to Bingham's. She was standing behind her half-opened door.

'Are you a doctor?'

'A friend.'

'Is he all right?'

She released her hold on the door and clasped herself in an anxious embrace. Bingham's corruption soured the air. He shook his head.

'No.'

She put a hand to her mouth, stepped back and closed her door.

Back inside the apartment Lorrimer took out his camera and worked through every room taking two exposures in each, then one of the body and two of the kitchen table. One with everything as Bingham had left it and the other with the butcher's paper missing. Lorrimer took it with him.

Vodka

The air in Bingham's office was stale. The files that had been placed against the wall by the MI5 agents had slid away onto the carpet, spilling their contents. His filing cabinet drawers were partly open and all the chairs from the meeting table had been dragged aside.

Lorrimer glanced at the windows as a sudden gust of wind smacked a sheet of rain into the corner of the building. Sydney was being lashed by a second gale in a week.

He called the Sydney Port Authority and asked for the telephone number of *Lady Ruth*'s shipping company. They were unwilling to give Lorrimer any details, eventually telling him that the boat would be sailing to Williamstown where the crew would be paid off and the ship scrapped.

Lorrimer found Bingham's quarter-full bottle of vodka in his desk drawer, carried it to the table, unscrewed the cap and took an exploratory belt, liked it enough to have another, set the bottle and cap on the table, slipped Bingham's butcher's paper from his coat pocket, unfolded it and laid it out on the glass.

Ed Baxter. Lorrimer wondered how the tough old coot was travelling.

Hocus-Pocus

The Randwick Municipal Tramway works entrance was one of several in a long road lined with the ornate brick facades of bond stores and breweries, their towering walls overshadowing the street's few shuttered houses, built with front gardens the size of two small graves and porches with space for one chair.

Ed Baxter spent his weekdays working inside a high-ceilinged iron-walled shed amidst the ceaseless roar of heavy machinery. The war had faithlessly deposited him back into the same job it had taken him from and at the same rate of pay, though his return to work had been celebrated with great affection among the younger returned soldiers, who regarded him as a war relic and worthy of constant, disrespectful banter. Baxter, happy enough to be back working with his own tools and at his old workbench, returned their youthful jibes with interest.

All the machinery powered down when the knock-off whistle sounded through the shed and the constant day-long percussion quietened into solitary bangings as the mechanics and engineers, boilermakers and apprentices packed away their tools before leaving the building and making for the gates.

Pushbike riders flickered through the walkers before powering into the afternoon stream of cars and buses. Baxter pushed his Harley Davidson out with the last and oldest of the hands. As he mounted, somebody whistled from across the street. He looked up to see George Lorrimer leaning against a car on the other side of the road.

Baxter kick-started the Harley, waited for a gap in the traffic and accelerated across, pulling in behind Lorrimer's car. He propped up the bike and climbed off to shake the American's hand.

'The people you see when you don't have a shotgun. How're you going, George?'

Baxter stooped to look through the car windows, saw nobody inside, straightened up and turned back to Lorrimer.

'Just the two of us?'

Lorrimer opened the passenger door for Baxter, walked around the car and got in the driver's side. He looked over at Ed.

'What do you say, happy to be home?'

'Is the pope a Catholic?'

Lorrimer laughed and reached into his coat pocket, took out a square of folded paper and passed it over.

'The left-hand panel.'

Baxter unfolded the sheet and held it up against the dashboard.

'Not a bad likeness. Under full steam too. Who did this?'

'Bingham.'

'Nice pencil work.'

Baxter refolded the sheet and handed it back to Lorrimer.

'When did you last talk to him, Ed?'

'The other day, I passed on a message.'

'From who?'

'A friend on the *Ruth*. He got in touch, wanted me to sound the Major out.'

'About?'

'Didn't the Major tell you?'

'No.'

'He wants to unload something.'

'Unload?'

'Sell.'

'You're being pretty tight, Ed. What does he want to sell?'

'Some film came his way.'

'Has he developed it?'

The car was getting hot as heat radiated off the dashboard. Ed rolled down his window.

'We should do this in the pub.'

'How did you get onto Bingham?'

'I called my old CO, Bill Stanner.'

A couple of men walked across the road in front of the car, squinting at Baxter and Lorrimer through the windscreen, one gave Ed a thumbs up.

'They probably think you're a walloper.'

Baxter opened his door, leaned out and looked towards the back of the car; a couple of boys were standing by his bike, attracted by the gleaming paintwork and glistening chrome. He shifted back inside and part-closed his door.

'Where's your friend now?'

'Due in Sydney tomorrow.'

'For how long?'

'A day and a night, the boat's on its way to the scrapyards.'

'Do you know where he's heading when he gets paid off?'

The bike collapsed onto its side in a splintering crash of breaking glass and protesting metal as Baxter leaned out of his door to see the two boys haring off down the road. He climbed out of the car and walked around the Harley inspecting the damage, one headlight smashed and no doubt more ruin on the underside. Lorrimer joined him on the footpath trying to look sympathetic.

'That bloody globe is going to be hard to find.'

Baxter grunted as he heaved the bike back up onto its stand; he walked around and stood looking at it with his hands on his hips, shaking his head.

'You'd have more than one wouldn't you, champ?'

Baxter wasn't amused; he squatted down and ran his fingers along the scratch lines on the bike's petrol tank.

'Six, this is the flash one for riding to work.'

'What's your friend's name, Ed?'

'Tom.'

Baxter stood and looked in the direction the boys had fled.

'Little *bastards*!'

'Tom? Is that it?'

'Tom, the bookmaker; we ran a few rings around you blokes in Rabaul once.'

Lorrimer took his hat off and wiped away the perspiration gathering on his forehead.

'I'll take you up on that beer.'

Lorrimer followed in his car as Baxter rode to the nearby Orient Hotel, crowded from the roadside to the bar doors with men waylaid as they walked home from work, their empty glasses littering the footpath. A couple turned when they heard the rumble of Ed's Harley and watched him ride past to stop a little way up the street. Lorrimer parked behind the bike and left Baxter to fight his way in and out of the hotel.

They stood on the footpath in the shade of a high brick wall that stretched the length of the block. Lorrimer examined the colour of his beer.

'What am I drinking?'

'Resch's.'

'Resch's?'

'Drink it, that's all you need to know.'

Two men walked towards them from the hotel, one short and unsteady on his feet, the other bigger, dark-skinned and wearing a weather-beaten hat on black curly hair.

The smaller man looked up and sneered at Lorrimer, then stopped and glared.

The taller man nodded to Baxter and walked on.

'Piss off, Evans,' said Baxter. 'You're a nuisance.'

The little man looked angrily at Baxter and stumped off, muttering.

'He thinks you're a cop.'

'The suit?'

'Maybe the tie.'

Lorrimer placed his glass between his feet, undid his tie, rolled it up and put it in his coat pocket.

Both men leant back against the wall, taking the occasional mouthful of beer and watching the traffic.

'Was Rabaul the last time you saw him?'

'Ambon, north of Darwin. Getting patched up in the boat's aid station after a stink onshore, and talking about getting home with enough money to settle down.'

'The film, did he say how he got it?'

'No, but he said it got him into a little trouble in Hong Kong. Ever been there, George?'

'A couple of times.'

'Then you know more about the place than I do.'

'What was the trouble?'

'A problem with his skipper, cost him his job.'

A car slowed as it passed Ed's Harley and a youth in the front passenger seat leaned out of the window and stared at the bike before the driver accelerated away.

'What boat was he on?'

'The *Cycle*.'

Ed finished his schooner.

'Adelaide, George, ever been there?'

'Is that where he's going?'

'Sounded like it.'

'Any special reason for Adelaide?'

'Remember the little nurse you paired me up with a couple of years ago?'

Lorrimer nodded.

'Did he say how they met?'

'He was a bit cagey about that.'

'Can you get a message to the boat after it leaves Sydney?'

'It'd mean a ride across to the Georges Head radio room.'

Lorrimer drank the last of his beer and put his glass on the ground by the wall. He stuck out his hand.

'I'll be in touch.'

Lorrimer watched Baxter ride into the traffic, weaving smoothly through the slower vehicles before taking on a yellow light at the second intersection in a loud blat of acceleration.

The Forklift Driver

The worst of *Ruth*'s cargo was the unused sheet iron repatriated from Bougainville and Rabaul, jagged-edged and unsteady in the nets as the ship's gantry lowered them to the dockside. The stevedores stood away from the swaying loads and leant against the warehouse walls smoking, distrustful of the old tub's chains and wary of the complaints that issued from the gantry as the structure flexed.

Keyannik quickly backed his forklift truck into the mouth of the nearest warehouse when he spotted a man standing by the boat's rail who looked to be idling but was carefully watching the gangway movement and the men standing in the shade of the warehouse wall. Any movement along the wharf turned his head.

Tom caught the forklift's movement and watched as its driver reversed into an open shed door one hundred feet away, stopping just inside.

The only thing that fitted Keyannik was his cloth cap; the lungful of oil he swallowed in Hong Kong had blistered a dead path through his body, reducing his weight by a quarter.

Tom looked away.

When Keyannik finished his shift he made his way across the city to Rostov's Potts Point apartment and left a note in his mailbox before going home to wait by the phone.

Rostov rang within the hour.

'He is back.'

'Where?'

'We are unloading his boat, the *Lady Ruth*.'

'How long is it in port?'

'One more day.'

'Then?'

'It sails for Williamstown.'

'You are sure of this?'

'I know who to ask, Oskar.'

A harsh sound from Rostov, a series of small dry barks.

'Excuse yourself from work.'

Keyannik hung up and walked out the front door. The boarding house was built on a small rise overlooking a cove west of the Harbour Bridge, its front steps catching the afternoon sunshine. Some of the boarders sprawled there, drinking beer and leaving just enough room for one person to pass through at a time.

Most were Australians, genially mocking each other in drab monotones. Many were returned servicemen, reluctant to share much more than civilities and a space on the bottom step with Keyannik. They called him Moscow, or Red Ted, and tried not to diminish him too much as he sat quietly in their midst.

When Keyannik asked them what the train fare to Melbourne might cost, one of them asked him if he was moving out.

'No, away for one week, maybe.'

The man called Terry leaned in.

'Goin' on holidays, Ted?'

Keyannik shook his head.

'No.'

'Got a job then?'

When Keyannik failed to reply, Terry winked at the other man.

'Dark horse, our Red Ted.'

A Message

At sea, 1948

Tom woke at 10.30pm when the door of the cabin he shared with the engineer opened and the radio operator beckoned him outside.

He followed the operator to his radio room, pulled on a pair of headphones and flinched at the sudden headful of roaring static. The operator pointed to the volume and wavelength knobs, held four fingers in the air, mouthed the word channel then left Tom to it and went out on deck for a smoke.

'Hello? Tom? Over … Tom?'

Baxter's voice was lost in a static burst.

'Come again.'

'Is that you, Tom?'

'Ed?'

'Yes, how're you doing?'

'Off Wilson's Promontory, good sailing.'

'When do you get to Adelaide?'

'Couple of days.'

'You'll be met ... Someone's ... *static* ... Adelaide.'

'Say again?'

'Someone ... wait for you ... Strathmore Hotel, opposite the train station.'

'Someone?'

'Buyer's man.'

'Got that.'

'He'll have a black case.'

'Got that.'

'Every day from Friday.'

'Okay.'

'What do you smoke?'

'Army Club.'

'Fill up with another type ... ask him for a light ... *static* ... Over'

'Why the rigmarole?'

'He'll take you to a house.'

'What?'

'Jessica's place, away … the city.'

'Why there? … Ed … come in.'

'Best option. I was told the Major cleared it.'

'Is she … ?'

Tom felt cold air on his back as the radio room door was opened.

'Say again?'

'Anyone else live there?'

'Everything is taken care of, the house will be empty.'

'Got to go, radio operator breathing down my neck. Thanks, Ed.'

'Watch your back, Tom. Out.'

Disembarking

During the voyage south, *Ruth*'s skipper gave instructions for everything below decks judged portable and salvageable to be boxed up and stacked on deck under tarpaulins in time for the boat's arrival in Williamstown. Tom volunteered to manage the deck operation then spent two days in the sunshine cutting stencils and marking up the boxes as the crew brought them up from the lower decks, one of them the Maori stoker he had fought with in Ambon.

Tom told him to make his pile as far away as the deck allowed, ignoring the murderous looks and blasphemy as throughout the day the Maori let drop each of his chests with a splintering crash.

The lower deck crew was paid off at midday, leaving the boat in the hands of a salvage company whose men had already started stripping out the bridge and captain's quarters. The binnacle and instrument stations were removed first, followed by the wheel and cabinet timber. Tom watched as a couple of navvies manhandled the skipper's bunk down the gangway, a teak bed made in Indochina before the war.

Tom stayed on the flybridge until he had seen all the stokers off the ship, then waited another ten minutes before collecting his pay from the skipper and going ashore.

The only other boat close by was deserted but for a long-faced watchman leaning over the rail, smoking. He looked down as Tom walked along the dock beneath him and blew a long, reflective stream of smoke into the air before flicking the butt away and spitting a gob of browned phlegm after it. He watched it fall into the water between the ship's hull and the dock's wooden piles, then hawked up another.

Melbourne was burdened beneath a mass of over-heated air that had moved in from the deserts of the northwest and been stationary over the city for three days. Tom stepped into it, invigorated and happy to be leaving the ship's confinement and the stink of the lower decks. He swung his seabag over his shoulder and strode through the yard gates.

A Landsman's Wardrobe

E ddie Mittelhausenn sat at a workbench at the back of his shop, Mittelhausenn's Menswear, The Best of Used, unpicking name tags from his new stock as he watched a man wandering among the trouser racks, wearing dungarees, boots, a jacket and carrying an old seabag. A seaman come ashore, no doubt, looking for a landsman's wardrobe.

Eddie priced his navy jacket at three shillings, the dungarees at one.

Tom bought an American-style sports jacket, a pair of trousers, repaired and clean, and a couple of shirts and ties. He asked Mittelhausenn to hold them and his bag until he returned with a suitcase. Eddie watched him disappear into the crowds of the market.

The leather dealer who sold Tom the suitcase said it had only been used on a one-way trip to Townsville by the sister of a good friend, and to prove it he showed Tom a newish Townsville Railway sticker stuck to its side. When asked how the case had got back down to Melbourne the dealer took a shilling off the fifteen, unpeeled the sticker and put it into his pocket.

The trousers felt good; they were Crusader Cloth with only a few repairs, none too visible. The jacket was snug on his shoulders.

Tom used Mittelhausenn's back room to change and transfer everything into the suitcase but his shoes. He would have liked a view of himself in a bigger mirror but was satisfied with the drape of his trousers and jacket, pleased to be wearing his street shoes which he buffed to a high shine with a singlet.

Mittelhausenn watched Tom leave the shop, drop his bag and old boots into a waste bin and turn towards the Peel Street exit.

Keyannik waited in the market doorway as Tom crossed Peel Street and walked in the direction of a tram terminus at the end of the block. Three trams were parked in the middle of the street taking passengers. Keyannik took a step off the footpath and was jolted when a taxi swept past sounding its horn.

Tom climbed into the rear door of the Spencer Street tram and took a middle seat. Keyannik followed and sat in the rear, watching the back of Tom's head through the shoulders and hats of the passengers sitting between them.

The Train from Melbourne

Melbourne, 1948

A thin, middle-aged man wearing a cloth cap and dark coat approached Tom as he walked from the street into the hall of Spencer Street Station. Tom made to walk around him when the man spoke.

'Photos? *French* girls?'

He moved to take something from his inside coat pocket but Tom was past him. The man turned and sneered at Tom's back, then scanned the crowd for another opportunity. A minute later he made a similar offer to Rostov, who hesitated just for a moment.

Tom wandered the hall end to end, a tourist examining the soaring metal structures that supported the roof, turning quickly when a clatter of pigeons sounded in a corner.

Boys loitered in wall recesses of the station, eyeing back pockets and open coats, telegraphing to each other with their pickpocket's tic-tac before slipping into the crowds. Nimble, sharp-eyed kids.

Tom knew he was being followed. Rostov unmistakable, although looking older than when Tom last saw him on the *Cycle*, and the man in a blue cap who had followed him onto the tram after almost being run over crossing Peel Street. Tom bought a ticket for the Adelaide Express before walking over to the kiosk and taking a stool at the counter.

He stayed at the kiosk for twenty minutes before getting up and passing through the ticket barrier, past a long, black locomotive butted up hard against an immense ironwood barrier. The engineer was leaning out of his cab watching the passengers go by, his back to a man shovelling coals into the flickering mouth of the train's furnace. A couple of boys stopped and shouted up to him, their words lost in the general uproar. The engineer winked at them, raised his arm and pulled the imaginary cord of a steam whistle.

The night had brought colder weather and winds that promised rain from the south.

Two schoolboys in uniforms and caps were being shepherded into their carriage by a stout, grey-haired woman wearing a long beige coat; both boys looked fearful and the younger one was crying.

Tom climbed into the last carriage and walked along its corridor until he saw a vacant seat in one of the compartments. He stepped around the occupants' legs and feet, lifted his case into the rack, took off his jacket, laid it on top of the case and sat down.

Two of the men opposite nodded at him, the other was reading a book. The men either side gave him a few inches.

Tom slept intermittently for the first three hours then got up to find the lavatory. The bowl was full and slopping its contents into a slowly moving pool on the floor. He shut the door and walked to the end of the carriage, let himself out and took a stance on the narrow coupling platform.

He saw two buildings in an open field, one a large shed with the silhouette of a man standing in its illuminated doorway, hands on hips, and inside a rearing horse with a man on either side, grasping its bridle.

A moment later the train passed through a small town and over a road crossing, its lights flashing and alarm bell clanging. One car was waiting for the train to pass and Tom glimpsed the red arc of a lit cigarette as the driver flicked it away through the half-open window.

When the train stopped at Horsham to take on coal and water Tom was the only passenger who left the carriage to walk in the rain, a fine cold mist that soaked his hair and made his cigarette hard to light. He heard a boobook's low song while he smoked, then the rustle of feathers above his head. Tom finished his cigarette, climbed back into the carriage, found his seat and waited for daylight.

The Coquette

Ina Harvey ran the desk at the Strathmore Hotel and watched as Nick Bellantoni signed himself into the register on the afternoon of 27 November. Mr S. Cramer of Melbourne. Traveller. He looked up when he had finished and smiled.

'Do you have a room that opens onto the front balcony?'

Bellantoni had a mouthful of very good teeth and Ina Harvey liked them as much as she did his broad suntanned hands and open-necked shirt. She anticipated a chance meeting in the bar later that afternoon after her shift, when she usually enjoyed a gin and tonic before catching the bus home.

Ina turned and unhooked a key from the wall behind the counter giving Bellantoni a moment to appreciate her new American hosiery.

Bellantoni let himself into his room, locked the door, put his case in the wardrobe and used the same key to unlock the double doors that opened onto the balcony. The railway station concourse faced almost square on across the street and a stairway at the end of the balcony led down to a side passage and the street where he had left Lorrimer with the car. Bellantoni locked the balcony doors and left by the stairway.

The trip from the city to Glenelg took twenty minutes and Bellantoni gave up looking for an Italian restaurant after five. Lorrimer seemed to know where he was going and Bellantoni rested his head on the back of the seat and closed his eyes.

Lorrimer finally turned the car into Moseley Street, slowed down and parked. He turned off the engine.

'Wakey-wakey.'

Nick sat up, stretched both arms and rested his hands on the dashboard. He yawned.

Lorrimer took off his tie, folded it and put it into his coat pocket. He sat forward and worked his coat off, handed it to Nick, then rolled up his shirtsleeves and got out of the car.

'Back in about an hour,' he said before closing the door.

Lorrimer walked down Moseley Street with his hands in his pockets, passing a man seated in his garden with a glass of beer in one hand and a hose-end clamped in the other pretending to ignore a couple of small boys as they scampered about the hydrangeas in the borders. He looked up and with a rabbit shooter's accuracy hit one with a sharp squirt of water. The boys yelped with excitement and ran up closer, daring him to fire another shot. The man glanced over his fence at Lorrimer and winked.

90A Moseley Street was a single-storied maisonette with a small, ordered garden behind a low brick wall; the homes on either side were hidden behind tall hedges of lilly pilly myrtle. Lorrimer heard the sounds of a push mower.

He opened the wrought iron gate and walked up to the front door, knocked once, waited, then knocked again. He took a half-step closer to the door and listened. Nothing.

Lorrimer stepped back and looked around; there were a few toys swept into a corner of the porch and a straw broom leaning against the wall.

He walked back to the footpath, closed the gate and resumed his leisurely pace along the footpath until he could see the ocean at the end of a side street. He turned towards it and strolled past the small homes and maisonettes, some with their front gardens in flower, others where the stakes of a vegetable plot could be glimpsed in the backyard.

Lorrimer reached Somerton Beach and found a vacant seat on the esplanade, took off his hat, placed it beside him and sat with his hands on his thighs. The sight of a thousand acres of passive sea and the warm sun on his face kept him there for ten minutes before he returned to the car by a roundabout route. Nick had moved over to the driver's seat and looked asleep under his hat. Lorrimer climbed in the passenger side.

'Where to?'

Lorrimer wound his window down.

'Food.'

Bellantoni sat up and scratched the stubble on his chin, leaned forward and smiled into the rear-view mirror, checking his teeth both sides.

'You know something, George?'

'What?'

'I don't think they heard of garlic in this town.'

'Or hamburgers.'

Both men sat in silence. Nick reached for the ignition key.

'Where are we eating?'

'The Grosvenor; they have oysters.'

Bellantoni laughed, swung the big car out into the road and drove back into the city.

Adelaide Central Station

Tom waited until all the men in his compartment had left before following them off the train and into the main hall.

The Broken Hill express had arrived a couple of minutes earlier and the concourse was busy with travellers. Small groups stood about in the hall barricaded by their luggage, some pointing to the chalkboard timetables overhead.

Tom walked into the middle of the hall and looked around for a sign to the gents.

He spent twenty minutes in the station's restroom, shaving and sluicing himself down at one of the sinks, taking his time before deciding whether to keep his pullover on as well as his coat. It could be a long night.

When he emerged, the hall was quieter with only a couple of people at the ticket queues and on the concourse. He walked over to a newspaper stand, bought a copy of the morning's paper, found an empty bench and sat down to read it. An advertisement at the bottom of the front page caught his eye. *You buy more than an engagement ring at Sheppards.*

Ed hadn't known if Jess was married, and the fifteen pounds for the ring would have emptied Tom's pockets.

He carried his suitcase and paper over to the station kiosk, took a stool and waited for the waitress to walk over and serve him.

Tom dawdled over his food and accepted another cup of tea before smoking his cigarette down and getting up to leave. He picked up his suitcase, walked over to the ticket office, looked up at the departure board and asked for a single on the next train out of the city, then joined a line of people waiting to be checked through the ticket barrier and onto the platforms. When he reached the front of the queue Tom handed over his ticket and asked if he could leave his suitcase for a moment while he visited the washroom. The railwayman sighed, looked at the ticket then handed it back.

'You've got four minutes.'

The railwayman took Tom's case and placed it behind his stool.

Tom turned and walked along the line of waiting passengers, Keyannik among them, behind a man in naval uniform. Once Tom had passed by, Keyannik glanced at Rostov who was standing beside a steel column fifty feet away. Rostov gestured him through the ticket barrier.

Keyannik reached the head of the queue, looked down at Tom's suitcase, hesitated, then offered up his ticket, walked through to the train and climbed aboard.

The railwayman was enjoying a cigarette when Tom came back to claim his case five minutes later.

'You're out of luck, mate, train's long gone.'

'Any chance of a refund?'

Tom waited as the railwayman took a long draw of his smoke before pinching the butt out and flicking it into a nearby waste bucket.

'You'd be the first.'

One senior porter was working the luggage office counter, dealing with the incoming luggage. His subordinate, a small, round-shouldered man, was working among the corridors of metal shelves, busy unloading a small trolley loaded with canvas sacks, lobbing them up into one of the higher racks. Tom watched from the queue as one of them tumbled back down and landed on the man's shoulder. The porter looked up at the racks with rancour.

A young woman at the counter with two children among her skirts and two large suitcases at her feet was talking to the senior porter. She had not been met and would now have to catch a bus to her sister's place. She only had enough money for the fare, none for storage, and the bags were too heavy to carry beyond the station.

The porter leaned over the counter and looked down at the two little girls who both peered back at him, bright-eyed, freckle-faced and sun-struck, only days away from the farm. He sat back and tore off a luggage ticket, initialled it and gave it to the woman.

'See me when you come back to pick them up. I'll get Eric to put them in the day racks, down the other end.'

Tom, who was next in line, left his suitcase and came to the counter, smiled at the woman, nodded to the senior porter and heaved both of her suitcases up to the counter top in one swift, double-armed movement.

The porter looked at Tom.

'Very good of you.'

Tom resumed his place as the porter asked if the woman had change for the telephone. She nodded, and he pointed to his right.

'Behind the kiosk. Next?'

Tom asked for a twenty-four-hour ticket.

'Can I get access to it during the day?'

The porter grunted.

'You won't be popular.'

'How much?'

'Fourpence.'

Tom lifted his suitcase onto the counter, sorted four pennies from the change in his pocket and handed them to the porter who wrote the ticket, gave Tom his half, tagged the other onto the suitcase and punched the desk bell to summon Eric.

Tom left the station and walked out into the Adelaide sunshine. The enquiries desk had told him where to find the nearest bus stop and he set off across the street towards the Grosvenor Hotel, glancing at the Strathmore's entrance as he walked by.

Rostov, more cautious since Keyannik had been duped, followed Tom as he left the station, crossed the road and walked towards the city centre. Two blocks on, Tom stopped and joined a short bus queue, lit up a smoke and grimaced; he had none of his own left in the pack and vowed never to smoke Kensitas again.

Rostov waited in a building doorway until more people joined the line.

Tom reached the driver who was collecting money at the bus door, bought his ticket then stepped aside to let the next person through while he finished his cigarette. He let more passengers past before re-joining the queue, walking past Rostov who turned his head just enough to see him stop at the end of the line.

Rostov reached the head of the line, bought his ticket and got on the bus. He took a seat and glanced over at the far side window. Tom was still outside, taking a draw on his cigarette as the conductor dealt with his last few passengers.

A woman walked down the aisle and sat beside Rostov. Dressed for town in a crisp floral dress and large straw hat, she smiled at Rostov as she settled herself. He tipped his hat and looked away.

The driver climbed aboard, closed the door, settled himself in the driver's seat and pulled the bus away from the kerb.

Rostov turned to see Tom walking back the way he had come.

The Second Morning

Adelaide, 29 November 1948

Bellantoni thought he was being stood up and told Lorrimer as much over a plate of Coffin Bay oysters on the second night. They were eating dinner at the Grosvenor Hotel again and Bellantoni was on his third dozen.

'Waiting in that lobby with a flute case on my knee. Some of the looks I'm getting aren't too hard to figure out.'

Lorrimer squeezed lemon juice over his oysters.

'Remember the club I dropped you at, in Sydney? They were probably eye-balling you the same way in there, but you were too busy to notice.'

'Put your pistol in there if it makes you feel better.'

'We don't even know if he's in town.'

'He'll show; he wants the money.'

Bellantoni picked up a half-shell and freed the oyster from its anchoring tendon with his thumbnail. He tipped his head back, lifted the shell to his lips and eased the oyster into his mouth before crushing it against his pallet and letting the remains slide down his throat. He sighed.

'Too many of these is never enough.'

A waiter passed their table holding a large plate covered with a bright metal dome.

'Speaking of which.'

Lorrimer looked up from his plate.

'We never spoke about money, apart from you footing the bill for the plane tickets and hotel.'

Bellantoni ate another oyster and took a sip of beer looking at Lorrimer all the while.

'What does Alex pay you?'

'This is something else.'

'What's on your mind?'

'A grand, at least.'

Lorrimer laughed.

'Five hundred, more if it gets complicated.'

Bellantoni turned back to his oysters.

The Meeting

Two women were sitting at a table in the Strathmore Hotel lobby drinking tea and choosing pastries from a small plate when an American naval officer followed by a man carrying a camera entered the hotel through the front doors. The women both looked up as the men walked through to the front desk, crossing Tom's path as he walked into the lobby from the bar. Tom stood by a window close to a dark-haired man wearing a jacket and shirt with no tie who was fidgeting with the locks of a small black case on his lap.

Tom pulled his cigarette pack out and patted his coat pockets before leaning into the seated man.

'S'cuse me, mate.'

Bellantoni ceased his fiddling and looked up.

'Haven't got a light, have you?'

Bellantoni sat up in his chair, searched through his jacket pockets and pulled out a packet of matches.

'Thanks.'

Tom lit up a Kensitas, drew back the smoke, held the cigarette pack in front of his face and looked at it with distaste. He gave the matches back to Nick, turned and stared out of the lobby window.

'What happens now?'

Bellantoni pocketed the matches and shrugged.

Three men wearing suits and ties walked into the hotel and crossed the lobby to the bar entrance. They were laughing as if they had just shared a joke.

Tom turned away from the window, looking for an ashtray.

'Play that thing, do you?'

'What?'

'Whatever's in the case – what is it? A flute?'

Bellantoni smiled.

'My mother's.'

Tom leant over and crushed his cigarette out in the ashtray on Bellantoni's table.

Neither spoke for a moment as they watched an elderly couple walk through the lobby to the street.

'She plays the flute, does she?'

Bellantoni barely nodded.

'Like I said.'

The lobby lit up with a camera flash. The naval officer was at the reception desk; he was standing next to a red-faced man with white hair. They were shaking hands and smiling at each other.

Tom looked down at Bellantoni; with all that hair he had to be Italian as well as a smartarse.

Nick stood up, holding his case in one hand.

'I'm parked a block away. What do I call you?'

'Whatever you like.'

Tom took a last look around the lobby then followed Bellantoni outside.

The Deal

Neither man spoke until Nick pulled up in Moseley Street and turned to his passenger.

'This is where you get out.'

Tom looked up at Jessica's home. A man was standing in the open doorway, filling it.

Bellantoni cut the engine and sat back, turning his head to watch the welcome.

Tom climbed out of the car, shut the door and walked through the open gate up to the small porch. Lorrimer stepped aside.

'Let's do this without names,' he said as Tom passed him and entered the house. 'Take the first door on the left.'

The American.

Lorrimer followed Tom into the small living room where a couch and two armchairs were arranged around a low wooden table. Their eyes met for an instant in the mirror over the fireplace before Tom looked away to a bookcase and the framed photographs arranged on the top shelf.

Lorrimer sat in one of the chairs and waved his hand at the other. The room smelt a little stale and the windows were closed. Tom looked around for an ashtray, then remembered he had none of his own cigarettes. He sat back and waited. What would it be like if Jess walked in now? How would that go?

Lorrimer slipped an envelope from his inside coat pocket and placed it on the table.

'What did you bring?'

Tom reached inside his jacket pocket, took out his wallet, removed two folded sheets of paper and placed them next to Lorrimer's envelope. He leaned back as Bellantoni entered the room and dumped the flute case on the couch.

'Everyone happy?'

Lorrimer glanced at Bellantoni.

'I could use a coffee.'

He looked at Tom.

'You?'

'Black.'

Lorrimer read through the sheets, going forward and back a few times.

'This is it? Two sheets?'

'There's more.'

Bellantoni came in with the coffee, played the waiter then sat on the couch.

'Don't ask me what was in the coffee jar.'

Lorrimer tapped his envelope.

'The thousand in there is for everything.'

Tom drank a little of his coffee. It was better than the *Ruth*'s.

'It won't even get you what's on the table.'

He looked over at Bellantoni and tilted his cup.

'You an Italian, Driver?'

Bellantoni shrugged.

Tom put his cup down and pushed the envelope back to Lorrimer.

'I'm owed more than that.'

Lorrimer held Tom's eye as he put down the two

sheets. He picked up his envelope, stood and smiled.

'Nature calls.'

Bellantoni and Tom finished their coffee in silence as they waited for Lorrimer to return. After two minutes Nick took his cup and strolled into the kitchen.

Tom got up and walked over to the bookcase. Jessica was in most of the framed pictures on the top shelf. He looked closely at one of her standing beside a roadster with a dark-haired man, one of his arms around her waist and the other encircling a large silver cup.

He picked up a photo of a little boy smiling as he held onto the edge of a canvas wading pool, put it back and stooped to look through the small collection of books that half-filled the second shelf. He took one to his chair, sat and flipped through the pages.

The toilet flushed.

Tom closed the book and looked around the room.

The walls needed fresh paint and there were cracks in the plaster ceiling. A radio was sitting on a corner table under a lamp with a beaded shade. Two pictures were hanging on the wall, one an indistinct landscape, the other a clown's face. He could hear intermittent traffic noise and the shouts of children from the street outside. Tom's eyes rested on the small boy. He wondered who had taken the photograph. Such a wide grin.

He could see a closed door across the hallway, possibly the main bedroom. There would be a wardrobe, her clothes.

Lorrimer came back into the room, sat down and rubbed his hands together.

'You brought a book?'

Tom showed him the cover.

'A jug of wine, a loaf of bread.'

'How many sheets have you got, all up?'

'Another seven.'

'Where?'

'Four hundred per sheet.'

'Three.'

'Show me.'

Lorrimer reached into his inside pocket and took out a wad of American notes, counted off two thousand seven hundred dollars and put the rest back into his pocket.

Tom held his hand out and Lorrimer laughed.

'Where are they?'

'Luggage office.'

'Ticket?'

Tom put the book down, sat up, took his wallet from his trouser pocket and slid out the ticket. He stood and fished a small key out of his fob pocket.

'It's locked.'

Nick drove into town. Tom went back to the book and Lorrimer picked up his coffee, took a sip and grimaced.

'Cold. You want another one?'

'No. ... The woman who lives here, she works for you?'

The Luggage Office

Adelaide, 5.30pm, 30 November 1948

The senior porter looked up as Bellantoni approached, took his ticket and gestured to the end of the counter where Eric was working.

'Day racks.'

He handed the ticket back and looked at his watch; Harold always allowed himself two schooners in the public bar of the Grosvenor before catching his bus home and the police were overdue. A traveller who had lodged his suitcase three weeks ago and retrieved it yesterday had reported that it had been comprehensively burgled while under the railway's care. That the police might think either he or Eric were light-fingered was unsettling.

Bellantoni waited for Eric to look up from his ledger book. He was filling a column with numbers using a sharp pencil, an eraser ready by his elbow.

'Help you?'

Bellantoni offered up his ticket.

'Okay if I just take something out?'

Eric had coveted Harold's job and chair for eleven years. Soured by this long apprenticeship he took advantage of whatever came his way

'Threepence.'

Harold caught the sound of a coin on the counter. He allowed Eric some small opportunities in order to placate his ambitions and turned his head a degree or two to watch Bellantoni unlock the suitcase and open the lid. Harold had been handling baggage for over thirty years and when he saw Bellantoni put his hands on his hips as he surveyed the contents of the suitcase he knew the bag wasn't his.

Harold glanced over at the main entrance, looking for a uniform.

Bellantoni pushed his hands through the clothes to the bottom of the case.

A razor strop and glass dish, pencils and letterforms, a travelling man's shrapnel. And underneath them all a pair of socks, each containing a bundle tied with light twine.

Nick took out the cleaner of the two shirts and placed it beside the case, picked out a couple of the ties, chose one and put it on the shirt. He wrapped the socks into a singlet, closed the suitcase lid and gave it back to Eric to take away.

The police arrived, a constable and weatherworn detective. Harold sighed and got to his feet as Bellantoni walked away with another man's change of clothing.

The Wait

Lorrimer opened the front door and walked onto the darkened porch, standing there for a minute before coming back inside and quietly shutting the door behind him. He walked into the living room, sat down and looked at his watch.

'He's late.'

Tom was reading a magazine he'd found on the hall table.

'Maybe he's getting dinner. Anything in the fridge?'

'Nothing I'd eat.'

Tom stood up and stretched, picked up the two code sheets from the table, refolded them and put them back into his wallet.

'Get you anything?'

Lorrimer shook his head.

Tom took his cup, walked into the kitchen and opened

the refrigerator door. Eggs and milk on the right and something wrapped in butcher's paper on the top shelf. A bowl of cooked peas, another of boiled potatoes. A brown paper bag on the middle shelf. Tom put his cup down, took the bag out and opened it. One pasty, fresh enough to have been bought today.

Tom took it to the kitchen table and ate it out of the bag.

Lorrimer was getting antsy and regretted not giving Bellantoni Jessica's phone number. He waited until Tom returned before picking up his hat and heading to the front door.

'I'm going to take a walk around the block.'

The Shared Wardrobe

Tom waited a moment, motionless, ears straining, before getting up and walking into the hallway. He half-opened the door he'd seen earlier from the living room and glanced inside, then waited again, fingers resting on the handle, listening for the sound of anyone approaching the front door. Silence. He pushed the handle and the bedroom door swung wide.

There were two single beds in the room, both neatly made and separated by a polished wooden table with a small lamp placed in the centre. A chest of drawers and chair stood to one side and a wardrobe the other. The only picture on the wall was a framed sketch of a Tualinbari boy's head and shoulders. Tom walked to the wardrobe and opened both doors. There were three hatboxes on the top shelf and a couple of dresses hanging on the right. A jacket, suit and two shirts took up the left-hand side.

Tom stood there a moment, a hand on each door, looking at the man's clothes, the smell of mothballs in his nostrils. He closed the wardrobe and turned to look at the two beds.

That was that.

The Drunk

Lorrimer took the same path to the beach as before. He crossed the road and strolled to the edge of the esplanade, stopping to look at the sea.

A pale, lightly built man sprinted from the shallows, threw himself down onto the sand then began an intricate series of exercises, starting with rapid one-armed push-ups. Further north, towards the Children's Home, two women wearing wide-brimmed hats were standing in knee-deep water, dresses gathered up in their hands.

Lorrimer walked towards a set of steps leading down to the beach. A young man and woman were sitting on a bench below the esplanade; she was talking very quickly and looked excited. As Lorrimer passed above them the man patted her on the knee.

A little further on he stopped and turned around. A man was sprawled on the sand at the bottom of the steps, his head resting awkwardly against the sea wall. Lorrimer watched him until he moved an arm then continued walking for a half a minute before turning back. The couple had mounted a small motorbike parked by the side of the road.

Lorrimer waited until they had driven away before walking over to the top of the steps; the man was still there. Lorrimer used the toe of his shoe to scuff some gravel from the top of the sea wall onto him, followed by a few small pebbles.

The man awoke brushing at his head and shoulders, then rolled onto his stomach and clambered slowly to his feet using the sea wall for support.

He looked up at Lorrimer and almost fell over, then with a defiant tug at his belt, staggered up the beach towards the lights of the Pier Hotel.

Not of his Choosing

Lorrimer had taken the two empty coffee cups to the kitchen when he heard the sound of something heavy hitting the floor. He put them in the sink and walked back into the living room. Tom was on both knees beside the table, retching, his hands on the floor. Lorrimer quickly helped him to his feet, lifted one of Tom's arms over his shoulder and walked him to the bathroom.

Tom rushed towards the toilet bowl, jamming both of them in the doorway for an instant. Lorrimer manoeuvred him through, supporting Tom until he reached the pan, bent over and lost his teeth in a hot rush of vomit. Lorrimer heard the clatter as they hit the porcelain.

Tom knelt low over the toilet pan, both hands grasping the rim. He retched again and threw up more food, then a great gob of mucous. Foam bubbled over his lips. He retched again.

He pushed himself to his feet using the toilet bowl for support, turned and steadied himself with one hand on the cistern. He searched for Lorrimer in the kaleidoscope of colours and fragments that screened his vision then slowly collapsed to his knees, shuddering. A deep moan escaped his throat and Tom retched once more, dry this time.

Lorrimer bent over the toilet bowl and plucked out Tom's dentures. He dropped them into the sink, ran some water over them and rinsed his hands. With a wodge of paper pulled from the toilet roll he wiped the bowl and seat clean, threw the soiled paper into the pan, flushed the toilet, wrapped the teeth in his handkerchief and put them in his coat pocket.

Tom was still on his hands and knees, breathing quickly and grunting as he fought to control the spasms in his stomach. Lorrimer put his hands under Tom's arms and sat him back on his haunches, then got him to his feet and sat him on the toilet pan.

Steadying Tom with one hand, he unrolled another length of toilet paper to catch his drool. He still looked clean enough, no splatter on his clothes, no bumps or bruises from his fall, just a little blood on the knuckles of his right hand from the door jamb.

He lifted Tom to his feet and half-carried him back to the couch in the living room, laid him flat then stood and watched as shudders coursed along his body. Tom was tossing his head around and whispering an urgent monologue between his convulsions. He tried to sit up and Lorrimer put a hand on Tom's chest until the moment passed.

He looked at his watch. Almost ten. Bellantoni was four hours late.

Lorrimer turned off the living room light, went to the kitchen and made himself more coffee. He took it into the darkened living room, sat down opposite Tom and listened as his breath became shallow and ragged.

Tamám Shud

Lorrimer opened the front door for Bellantoni and followed him into the living room where Tom was stretched out on the couch.

Bellantoni leaned over and looked at Tom's right hand.

'What happened?'

'You were so long he got restless.'

Bellantoni looked at Tom's fluttering eyes.

'He's out of it. What did you do?'

'Slipped a mickey into his coffee.'

Bellantoni took the socks from his jacket pocket, slid out the bundles, untied them and put the documents on the table. Lorrimer sat down and picked through them until he had the seven code sheets in a pile.

'Film?'

Nick shrugged.

'I looked.'

Lorrimer looked up at Bellantoni.

'So what happened?'

'The car you hired, the '39 Buick? Try getting a tyre for one of those at dinnertime in a strange town.'

'No spare?'

Bellantoni shook his head.

Lorrimer shrugged, folded the papers into two bundles and stowed them in his inside coat pocket.

Tom startled Bellantoni by suddenly flinging both his arms into the air, only for them to collapse and fall back by his sides. He was breathing quickly now and small bubbles of grey foam were leaking from the corners of his mouth. Both men watched in silence for a moment.

'Is this a complication?'

'Only if he's too big for you to carry.'

Bellantoni ran his eyes down the length of Tom's body.

'How far?'

'Maybe a hundred yards.'

'When?'

'Soon.'

'My mother has this.'

Bellantoni picked up a small book from the floor. Lorrimer was leaning in the kitchen doorway watching Tom.

'She never knew what the last two words meant.'

Bellantoni flicked through to the end of the book.

'Tamám Shud.'

'It's right at the end?'

'Yep.'

'The last two words?

'Yep.'

'How about it means "the end"'?

Bellantoni laughed.

Somerton Beach

'You'll have to carry him along the beach and dump him by the steps that lead up to that big house on the corner.'

'Big house?'

'The Children's Home, biggest house on the street. Leave a cigarette in his mouth; it'll look like he's sleeping off a bender. Where did you park the car?'

'Right out front.'

Lorrimer quietly opened the front door and stepped outside as if to take in the night air. He paused at the front gate looking in both directions before slowly opening it and stepping out onto the footpath. The street was deserted. He eased open the Buick's nearside back door.

Bellantoni had tidied the kitchen and was ready when Lorrimer returned, standing by Tom's feet at one end of the couch. Lorrimer gripped Tom's upper arms and with Bellantoni holding his legs they lifted him over the back of the couch, through the small hallway and out of the house to the car, first stopping behind the half-open front door to listen for any activity on the street before Bellantoni pushed it back with his heel.

Lorrimer rested Tom's head and shoulders on the back seat, climbed in around him, put his hands under Tom's arms and pulled him along the seat while Nick held his legs clear of the car and pushed. Once Tom was inside and the car door closed, Nick got into the driver's seat and Lorrimer went back into the house to straighten the living room furniture and turn the kitchen light off. He locked the front door behind him and dropped the key through the letterbox.

The drive to the beach took less than five minutes and Bellantoni parked on the ocean side looking north, a couple of hundred feet from the Children's Home. He turned off the lights and engine. Two men were strolling towards them on the opposite footpath; another loomed in Lorrimer's wing-mirror. They waited.

Only a few lights were visible in the boarding houses and homes on the other side of the street. A small terrier trotted out of an open gate to bark at the Buick before marking its territory and retreating into the darkness. Lorrimer turned and looked through the rear window.

'All clear.'

Bellantoni got out of the car, opened the rear door and with his back to the ocean, eased Tom forward until his legs were free. Gripping Tom's jacket by the lapels he pulled him into a sitting position, bent into his midriff and took Tom's weight on his right shoulder. Bellantoni took a breath, put his right arm around the back of Tom's thighs and stood up with a grunt, adjusting his shoulder until he was comfortable under the weight. He stepped back onto the kerb and closed the car door with his free hand, shifted his load once more and turned to Lorrimer's open window. He jerked his head in the direction the car was facing.

'Up there?'

Lorrimer nodded, slid over to the driver's seat and watched Bellantoni as he slowly carried Tom through the soft sand to the shoreline, then turn north towards the Children's Home. Lorrimer waited until Bellantoni was halfway to the Home before starting the car and slowly driving after him, lights on half beam, stopping at a pedestrian crossing to allow two couples to cross the road and reach the beach.

Bellantoni slugged it out, sinking to his laces with every step and was glad to be rid of Tom's weight as he settled him against the sea wall. The cigarette wouldn't stay in Tom's mouth and Bellantoni wedged it under his chin, got to his feet, brushed his hands on his trousers and climbed the steps to the path. Lorrimer had parked at the top, engine running, radio on low, the glow of his cigarette visible.

Kay Kyser was singing On a Slow Boat to China.

Saint Francis Xavier's Cathedral

Six months later

Jessica sat outermost in a line of five penitent women who all slid a place closer to the confessional door every time it opened to discharge an unburdened soul into the dim light of the cathedral. She only attended Catholic churches for weddings and funerals and had little knowledge of confessional rites. Jessica waited uncertainly, the elderly woman beside her whispering prayers as she passed rosary beads through her gnarled fingers, both hands bent and swollen with arthritis.

When Jessica's turn came she stood, entered the darkened booth and closed the door. She saw a small, gauze-covered opening at waist height surmounted by a crucifix, a carpet-covered kneeling bench below.

Padre Pearce, the visiting priest, was at the end of another four-hour roster attending to Adelaide's elderly women, all intent on scouring themselves of every hard-remembered blemish that might shadow an illuminated journey from their deathbed. The depth and detail of their memories astonished him at times.

He sat behind a curtain on the other side of the gauze. Jessica knelt.

'Good morning.'

'Good morning, Father.'

'Call me Padre, please.'

Jessica waited.

'Do you wish to make a confession?'

'I wish to talk to a priest.'

'Well, here I am.'

'Not a confession ... I ...'

'Are you familiar with the true purpose of a confessional?'

'No, Padre. Only that whatever is said is kept secret.'

'You're not Catholic?'

'No.'

Pearce unclasped his fingers, raised a hand to his vestment and straightened it.

'I have to talk to *someone*.'

'About what?'

Jessica hesitated. Pearce sat back and scratched his forehead; not all who knelt on the other side of his curtain were of sound mind. He prepared to be patient.

'It concerns the war … and my … what I did.'

'What did you do?'

'I was a courier.'

Pearce bent forward, drew the curtain and looked at Jessica through the gauze. She met his gaze.

'Go back outside and wait for the last to leave. I'll turn off the light and follow in a few minutes.

'Thank you, Fa … Padre.'

'Now you're getting the gist.'

Jessica left the confessional and sat a few pews behind the two women waiting their turn. One stood, adjusted her veil and walked in. She emerged three minutes later and the next took her place, reappearing shortly after with a handkerchief pressed to her cheek, looking slowly from side to side before walking towards a dimly lit prayer niche set deep into the cathedral wall.

An elderly man was making his slow journey around the Stations of the Cross and a few scattered figures occupied the pews as Pearce and Jessica made their way to the middle of the nave and sat down.

Pearce was a slightly built man with very little hair and a deeply corrugated brow. He leaned back and turned to Jessica.

'Do you want to tell me your name?'

'I'd rather not.'

Pearce waited.

'Are you called Padre from your war service?'

'It wasn't the only thing I was called. And you? Were you at home? Abroad?'

'Home, in Sydney, training to be a nurse. I never managed to finish.'

'Where were you?'

'The Royal North Shore.'

Pearce scratched the back of his neck.

'How can I help you?'

Jessica opened her handbag and withdrew a folded sheet of newspaper.

Pearce patted his shirt pocket and retrieved his glasses.

'What am I looking at?'

'It's today's paper.'

Pearce unfolded the sheet and read the front-page article.

'I remember this. He was never identified, was he?'

'No.'

'You know him?'

Jessica didn't reply. She took a small book from her bag and handed it to Pearce. He took it and turned it over in his hands.

'Is this the million to one chance they're talking about?'

Jessica nodded

Pearce opened the book at the last page and examined the tear.

'How did you come by this?'

'It was given to me, years ago.'

'Like this?'

'No.'

Pearce looked at the newspaper page once more,

folded it and handed it back to Jessica with the *Rubaiyat*.

'It's a police matter; I don't see what I can do.'

Jessica sat back and watched two black-robed nuns enter the cathedral from a side door.

'Where were you during the war, Padre?'

'Singapore.'

'How was that?'

'A fair bit bloody; I spent a bit of time ferrying various personnel around the country before the Japs came down.'

'Were you taken prisoner?'

'Almost. I pinched a Bentley to get some wounded pilots down to Singapore from Ipoh, then a couple of us took over a merchant steamer and sailed for Darwin a day before the Japs marched in.'

'How do you take over a ship?'

Pearce laughed.

'Put it down to plain talking and a sky full of Japanese bombers; the skipper was happy enough to be going anywhere.'

Jessica put the newspaper article back into her handbag, then took out a pencil and wrote on the outside back cover of the *Rubaiyat* before placing it on the pew between them.

'Give it to Detective Leane; he seems to be the one in charge.'

Pearce picked up the book and looked at the back cover.

'Your phone number? Then why not give the book to them yourself?'

'They'll ask me where I got it.'

Pearce gazed up at the stained glass windows behind the altar. Their colours were glowing richly in the afternoon light.

'Just the one thing I don't understand.'

'What?'

'This story has been in and out of the papers for months.'

'Yes.

'With his picture.'

Jessica looked up at the altar; a woman was removing the part-burned candles from their holders and replacing them with new.

'You know the police will take you to see him.'

Jessica nodded.

'Is there anyone else who can help?'

'Will you?'

The Francis Rubaiyat

Monday, 25 July 1949

Detective Sergeant Leane saw Pearce to the door and thanked him, walked back to his desk and picked up the manila envelope the priest had given him. Leane, who attended the cathedral regularly, knew Pearce by sight and sermon, usually dry affairs, he thought, that relied too heavily on his war service anecdotes.

The book, Pearce told him, had been left on a pew.

Leane picked up his letter opener, slit the envelope and let the small soft-covered book slide out onto his desktop. He considered calling the fingerprint division and telling them he had something that may have been handled a hundred times, thought better of it, picked the book up and turned to the back page.

Whistling softly, he took out his notebook and pencil and made a quick note before locking the book in his desk drawer and leaving his office for the detective's room.

The only men on duty were Detective Errol Canney, with his feet up on his desk reading a newspaper, and

Detective Len Brown who was on the phone. Leane caught their attention and beckoned them over to the vacant desk beside him. Canney folded his paper, stood up, tucked in the front of his shirt and ambled over. Brown hung up and joined them.

'The Somerton case, where's the slip of paper?'

Brown shrugged. 'Evidence room, last time I saw it.'

'Which was when?'

'When the papers wanted a picture.'

'Fetch it and bring it to my office, will you, Len? And don't muck about yapping on the stairs.'

Leane took his notebook from his jacket pocket, tore out a page and handed it to Canney.

'Have this traced.'

Leane looked about the detectives' room on his way out, noting the misarranged desks and cabinets, the overflowing bins and scattered, overfull ashtrays. He wondered if Brown still kept a bottle of Corio whisky in his desk drawer. The higher you climbed in the South Australian Police Force the better the whisky in your desk. Leane had been drinking Johnny Walker Red Label for years.

When the two detectives reappeared back at his office, Leane rang the switchboard and asked them to hold his calls then motioned Brown and Canney to take a seat. He held his hand out for the evidence envelope, opened the book and attempted to match the Tamám Shud slip of paper with the small rectangular hole torn out of the last page.

Leane looked up.

'What do you think?'

'Give us a squiz, Skipper.'

Leane handed the book and the slip to Brown and watched as he repeated the process. Brown had small hands and kept his nails short and clean. He put the book down and lifted the slip to eye-level.

'Anyone got a magnifying glass?'

'What do you *think* is what I asked.'

Brown shrugged.

'Could be.'

'Errol, the phone number, whose is it?'

'Jessica Beecham, Mrs, domiciled at 90A Moseley Street, about two hundred yards from where the body was found.'

Leane sat back, switched his gaze to Brown and held his hand out. Brown handed back the slip.

'Boss?'

Leane glanced at Canney.

'Where did you get it?'

'Half the time you're better off not knowing what's going on, Errol.'

Canney folded his hands under his arms; he picked at his fingers when denied a cigarette and the only smoker Leane allowed in his office was his father when he visited.

'A local businessman handed it in this morning.'

'This businessman got a name, Boss?'

'Francis. Mister.'

'Is that what I'm to tell the newspapers?'

'Yes.'

Canney bent to his notepad and pencilled a few notes.

'Detective Canney?'

Canney looked up.

'Boss?'

'Go down and have a preliminary chat with this

Beecham woman, and take the book.'

Canney picked up the book and examined the cover.

'Ru – bay – at, is that how you say it?'

'Close enough. Show her the phone number on the back.'

Canney turned the book over.

'What's the other one?'

'You tell me and we'll both know.'

A Detective at the Door

Errol Canney, middle-aged, sandy haired and pot-bellied, had a great liking for the comfort of the new radio car, a Vauxhall Velox, and drove from the city to Somerton the long way via Henley Beach, enjoying the coastal scenery as he travelled south.

He turned into Moseley Street and cruised half its length before coming to 90A, parked the car, got out, retrieved his coat from the back seat and approached the house. The gate was open. Canney walked up to the front door and knocked twice, waited fifteen seconds then knocked twice again.

Jessica opened the door, a small boy at her knees squinting up at the silhouette blocking the light.

'Mrs Jessica Beecham?'

Canney showed his badge.

'Adelaide CIB. Can I come inside?'

He looked over Jessica's shoulder, a practised switch of his eyes.

She bent and had a quiet word with the little boy, then watched as he walked back into the house before turning back to Canney.

'This is rather important, Mrs Beecham, it would be better done inside.'

Jessica held up her gloved hands.

'I'm in the middle of a spring clean, everything is in a muddle.'

Canney thought Jessica about twenty-five and although diminutive her quietly challenging gaze told him he wouldn't be getting inside the house.

He slipped the *Rubaiyat* from his jacket pocket and held it out to show her.

'We believe this book is connected to a deceased person found in this vicinity last December.'

Jessica glanced at the book.

Canney gave a small cough.

'Do you know of any reason as to why your telephone number is written on the back?'

'How could I?'

'Mrs Beecham, does this book belong to you?'

Jessica took the book from Canney, flicked through the first couple of pages then turned it over and looked at the back cover before handing it back.

'No.'

'Have you ever had a copy?'

'Yes.'

'Do you still have it?'

Jessica shook her head.

'I gave it away years ago.'

Canney put the book back into his pocket and straightened his jacket.

'Where was this?'

'Sydney.'

Canney took a moment to fumble his notebook from his coat pocket then poke around in his shirt for a pencil.

A woman slowed as she walked passed the front gate, glanced at the Vauxhall then looked over at Jessica and the detective on the porch.

'Do you have the person's name handy?'

'Baxter. Ed Baxter.'

'His address?'

'Inside … a letter from him somewhere.'

Canney hesitated.

'Was Baxter … how well do you know him?'

'Well enough, why?'

'His address, please?'

Jessica turned and walked into the house, leaving the door ajar. Her son was sitting on the living room floor playing with a large stuffed dog and he looked up as his mother passed by, raised one of the dog's paws and waved it at her back.

'Bye-bye, Mummy.'

Jessica found Ed's letter in the suitcase with all her other correspondence and took it out to Canney. He copied the address into his notebook and added a comment, noting Baxter as a friend of the woman and a possibility for the dead man.

Canney asked Jessica whether she wouldn't mind coming to the museum with him to view the bust.

'I can't leave my son.'

'Perhaps a neighbour?'

Jessica shook her head.

'He'll have to come, but I don't want him to be with us ...'

The Viewing

Detectives Canney and Brown were waiting with the museum's taxidermist in his office when DS Leane arrived with Jessica. Leane gestured at one of the chairs in front of Logan's desk.

Jessica shook her head.

'No, thank you.'

A faint smell of corruption hung in the air coupled with a lingering chemical odour. Jessica looked around at the crowded walls, the shrouded object on a bookshelf behind the desk, the only window, almost opaque with grime.

'We all set, Henry?'

Leane moved to Jessica's right and the other two detectives her left. They watched Logan walk behind his desk and quickly slide off the shroud to reveal the plaster cast.

He stood back, balled up the material and watched closely as Jessica quickly lowered her gaze to the floor. Canney and Brown's eyes were fixed on the bust. Leane looked away from Jessica and caught a questioning glance from Logan.

Jessica waited for it to end.

DS Leane was asking a question.

He spoke again.

'Do you know this man?'

The detectives had dusty shoes and the one called Brown a ragged edge to one of his trouser cuffs.

'No.'

'Would you please look at the bust? Is this man Alfred Baxter?'

'No.'

Leane exchanged glances with Canney.

'Mrs Beecham?'

'She's going over.'

Brown moved in to take Jessica's arm.

'Mrs Beecham.'

Jessica straightened, her eyes still fixed on the floor.

'This man was found two hundred yards away from

your home, most probably murdered, and the slip of paper found in his pocket came from a book that has your telephone number written on the back.'

Leane waited, then softened his voice.

'Do you know him?'

The taxidermist's office had a floor of nailed planks, not unlike a ship's deck, a ferry, the one she sometimes took from Manly to the city. A merchant steamer.

'No.'

Leane nodded at Logan and the taxidermist walked over to the bookshelf and covered the bust, twitching the corners of the shroud to straighten it.

'I think we're done.'

Leane turned to Jessica.

'I'll take you home.'

She looked up at Leane when he took her elbow.

Logan showed them out, shut the door and walked back to the bookshelf. He slid off the shroud again, stood back and allowed himself a small smile.

The little boy was crying, his minder, a young policewoman, had been unable to interest him in a tour of the museum and gladly handed him back when

Jessica reached the lobby with the three detectives.

DS Leane drove Jessica home and sat in his car watching as she and the little boy walked through the gate and up the path to the porch. The boy, standing behind his mother as she unlocked the front door, looked back over his shoulder at the policeman. Leane waved.

Jessica turned her son's head away from the street, opened the door and led him into the house.

But helpless Pieces of the Game He plays
Upon this Chequer-board of Nights and Days;
Hither and thither moves, and checks and slays,
And one by one back in the Closet lays.

The Rubaiyat of Omar Khayyam
Fitzgerald version

Afterword

Adelaide, the capital of South Australia, can experience summer temperatures as high as 43 degrees Celsius in November when hot winds blow down to the sea from the dry interior. The city's long, sandy beaches, including Somerton Beach, Glenelg, face west across Gulf St Vincent and are protected from the great Southern Ocean swells by the bulk of Kangaroo Island to the south, giving the people of Adelaide much calmer waters to enjoy than are found on the open coast.

In April 1948, one of the strongest hurricanes on record blew into the Gulf St Vincent, generating high waves and winds so severe that both the Glenelg and Brighton Piers were washed away and the 1,420-ton HMAS *Barcoo*, a River class frigate, was driven ashore just north of Glenelg after being unable to turn into the wind. The residents of the city and nearby beach suburbs also suffered badly as the storm damaged many of their homes and uprooted dozens of large trees throughout the city and its parks. Wind gusts were measured at 130kph and over 70mm of rain fell on the day.

In December 1948, Glenelg was in the news again when a body was discovered on Somerton Beach. A man, overdressed for hot weather and no clue as to his identity.

DEAD MAN FOUND LYING ON SOMERTON BEACH

The fully clothed body of a man was found on the beach at Somerton, opposite the Crippled Children's Home, at 6.30 a.m. today. Up to noon police had no clue to his identity.

The body had not been in the water.

The man was lying on his back against the sea wall. The legs were crossed, and death appeared to have occurred while the man was sleeping.

A thorough search of his pockets revealed no papers or anything that would give a clue to his name.

The man is thought to have been about 40. He was 5 ft. 11 in. in height, and well built. He was clean-shaven, with fair hair slightly grey over the temples, hazel eyes, and was wearing a grey and brown double-breasted coat, brown trousers, socks, and shoes, and a brown knitted woollen pullover, white shirt and collar, and red-white-and-blue tie.

The discovery was made by Mr. John Lyons, jeweller, of Whyte road, Somerton, who called Constable Moss, of Brighton, and Det. Strangway.

The (Daily) News, Wednesday 1 December 1948

The Crippled Children's Home

Around 1880, William Bickford of A. M. Bickford and Sons built a large residence at Glenelg, a coastal suburb about fourteen kilometres from Adelaide in South Australia. He named it Alvington after West Alvington, the home village of his grandparents in Kingsbridge, South Devon, UK.

The Bickfords lived in their big house on the corner of The Esplanade and Madge Terrace, with its good verandahs, sea breeze and ocean view, until William's death in 1918 when he left it to his widow, Margaret, and son, Harold.

In 1938, Alvington was sold to a charitable institution called the Crippled Children's Association of South Australia and used as a home for children with poliomyelitis (commonly known as polio) until it was demolished in 1976. Its official name was The Somerton Home, but it was generally known as the Crippled Children's Home.

The Witnesses

On the evening of 30 November 1948, four people saw a man lying near the bottom of a set of wooden steps that led down to the beach from the street, opposite the Crippled Children's Home. The drop from the road to the beach was about four and a half metres.

The cross marks the spot where the Somerton Man was found

John Bain Lyons, a local man and jeweller with a

business in Adelaide's King William Street, and his wife were taking one of their regular walks along the Somerton Beach shoreline in front of the Crippled Children's Home. At about 7pm, from a distance of about eighteen metres, they both saw a man slumped near the bottom of the steps with his back on the sand and his head and shoulders supported against the sea wall.

John saw the man fully extend his right arm vertically before letting it fall by his side. He thought the man was drunk and trying to smoke a cigarette. He and his wife did not suspect anything unusual and continued to their home at 52 Whyte Street (the reference to 'road' in the newspaper article is incorrect), Somerton, which was within easy walking distance.

Olive Constance Neill, a typist and telephonist of 54 East Parkway, Colonel Light Gardens, Adelaide, arrived at Somerton Beach at about 7:30pm on the back of a motorbike driven by her boyfriend, Gordon Kenneth Strapps, of 5 Seymour Terrace, Adelaide.

After parking the bike by the roadside they walked down the steps (pictured above) to a bench on a pathway a little south of the Crippled Children's Home where they sat to watch dusk approaching over the sea.

They also observed a man lying on the sand about nine metres from where they sat. They could only see him from the waist down because the sea wall obstructed their view of his upper body.

'Where he was lying was a fairly public place,' said Olive, 'not the sort of a place a man would be likely to choose if he wanted to go somewhere and die quietly.'

Police Constable John Moss later told the inquest that there would have been many people about as it was a warm night.

Olive also saw another man standing above them at the top of the steps looking down for a full five minutes at the man lying against the sea wall. The watcher was about fifty years of age, she said, of stocky build, not tall, and wearing a navy suit and grey hat.

Gordon noticed that the position of the man's legs changed while they were there, but he didn't actually see this occur.

'They (the legs) were straight out when we got there, not crossed,' he said. 'I only took a casual glance (and) when I walked (back) up the steps his left leg had been drawn up, taking it up the sand a bit. I made a remark to my girlfriend that as there were mosquitoes there he must have been dead to the world in not noticing them.'

These witness statements were made at the coronial inquest held on 17 June 1949.

No one reported seeing a body by the steps before 7pm or after 8pm on the night of 30 November.

The Next Morning

John Bain Lyons had unshakable swimming habits in the warmer months and at about 6:35 on the morning of 1 December 1948 he walked down to the sea from his Whyte Street home, looking forward to seeing the familiar glitter of the ocean as he drew closer to the beach.

After he had completed his swim he dried off and strolled along Somerton Beach towards Glenelg to meet a friend, another regular. While they were talking, John noticed that a couple of horses and their jockeys had stopped by the sea wall, near to the steps that led down from the road opposite the Crippled Children's Home.

One of the jockeys had dismounted and was standing above a body lying on the beach where John had observed a man the previous evening. Realising that his earlier sighting might be important to the police, John returned to his Whyte Street home to call Brighton Police Station before returning to the beach where a small crowd had gathered.

Police Constable John Moss of the nearby Brighton Police Station arrived at Somerton Beach at about 6:45am on 1 December 1948 after receiving John Lyons' phone call. PC Moss examined the body of the fully clothed man who was lying on his back with his head resting against the sea wall. In his deposition at the inquest, he stated that there were no signs of violence and a partly smoked cigarette was resting on the right collar of the dead man's coat, wedged in position by his cheek.

PC Moss said he did not check if the partly smoked cigarette on the man's collar was the same brand as those found in a packet in his pocket. He also stated: 'There was no visible scorching or blistering on the deceased's cheek.'

The cigarette was left on the beach.

Constable Moss's deposition on oath at the coronial inquest described the items he found in the deceased's clothing on the morning of 1 December 1948 before the body was taken to the mortuary:

'I searched the clothing, found a railway ticket to Henley Beach, also a bus ticket, a tramway bus ticket. There were cigarettes on the body, which were in a packet. I did not compare them with the one that was partly smoked.

'The packet produced (at the inquest) looks like the cigarettes I found. The comb produced (at the inquest) was on the body, also the chewing gum and the metal comb. The bus ticket produced and the railway ticket produced (at the inquest) are similar to the tickets I found on the body. I did not find the slip of paper with the words Tamam Shud.'

List 1 of items found on the body according to PC Moss's deposition:

A train ticket
A bus ticket
Seven Kensitas cigarettes in an Army Club packet.
One part packet of Juicy Fruit chewing gum.
A metal comb

A subsequent list of items found on the body included a pair of underpants and a singlet in addition to the ones he was wearing. The conclusion is that the Somerton Man was carrying them in his pockets and they were missed by PC Moss and later consolidated with the clothes from his suitcase.

List 2 of items found on the body according to Gerry Feltus*:

A handkerchief.
A pair of underpants (jockey type).
A singlet.
A train ticket.
A bus ticket.
Seven Kensitas cigarettes in an Army Club packet.
One part packet of Juicy Fruit chewing gum.
Two combs.
A box of Bryant and Mays matches (quarter full)

The disparity may be attributed to PC Moss becoming flustered as he dealt with the body and the many onlookers, including John Lyons. It became apparent during the inquest that PC Moss and John Lyons may have had a lively discussion on the beach resulting from their differing opinions as to whether the cigarette on the collar had been partly smoked or not. John Lyons swore it had not. It is not known why the cigarette was left at the scene.

*Gerry Feltus is the author of *The Unknown Man*; he is a retired South Australian criminal branch senior detective and was the last official investigator into the Somerton Man case.

The Train Ticket

The 7d second-class, one-way railway ticket found on the body – number 091172 – was purchased at Adelaide Train Station from ticketing clerk Douglas George Townsend on the morning of Tuesday 30 November 1948. It was his first ticket of the day for the 10:50am train to Henley Beach, a destination about 11 kilometres north of Somerton Beach and about the same distance from Adelaide Railway Station.

The railway's ticketing records showed that Townsend sold only two more tickets for the 10.50am train before it left the station. The train tickets were not time-stamped and he was the only railway employee issuing them on that day.

The 10:50am train ran on time and the ticket of every

passenger who got on board was punched at the barrier. The ticket found on the body had not been punched.

The Bus Ticket

The bus ticket found on the body – number C 88708 – was sold by Municipal Tramways Trust (MTT) conductor Arthur Anzac Holderness on 30 November 1948 at 11:15am at a bus stop between Adelaide Railway Station on North Terrace and the intersection of West Terrace and South Terrace. The bus was scheduled to terminate at St. Leonards, a beachside suburb eleven kilometres from Adelaide Railway Station and four and a half kilometres north of Somerton Beach. Tickets issued during this part of the journey cost 7d; after South Terrace, 6d tickets were issued to boarding passengers. Arthur's daily ticket log for 30 November showed that nine 7d tickets were sold on that scheduled journey and ticket number C 88708 was the sixth.

It was established at the inquest that on 30 November, facilities were not available at Adelaide Train Station for arrivals from the country who wanted to bathe. Harold Rolfe North, the senior cloakroom porter, stated at the inquest: 'He would have to go to an hotel or to the city baths.'

The police later conjectured that the man missed his train after taking too long to wash and shave at the nearby public baths, and after lodging his suitcase he left the station and took the bus from the city.

The Initial Medical Examination

Constable John Moss arranged for the body to be transferred from Somerton Beach by police ambulance to the Royal Adelaide Hospital on North Terrace.

On arrival at about 9.40am, Dr John Barkly Bennett briefly examined the body in the ambulance while it was parked in front of the hospital's emergency department. He concluded that the time of death could not have been earlier than 2am.

At the inquest held on 17 June 1949, Dr Bennett stated that in his opinion death could have occurred up to eight hours before his examination but no longer. His opinion was not questioned at the time, but it is known that the onset of rigor mortis can be delayed for up to four hours after death.

The body was not removed from the ambulance at the hospital. Immediately after Dr Bennett's examination, Constable Moss accompanied it to the city mortuary where it was stripped and placed in a large refrigeration unit.

The Autopsy

The government pathologist, Dr John Matthew 'Barb' Dwyer, of 105 Port Road, Hindmarsh, an inner suburb of Adelaide, was asked to conduct the post-mortem and he began his task at the city mortuary on 2 December 1948 at 7.30am.

The body had been stripped of clothing and was lying face up on the examination table: a circumcised, wide-shouldered, middle-aged, muscular man with athlete's calves.

At the inquest held in June the following year, Dr Dwyer described the dead man as tallish, about forty-five years of age, with greying hair and in good physical condition. His fingernails were carefully trimmed, probably with scissors, and his general appearance was of a man whose 'bearing would be noticed'.

The congestion of blood above the ears and neck was particularly intense, said Dr Dwyer, and many teeth were missing from both the upper and lower jaw. The small patch of dried saliva at the right of the mouth must have run out at some time before death, he said, probably when the man's head was hanging to the side and he was unable to swallow.

On emptying the man's stomach and bowels, Dr Dwyer found blood mixed with what he thought was partly digested vegetable from a recently eaten pasty.

The vessels in the liver contained a great excess of blood. The spleen was strikingly large and the heart, if anything, was contracted. Dr Dwyer thought the food may have been in his stomach for up to three or four hours before death but found nothing to suggest the presence of an irritant or poison.

Two marks in the hollows of the knuckles of the deceased's right hand were probably abrasions made just before death, he said. His legs were tanned up to the crotch, but his torso was untanned. Dr Dwyer thought the man had worked outdoors wearing a shirt and bathing trunks in the year prior to his death.

Constable Scan Sutherland of the Metropolitan Station assisted Dr Dwyer with the autopsy and at its conclusion took possession of four glass jars which he delivered to Robert James Cowan, the South Australian deputy government analyst, for further examination. The jars contained the following specimens:

Jar 1: stomach and contents.
Jar 2: liver and muscle.
Jar 3: urine.
Jar 4: blood.

By Friday 3 December 1948, *The Advertiser*, a local daily newspaper, was reporting that the identity of the man found on Somerton Beach was still unknown. No poison container was found near the body, it reported, and there were no signs of violence.

On the same day as this report appeared in *The Advertiser*, Adelaide-based police photographer and fingerprint technician, Patrick James Durham, accompanied by Mounted Constable Knight, attended the city mortuary to obtain fingerprints from the corpse and take photographs. Knight, who was present at the beach the morning the body was found, confirmed it was the same man.

Durham and Knight were faced with the unpleasant and difficult task of manoeuvring the dead man's clothes back onto his body before Durham could take suitable pictures of his head and upper torso for release to the press and inclusion in the local *Police Gazette*.

By 7 December 1948, the police had ascertained that trousers similar to the deceased's, distinctively labelled 'Stamina', a popular brand at the time, were manufactured in Coburg in the neighbouring state of Victoria. However, the manufacturer said it produced over three thousand pairs a week for both the home and export markets and would be unable to assist in any way.

On 22 December 1948, Detective Hector 'Hec' Gollan, of the Adelaide Metropolitan Station, compiled another report about the dead man, which included details about his teeth. The autopsy examination of the body had determined there were four missing from the upper left side, five from the upper right, five from the lower left and four from the lower right: eighteen in total.

Appeals to the Public

After the pictures taken by the police photographer appeared in the local papers, a number of people either telephoned the police or showed up at Adelaide's Metropolitan Police Station, resulting in a regular flow of visitors attending the morgue to view the corpse. However, no one recognised him.

On 2 January 1949, a man from Edwardstown, eight kilometres from Adelaide, contacted the police to say he thought the unidentified dead man was a seaman missing from a Dutch steamer, the *Thedens* of the KPML line. This was later disproved.

On the same day, a woman from Torrensville, four kilometres from Adelaide, rang the police to claim that the dead man resembled her co-worker at the British Tube Mills factory, Kilburn, a suburb eight kilometres from Adelaide. On 5 January 1949, a man from North Adelaide visited the Adelaide Metropolitan Police Station to make the same claim, but when taken to the morgue he stated the dead man was definitely not the British Tube Mills worker.

The last viewing was in June 1949 by two crewmen of the SS *Cycle*, which was in port at the time and known to have employed a Tommy Reade some years previously. However, after viewing the rapidly deteriorating body they were convinced it wasn't Reade.

Further Enquiries

On 21 December 1948, dossiers of information, including photographs and fingerprints, were posted to missing persons bureaus in New Zealand, the UK, America and Canada.

On 3 January 1949, another detailed dossier about the case was prepared by the South Australian Criminal Investigation Branch and sent to all state police headquarters in Australia.

During January 1949, the police received no positive leads in response to the dossiers sent around Australia and overseas. Replies included a personal note signed by John Edgar Hoover, director of the FBI, stating that a search of the FBI's Identification Division records had produced no result. (In 1949, Hoover was in the process of centralising America's fingerprint records, some of which were maintained by trusted prisoners in several federal prisons. He needed a warehouse to store them.)

On 8 January 1949, Detective Sergeant Lionel Leane, one of the most senior and experienced detectives in the Adelaide Criminal Investigations Branch, was placed in charge of the Somerton Man investigation team which also included Detective Hector 'Hec' Gollan, Sergeant Scan Sutherland and Assistant Coroner's Constable FC (Alf) Horsnell. The team was based in an office at Adelaide Metropolitan Police Headquarters.

The Embalming

On 10 January 1949, Laurie Elliott of FT Elliot & Son, funeral directors of 89-85 Port Road, in the Adelaide suburb of Hindmarsh, was appointed to embalm the body. The police were concerned that the identification of the body might take some time and given the expected summer temperatures they thought preservation by embalming would be the best option.

Elliott had only recently returned from England where he had been trained in advanced embalming techniques, including the use of both embalming fluid and formalin.

He became the first person in South Australia to use this new technique when he embalmed the Somerton Man. It was a slow process: to maintain the job to his satisfaction and to prevent further decomposition, Elliot averaged four visits to the morgue every week for the next three months.

He worked with both his nostrils stuffed with cotton wool and a dab of cloves for a clear head. He wore gloves, rubber boots, and an apron over his clothes and used carbolic soap and hard bristle at wash up.

Those who preserve the dead, men like Laurie Elliott, live with the smell of death. It's on their skin, in their mouth, on their clothes. It waits for them in their bed.

The Suitcase

On 11 January 1949, Detective Leonard Douglas 'Len' Brown joined the investigation team from the general duties division at the request of Detective Sergeant Leane. Len Brown, an avuncular and engaging man, immediately contacted the Adelaide newspapers to ask if they could publicise an appeal for owners of Adelaide boarding houses and hotels to report any abandoned luggage.

On 14 January 1949, DS Leane visited Adelaide Railway Station to ask if there were any unclaimed luggage that may have been deposited in late November. He met with immediate success and was shown an unclaimed leather suitcase that had been left on a 24-hour ticket, costing 4d, number G 52703, between 11am and noon on 30 November 1948.

The case was in good condition with no travel labels attached, although DS Leane noticed signs that a sticker or label may have been removed from the outside surface of the case.

After taking some items from the suitcase to

photograph back at Adelaide Metropolitan Police Station, DS Leane left the suitcase with the cloakroom staff for five days on the chance that someone might claim it. The railway staff were instructed to contact him if a claim was made, then wait until he arrived before handing the case to the claimant.

The items DS Leane took from the case to be photographed were: a card of tan Barbour thread; a white tie with the name T Keane written on the back in laundry pen; a particle brush; a cut-down table knife in a sheath; and a pair of cutting scissors in a sheath.

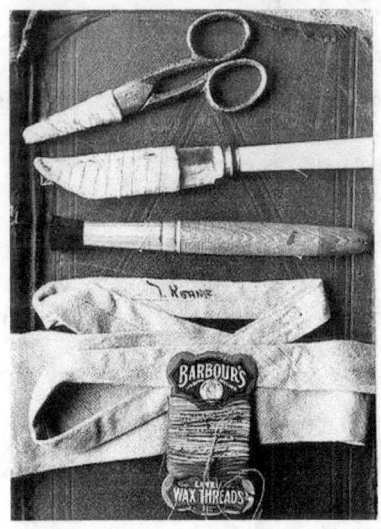

By 19 December 1949, no one had claimed the suitcase and DS Leane took it to the Adelaide Metropolitan Police Station where he made a close examination of its contents and listed the items it contained:

One dressing gown and cord.

One laundry bag (with the name 'Keane' written on it)

One scissors in sheath.

One cut-down table knife in sheath.

One small square of creased soft metal.

One particle brush. (Black particles were shaken out of the bristles by the police and sent to Robert James Cowan, the deputy government analyst who was experienced in analysing explosives. He was not able to identify the particles.)

Four singlets (one with a name torn off and one bearing the name 'Kean'.)

Four pairs of underpants

Two ties (including the white one mentioned above)

One pair of slippers (size 8)

One pair of trousers (Marco brand – Crusader Cloth) with three dry-cleaning or laundry marks written on the outside of a pocket: 1171/7 4393/3 305.3/1

One sports coat.

One coat shirt. (Coat shirts were designed to be worn outside of the trousers and were common in the warmer states; this particular one was of an unknown brand)

One pair of pyjamas.

One yellow coat shirt (Pelaco brand) with a label and its stitching removed.

One shirt

Six handkerchiefs.

One scarf.

One piece light cord.

1 cigarette lighter.

Eight large envelopes and one small.

Two coat hangers.

One razor strop.

One razor.

One shaving brush.

One small screwdriver.

Six pencils.

One sixpenny piece found in a trouser pocket.

One toothbrush and one tube of toothpaste.

One round, scallop-edged glass dish about three inches in diameter, its use unknown.

One green, plastic soap dish with a lid containing one hairpin, three safety pins, one front and one back shirt stud, one button (brown), one teaspoon, one pair of broken scissors, one card of Barbour thread (tan)

One tin of tan boot polish (Kiwi brand)

Two airmail stickers.

One rubber. (pencil eraser)

Apart from the names 'T. Keane' and 'Kean' all the name tabs had been removed from the clothes. It is conjectured that whoever removed them knew the man's name was neither Keane nor Kean. The police inspected some damaged labels under an infra-red ray lamp, but this revealed nothing.

DS Leane noted in his report that the suitcase was practically new and that the trousers found in it were the same size as those worn by the dead man. He also noted that the clothes in the suitcase were well-kept and tidy.

Although not noted at the time, it may be considered strange that no spare socks were found in the suitcase.

The Stencilling Tools

DS Leane interviewed Mr Gray, the headmaster of the School of Arts and Crafts at North Terrace, Adelaide, and after studying several catalogues there, DS Leane found a replica of the cut-down table knife found in the suitcase. Mr Gray also produced a piece of zinc similar to the one found in the suitcase and told Leane that in his opinion the knife was used to cut stencilling letters or numbers out of zinc plate and the scissors to trim and finish off the edges. It was conjectured that the tools were similar to those used by a ship's third officer when making stencils to label cargo.

The Clothes

In mid-April 1949, under the authority of the coroner's court, Professor John Burton Cleland LQMP, Emeritus Professor of Pathology at the University of Adelaide, and James Cowan, deputy government chemical analyst, took possession of the clothes the dead man was wearing and those found in the suitcase.

Professor Cleland had been a house surgeon at the Royal Prince Alfred Hospital in Sydney in 1900; a cancer research scholar at London Hospital, UK, in 1904; and a West Australian government bacteriologist in 1905 before becoming the principal microbiologist at the Bureau of Microbiology in Sydney in 1909. He was appointed the first Marks Professor of Pathology at the University of Adelaide in 1920 and was eventually to carry out over 7,000 systematic and meticulous autopsy examinations.

Professor Cleland, born in 1878, was in his early seventies when he was asked to help with the Somerton Man enquiry. By that time he was hugely experienced and knowledgeable with a reputation for being able to diagnose rare conditions after little more than a cursory examination. It was said that he used to stretch out the removed intestine and sniff its length for poisons.

One of Professor Cleland's more significant successes was his work on the newly discovered encephalitis, then called 'Australian X disease', and the proof that it was distinct from poliomyelitis due to its microscopic characteristics and the experimental transmission of virus strains to monkeys, sheep and other herbivores.

Given his illustrious career and the esteem in which he was held, his approach to investigating the unidentified man's clothes would not have been questioned or remarked upon at the time. Well over six decades later, his actions might be considered macabre and would certainly be prohibited simply to prevent cross-contamination and to safeguard evidence.

Professor Cleland tried on the dead man's clothes.

He wanted to satisfy himself that the clothes the dead man had been wearing and those found in the suitcase were of a similar size. James Cowan was not required to try on any of the clothing apart from the footwear.

At the inquest, held about two months later, Cleland stated in his deposition: 'I put on the deceased's double-breasted coat and it buttoned on me with some difficulty, and a sports coat in the suitcase similarly could be buttoned with a squeeze (Professor Cleland carried a little weight about his middle). The sleeves of each of these garments came down the hand about the same extent though perhaps the sports coat sleeves were not quite as long. The trousers in the suitcase and those worn by the deceased seemed to be of equal length. The shoes taken off the deceased were an excellent fit on Mr Cowan, but the slippers in the suitcase he thought a trifle smaller.'

Professor Cleland's deposition also stated: 'In the suitcase was an orange-coloured linen thread. I found a similar thread in the clothing on the body and in the clothing in the suitcase. (The thread) was examined microscopically and corresponded in colour and size of fibres to similar thread used to sew up a pocket in a pair of trousers found in the suitcase, buttons on the trousers taken off the deceased and to repair a coat collar where it had given way.'

Cleland further stated: 'I did not feel too convinced about the tags on the clothes – it appeared that they had been removed, but I did not find any thread to indicate they had been recently removed.'

The Tamam Shud Slip

It was while Professor Cleland was examining the trousers removed from the dead body that he found a small, tightly rolled cylinder of paper measuring about 35mm by 10mm tucked deep into the fob pocket.

He stated in his deposition at the inquest: 'In examining the clothes, in a fob pocket which was rather difficult to find, just to the right of the fly, I found a piece of paper.'

He extracted it with a pair of tweezers, unrolled it and saw it bore the printed words 'Tamam Shud'.

On 19 April 1949, Professor Cleland informed Detective Sergeant Lionel Leane about his discovery of the 'Tamam Shud' slip of paper. Once Leane had possession of the slip he delegated the task of finding the meaning of the two words to Detective Len Brown. However, it was not until two months later that Detective Brown met with success when a Mr C.T. Whiting of the Adelaide Public Library showed him a Persian-English dictionary compiled by Arthur Walleston. Detective Brown immediately reported back to DS Leane that the two words meant 'The End'.

Professor Cleland believed that the unidentified Somerton Man had killed himself, stating in his deposition: 'I have come to the opinion, taking all the circumstances into account, that death was almost certainly not natural, and in all probability that some poison had been taken with suicidal intent. I came to that conclusion before I found the piece of paper bearing the words Tamam Shud. Bearing in mind that those words mean something like 'the end' that supports my opinion considerably. I think the words were put there deliberately and indicated the intention that he was fed up with things.'

Cleland's Skull

In June 1949, the police approached the South Australian Museum on North Terrace in Adelaide to enquire about the possibility of creating a plaster bust of the head and shoulders of the dead man. This was yet another attempt in the quest to identify him.

The museum suggested Paul Lawson, a taxidermist, as the person most able to perform this task and on 2 June 1949, detectives from the Adelaide CIB took him to the morgue to view the body. It was now over five months old and badly decomposed, despite having been embalmed four months previously.

The bust was completed on 15 June 1949, two days before the inquest began, and given a final inspection in Paul Lawson's office by Professor Cleland, Detective Sergeant Leane and Detective Brown.

Professor Cleland was upset. He had asked Paul Lawson to saw a cavity big enough in the skull to withdraw the brain; his wish was to have the skull preserved and kept from burial. But the taxidermist had lacked the confidence to do any more than slit the skin of the body's forehead. Professor Cleland was not to have his skull.

The body was transported to Adelaide Metropolitan Police Headquarters on 16 June 1949 to be photographed by James Durham, a skilled police photographer who took pains to provide accurate images of the deceased's head and face from both front and sides.

At the inquest, Paul Lawson said: 'His feet were rather striking features, suggesting – this is my own assumption – he had been in the habit of wearing high-heeled and pointed shoes; I base that on the fact that the calf muscle was high and well-developed, such as found in women. The feet were comparatively broad at the joints of the toe and foot, but the big toe and the little toe were joined together towards a common apex, in other words wedge shaped. That peculiarity I found more pronounced than is usual.'

This may suggest that he had witnessed this physical condition on previous occasions, though he did not offer any details.

The author of this book was able to describe this 'peculiar and pronounced' condition to an eminent professor of neurology in his Sydney surgery, who suggested that the man might have had a condition called 'dystonia* of the toes.'

He added that the man's over-developed calves might have been the physical evidence of his valiant efforts to walk normally, despite the condition, as evidenced by the even wear on the soles of the shoes he was wearing.

*Dystonia is a neurological involuntary movement disorder.

Known only to God

On Tuesday 14 June 1949, just three days before the inquest began, the unidentified man was interred at West Terrace Cemetery in Adelaide. The funeral was conducted by Salvation Army Captain E. J. Webb and his eulogy included the words: 'Yes, this man has someone to love him. He is known only to God.'

Also present were funeral director, Laurie Elliott; funeral assistant, Claude Trevelion; journalist, Bob Whitington; and Sergeant Scan Sutherland. Leo Kenny, licensee of the Elephant and Castle Hotel, acted as a pallbearer. The Elephant and Castle was a popular drinking hole for cemetery workers, being situated on the opposite side of the road, and Leo Kenny was an avid follower of the case. No other members of the public were present.

Some days afterwards, a headstone donated by a monument mason, Mr A Collins of Keswick, Adelaide, was erected on the grave. Its simple inscription reads:

HERE LIES
THE UNKNOWN MAN
WHO WAS FOUND AT
SOMERTON BEACH
1ST DEC 1948.

The Inquest

The coronial inquest opened on Friday 17 June 1949. At the start of the proceedings, the city coroner, Thomas Erskine Cleland (a distant cousin of Professor John Burton Cleland) stated:

- the identity of the deceased was quite unknown;
- his death was not natural;
- it almost certainly was not accidental.

This was reported in *The Advertiser* the following day:

The unknown man whose body was found on the beach at Somerton was probably poisoned and his death was almost certainly not accidental, the City Coroner (Mr. T. E. Cleland) said at the opening of the inquest yesterday. This left the alternative that the deceased died by his own act or was murdered. After evidence of the discovery of the body, and medical and police evidence, the inquest was adjourned until Tuesday, when medical evidence will be given by Professor J. B. Cleland, Sir Stanton Hicks and Dr. R. B. Bennett.

In his evidence, Professor John Cleland said he was surprised to learn of the lividity around the ears and neck in view of the position of the body.

This was understood to mean that the body's lividity would be more commonly associated with a man who had died lying down, rather than one who died with his head and shoulders supported by the sea wall.

Sir Cedric Stanton Hicks, Professor of Physiology and Pharmacology at the University of Adelaide and expert witness, said he was inclined to conclude that a member of a group of drugs that can cause the heart to stop might have been used.

Hicks produced a piece of paper and handed it to the coroner, explaining that the first word he had written (glycosides) was the name of the group and the second and third words (digitalin and strophanthin) were members of that group. All are extremely toxic in relatively small doses.

Hicks went on to say that the drugs were easily procurable by ordinary people and no doctor's prescription was necessary.

Coroner Cleland adjourned the case *sine die* on 21 June
1949.

A Million to one Chance

The News, Friday 22 July 1949

A MILLION TO ONE CHANCE

*Although police realise they are acting on a million to one chance,
a search for a book with a torn page which may throw some light
on the Somerton body mystery is continuing throughout
Australia.*

*A torn page of Fitzgerald's translation of the "Rubaiyat of
Omar Khayyam" was found in the pocket of the victim.*

*Det.-Sgt. Leane and Det. Brown believe the torn book may still
be on the shelves of a library. They think that if they can find it,
they can trace the man to the city or town he was in before he
came to Adelaide.*

*With this information, it may be possible to establish his identity.
Melbourne police have made a search of public libraries and
libraries in Victorian provincial towns, but have failed to find
the torn volume. Although a number of city and suburban
libraries have been checked here, others in country districts have
not yet been investigated.*

The cause of death will probably never be known. A plaster cast of the victim's head and shoulders, which was exhibited at the inquest, is now in a store room at Adelaide Museum. No request for it to be displayed has yet been made by the authorities.

The Mail, 23 July 1949

Torn book gives new hope in body case

Fresh hope that the Somerton body mystery may be solved comes today with the finding of a copy of the 'Rubaiyat of Omar Khayyam' with the last page torn.

POLICE have been searching for such a book throughout Australia in the hope it might provide the missing clue to the body's identity. Last night an Adelaide businessman read of the search in 'The News' and recalled that in November he had found a copy of the book which had been thrown on the back seat of his car while it was parked in Jetty Road, Glenelg.

The book, the last page of which is torn, has been handed to police. If scientific tests, to be conducted next week, show the scrap of paper found on the dead man's clothing had been taken from the book, police will have brought off a million to one chance. On December 1, when the body of the mystery man was found on Somerton Beach, police discovered the name tags had been cut from the clothing and all he had in his pockets was a train ticket, a bus ticket, and a neatly trimmed piece of paper with the printed words 'Tamam Shud.' Investigators found these words had been used by Omar Khayyam at the end of his verses and meant 'the end' or 'the finish.'

A study of the printing indicated the words might have been torn from a copy of Fitzgerald's translation of Omar Khayyam. In the belief if the book could be found it might show the movements of the man before his death, police throughout Australia have been looking for it. The finder of the book today handed it to Det.-Sgt. R. L. Leane. On the last page the words 'Tamam Shud' had been torn out.

On the back of the book are several telephone* numbers and a series of capital letters, written in pencil, the meaning of which have not yet been deciphered. As the scrap of paper found on the dead man had been trimmed, police were unable to identify the book merely by fitting it into the torn page. Proof will now rest with tests on the paper and the print.

*In answer to one of the author's many questions to Gerry Feltus, he replied: 'Detective Brown made no mention to me of two telephone numbers.'

Mr Francis and The Rubaiyat

In 2010, the retired homicide detective sergeant Gerry Feltus published *The Unknown Man*, an account of his cold-case investigation into the Somerton Man.

In his book, Feltus refers to the 'Adelaide businessman' as 'Ronald Francis' and describes in detail the circumstances surrounding his discovery of the

Rubaiyat with the torn page, as recounted by Francis to Detective Sergeant Leane on 23 July 1949.

Francis told Leane he had read an item in *The News* on 22 July 1949 about the attempt by police to find a copy of the *Rubaiyat* with a tear in its back page. Francis immediately recalled that his brother-in-law had left a copy of the *Rubaiyat* in the glove box of his car, a Hillman Minx, at about the time the body was found on Somerton Beach. When Francis went to his car and found the *Rubaiyat* still in the glove box, he rang his brother-in-law to ask him where he had found it.

His brother-in-law told Francis he had seen it in the back footwell of the Hillman and as he got out of the car, he slipped the book into the glove box.

Francis took the *Rubaiyat* to the Adelaide CIB headquarters the next day and presented it to Detective Sergeant Leane.

To this day, the real identity of Ronald Francis remains unknown. When the author contacted Feltus in early 2016 and asked why the secrecy was necessary, his response was:

Police should not betray a confidence and if people request their identity not be revealed, they must respect their wish. Potential witnesses are not obliged to give their name and address (unless specified by law) or make and sign statements. If a witness specifically requests confidentiality it would be an idiot of a police officer who did not respect that wish. A police officer could also subject himself to possible external litigation, internal investigation or both as a result of his or her actions.

The author believes that finding the real identity of Ronald Francis would assist in identifying the Somerton Man.

The Code

Detective Sergeant Leane examined the Francis *Rubaiyat* and with the help of a large magnifying glass he discerned five lines of capital letters on the outside back cover:

(Line 1) WRGOABABD
(Line 2) ~~MLIAOI~~ *This line appears to have been crossed out and part repeated on line four.*
(Line 3) WTBIMPANETP
(Line 4) MLIABOAIAQC
(Line 5) ITTMTSAMSTGAB

Gerry Feltus writes in *The Unknown Man:* 'Some sources have suggested that there were indents on the rear of the *Rubaiyat* and were possibly caused when the book was used as a support to write on another piece of paper. The letters were exposed when police rubbed a lead pencil across the indents. The information is hearsay and cannot be confirmed.'

The Telephone Number

Detective Sergeant Leane also noticed what appeared to be a telephone number written in pencil on the outside of the rear cover of the *Rubaiyat* to the right of the lines of code.

He gave Detective Errol Canney the job of tracing the number in the Adelaide telephone directory. He soon found that the subscriber lived at 90A Moseley Street, Glenelg, a short walk from Somerton Beach and the Crippled Children's Home.

When Detective Canney visited Moseley Street, the occupant gave her name as Mrs Thompson. In fact, and as the police later ascertained, she was unmarried and her real name was Jessica Harkness.

Jessica lived at the Moseley Street address with her two-year-old son Robin and Prosper McTaggart Thomson, who had moved in after the birth of the child.

During their conversation, Jessica revealed to Detective Canney that she had given a copy of the *Rubaiyat* to an army lieutenant at the Clifton Gardens Hotel some years earlier. The lieutenant's name, she told the detective, was Alfred Boxall.

More Numbers?

Some commentators believe that another number was written on the back of the *Rubaiyat*. Gerry Feltus is non committal. Some researchers believe it may be an Australian bank account number and are checking through records dating from 1940 to 1950.

The *Rubaiyat* allegedly handed in by 'Ronald Francis', together with the deceased's clothing, his suitcase and its contents, were all said to have been disposed of during an evidence room clean-out in the late 1950s.

The fate of the Tamam Shud slip is unknown but some researchers suspect it is still in existence.

The Nurse

Jessica Harkness was born in 1921 in Marrickville, New South Wales, and after leaving school trained as a nurse at the Royal North Shore hospital (RNS) in Sydney.

Jessica was a regular after-work visitor to the Clifton Gardens Hotel overlooking Chowder Bay, Sydney, seven kilometres from the RNS but close to a convalescent hospital run by the Red Cross, housed in the old WW1 officers' quarters at Georges Head Army Water Base. The officers' quarters still exist, as do many others in the old army base, and are a popular destination for tourists and war historians. The Clifton Gardens Hotel was demolished in 1967.

It was at the Clifton Gardens Hotel that Jessica met Alfred Boxall, a lieutenant army engineer employed at the Georges Head Army Water Base. The hotel was close to where they both worked and was popular with nurses from the convalescent hospital and servicemen from the base. She was introduced to him by Heather Musgrave, a nurse and the wife of Tom Musgrave, a friend and fellow officer of Alfred's at Georges Head. Alfred was fifteen years older than Jessica and little is known about their relationship.

While still unmarried, she became pregnant at the age of twenty-five and in 1946 left Sydney for the Melbourne suburb of Mentone, Victoria.

After the birth of her son Robin in 1947 in Adelaide, Jessica moved to Glenelg, South Australia, and in 1950 married Prosper McTaggart Thomson, a recently divorced second-hand car dealer who had been discharged from the army for medical reasons and who, coincidentally, was living in Mentone with his first wife Queenie at the time Jessica was in Melbourne. Thomson's army records show he was suffering from haemoptysis (coughing up blood), an ailment commonly treated with digitalin.

Jessica had another child after Robin, a daughter called Kate. No details of her date of birth are available.

Gerry Feltus interviewed Jessica in 2002 and wrote that they had a lengthy conversation, although he thought her evasive and unwilling to share anything she might know about the case. She claimed not to remember Alfred Boxall and said that none of her family knew anything about the Somerton Man mystery. Jessica said she did not own a copy of the *Rubaiyat* (at the time of the interview) and questioned Feltus about its significance.

Prosper Thomson died in 1995.

Jessica Thomson died in 2007.

Robin Thomson, who became one of Australia's most celebrated ballet dancers, died in 2009.

Kate Thomson was interviewed by Sixty Minutes in 2015 and said her mother had a dark side and was secretive. Kate also mentioned that Jessica could speak some Russian.

Kate Thomson also quoted her mother as saying that she lied to the police and that the Somerton Man mystery was known only to 'a level higher than the police force'.

The taxidermist Paul Lawson, who created the bust of the Somerton Man, was interviewed on an Australian ABC TV programme in 1978 and described Jessica's reaction to seeing the plaster bust when she was brought into Lawson's laboratory by the police. Below are extracts from his description:

'Detective Leane brought Mrs Thompson (Jessica) into my lab.'

'Detective Leane stood over there (gesture) and the other two detectives over there (gesture).'

'I took the covering off the bust cast, stood back, and Jessica took one look at that bust and then looked down, and she didn't look up at that (gesture) again, for the whole of the interview.'

'Detective Leane was asking her questions, but they (the answers) were all no, no. Everything was no.'

The Centaur

The *Centaur*, 2/3rd Australian Hospital Ship was a Scottish-built passenger vessel converted in January 1943 for use as a hospital ship.

On 12 May 1943, the *Centaur* sailed from Sydney carrying her crew and medical staff. There were no patients aboard. The ship was sunk without warning by a torpedo from a Japanese submarine on 14 May 1943 at approximately 4am, about 50 miles east north-east of Brisbane.

Of the 332 people on board, only 64 survived. The survivors spent 35 hours on rafts before being rescued.

Sister Ellen Savage of Quirindi, the only one of twelve nursing sisters on board to survive, did all she could to help the other survivors despite being injured herself and was awarded the George Medal in recognition of her efforts.

The Engineer

Alfred Boxall was born in 1906 in Hammersmith, London, UK, and arrived in Australia as an infant with his parents and older brother Fred.

A severe bout of chicken pox prevented Alf from completing his school Qualifying Certificate and he was unable to enter high school. He studied mechanical engineering at a technical college near his home in Peakhurst, a Sydney suburb, and obtained employment as an assistant mechanic with Garratts Ltd in Elizabeth Street, Sydney. Garrats advertised their business as specialising in the repair of Yorkshire Steam Wagon Cars and English Karriers. The Garrats building was pulled down long ago and only a few photos of it exist.

In 1927, Alf was employed by the National Roads and Motorists Association (NRMA) as a patrolman based in Goulburn, a large provincial town 195 kilometres south-west of Sydney. He was given a Harley Davidson with a sidecar and very soon joined the Goulburn

Motor Club where, on a completely dry Lake George, he created a land speed record of 100mph. The lake, when dry, is a level, dusty strip sixteen miles long, six miles wide and it remains highly popular with local motorbike riders to this day.

Alf lost his job during the Depression and returned to Sydney but was unable to find permanent work until 1936 when he was offered a position with R Crealy Pty Ltd, cartage contractors in Haymarket, an inner-Sydney suburb, where he was responsible for the maintenance of a fleet of 24 delivery trucks. Despite the difficulties of the Depression years, Alf managed to successfully pursue his interest in motorcycle racing at the Sydney Speedway, an egg-shaped racing track claimed by the promoters at the time to be the fastest in the world.

In 1937, after a courtship of ten years, Alf married Dulcie Smith from Goulburn. In 1940, he was employed by the NSW Department of Public Transport as an engineer, a wartime-protected occupation. Alf was only allowed to enlist after proving to the army recruiting board that his skills were essential to the war effort. He completed basic training at the Cowra Military Camp in New South Wales before being sent to the Northern Territory of Australia as part of the 2/1 Nackeroo Force, an intelligence gathering unit formed by its commander, Major Bill Stanner.

'I wanted a highly mobile unit with good radio links, light weapons, and made up of men with a bush background and

adventurous spirit who could live outdoors for months at a time, operating in small groups on their own initiative.' ~Lt-Col Stanner, CO Nackeroos, 1942-45.

Major Stanner

Major Stanner was an anthropologist as well as a soldier and had secured an Australian Research Council grant in 1932 to finance what became a rigorous seven-month period documenting the traditional lifestyles of Aboriginal communities on the Daly River, in Australia's Northern Territory.

This was the first of several visits Stanner made to the Northern Territory between 1932 and the outbreak of war and during this time he became fluent in many of the indigenous languages. This was a rare skill for a white man and it later enabled him to recruit local blacktrackers to help in the search for early signs of the expected Japanese invasion.

The Blacktrackers

Blacktrackers were highly skilled hunters, able to search for signs of life in the hostile deserts and coastal swamps of Australia's Top End. Australia's early white settlers called on their skills to assist in hunting game for the table and navigating through the endless reaches of desert scrub; they were also indispensable in assisting the local police to track bushrangers* and escaped convicts.

*Bushrangers was the term used to describe outlaws who roamed the roads and highways that connected Australia's early settlements, stealing money and goods from travellers and stage coaches. Ned Kelly and his criminal gang were the most notorious examples.

When Mitamirri, a famous early 20th century blacktracker, was asked how he tracked, he said: 'I never bend down low, just walk slow round and round until I see more.'

While with the Nackeroos, Alfred met and became friends with Mordecai, one of the local tribesmen Stanner was using as a blacktracker. The trackers used by the 2/1 Nackeroo Force lived on the outskirts of the Timber Creek camp, preferring their own company to that of white soldiers. They used tribal dialects, knew little English other than a dozen or so commands and were very fond of Virginia leaf tobacco, preferring to unpack the ready-rolled cigarettes and remake them into cigar-sized smokes as a change from chewing the intoxicating bedgery (also 'pedgery'), a mixture of wood ash and local pituri leaves.

In June 1943, Alfred was transferred to the 4th Australian Water Transport Company (Small Craft) (AWTC), which comprised a fleet of war-requisitioned fishing trawlers, small, shallow-draft coastal steamers and in one case a Manly Ferry. The 4th AWTC had been given the task of supplying and maintaining the Nackeroos. A further posting saw Alfred transferred to the 13th Australian Small Ships Company under the Allied supreme military command of General Douglas MacArthur. In 1947, while serving as a lieutenant engineer on the MV *Crusader*, Alfred visited Ambon, a city in the Indonesian Malakulu Islands.

Keith Role served with him on the *Crusader* and Jack 'Bluey' Mayes, the great Bondi surfer, also served in the Small Ships Company in the South West Pacific. The author and Mayes spent some weeks together in 1962, travelling the roads of the Australian east coast, looking for waves.

Alf Boxall was an accomplished sketcher and occasionally included some of his drawings with the letters he sent home to his wife, Dulcie, who lived in their small bungalow in Maroubra.

Alfred was discharged from the army in 1948 and after his retirement from civilian work he visited Mordecai in the Northern Territory, intending to travel with him along Timber Creek to a distant tree Boxall had remembered from his service with the Nackeroos. However, during the trek, Alfred became too ill to continue and had to return home before they reached their destination.

Alfred Boxall's Rubaiyat
In 1949, two New South Wales police officers visited Alfred's last known place of work, a bus and tram maintenance depot in Randwick, a beachside suburb of Sydney. They initially thought Alfred might be the Somerton Man.

After finding him alive, they accompanied Alf to his home at nearby Maroubra where he showed them the hardcover *Rubaiyat* Jessica had given him at the Clifton Gardens Hotel some years previously. It was inscribed in pen on the inner flyleaf with a verse from the book

which includes the line 'my penitence a-pieces tore'.
The inscription was signed 'Jestyn'.

> *Indeed, indeed, Repentance oft before*
> *I swore – but was I sober when I swore?*
> *And then and then came Spring, and Rose-in-hand*
> *My thread-bare Penitence apieces tore.*

The book was printed by the Australasian Publishing
Company in Sydney and had been stamped as being
sold, possibly second-hand, from the Craftsman
Bookshop in Sydney

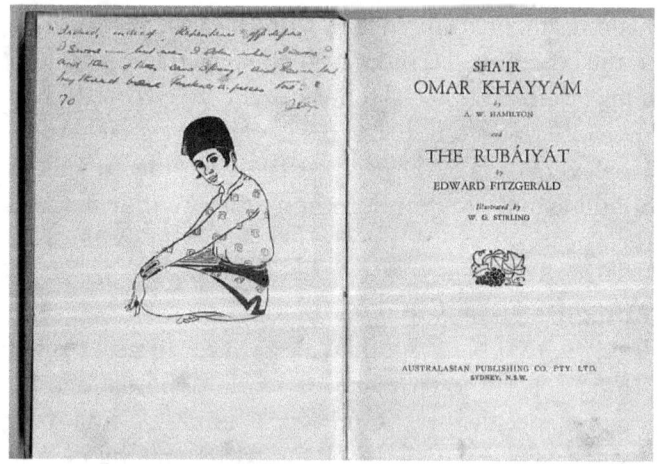

The Melodramatic Thesis
In an ABC documentary episode of Inside Story, called
The Somerton Beach Mystery, screened in Australia at 8pm,
Thursday 24 August 1978, Stuart Littlemore
interviewed Alf Boxall and asked him if he had been
involved in espionage activities during the war. A

transcript of their conversation follows:

'Do you see what I'm getting at, don't you? There is a theory about this whole affair that the man on the beach was a spy of some kind.'

Boxall takes a moment before replying:

'It's quite a melodramatic thesis, isn't it?'

Indeed, it's true to say that there wasn't a lot of scope for a lieutenant engineer to be a spy in WW2 – unless, of course, he was working in a place where intelligence was gathered. And it is known that Alf was involved in intelligence work: he was one of Bill Stanner's men, working in the heat and humidity of Australia's north west coast. The only intelligence the Nackeroo Force was interested in was the make of the Japanese aircraft they saw flying overhead and the origin of the footprints they found on otherwise desolate stretches of the mangrove-lined coast.

However, Alf later worked in another place where a different type of intelligence might be gathered: the Japanese changed everything when they sent their midget subs into Sydney Harbour in 1942, an affront that caused the wartime authorities to construct a submarine prevention barrier that stretched across the harbour from Watsons Bay to Georges Head. Even the Manly ferries were stopped and scraped on their way through, just in case a Japanese submarine was attempting to creep through under the shadow of their hulls.

The submarine prevention barrier; Watsons Bay is on the far side.

The author is familiar with Watsons Bay, its nooks and crannies, coves, caves and underwater gardens, its quiet depths. As a youth, he crawled through the defence tunnels, cut his feet on oyster shells and brought home bags of leatherjacket fish (delicious fried in butter), speared among the pilings.

Alf Boxall worked on the near side, the Georges Head side, and as an engineer had the right to board incoming steamers to be sure they had met their conditions of entry. You could almost liken him to a border guard in this duty, chugging out on a tender to a rusty old steamer waiting to be admitted to the harbour, a ship on someone's radar, perhaps, people aboard with notifiable backgrounds, their names in the ship's manifests. Could Alf have been asked to collect a different type of intelligence to be passed up the chain? The Clifton Gardens Hotel was just up the road.

Is it beyond the realms of possibility that Jessica Harkness might have been sitting in the beer garden with a few friends, taking a drink after work, waiting for him?

The Flowers on the Grave

Flowers appeared regularly on the Somerton Man's grave for many years, usually on the anniversary of his death.

A woman was observed leaving a jar of red gladioli, yellow antirrhinums and daisies on 1 December 1949. West Terrace Cemetery officials, when interviewed by *The Advertiser* on 2 December 1949, said the same woman had been noticed periodically visiting the grave to renew the flowers since the burial on 14 June 1949.

On 1 December 1952, *The News* reported that a wilted bunch of snapdragons was found on the grave. Gravediggers said they were left by a woman. Some said she was elderly, others thought younger. An overturned jar containing dead flowers was found on the grave on 1 December 1953.

For as many as thirty years after the Somerton Man was interred at Adelaide's West Terrace Cemetery, a woman left small bunches of flowers on his grave.

The Man Seen Carrying a Man

Over ten years later, on 5 December 1959, a witness came forward to report that at about 10pm on 30 November 1948, he and several companions had seen a man carrying a man on his shoulders, walking along the Somerton Beach shoreline.

The witness, whose name was suppressed, was interviewed by Detective Don O'Doherty of the Adelaide CIB. The lengthy statement was passed on to O'Doherty's superior.

Ex-Detective Gerry Feltus, the cold case investigator, found and interviewed this witness in 2003 and discovered that the police had never followed up O'Doherty's interview and had not visited him following his original statement.

The witness told Feltus that he had not reported the sighting to the police in 1948 because he thought others might have done so. The witness said he remembered the incident vividly; it was unusual, as the man doing the carrying appeared well-dressed and was walking along the shore where the sand was harder and easier to walk on. The witness assumed the man being carried was drunk.

The Mystery Endures

The Somerton Man case, also known as the Tamam Shud Mystery, remains alive in popular imagination in Australia and around the world. An article, titled The Lost Man, by Graeme Wood, appeared in *The California Sunday Magazine* in June 2015, and the popular Australian crime fiction writer, Kerry Greenwood, is the author of *Tamam Shud: The Somerton Man Mystery*, published by NewSouth Books in 2012.

Derek Abbott, a professor of engineering at the University of Adelaide, has been researching the case for many years and with the assistance of the university and his students has published his findings online at www.eleceng.adelaide.edu.au. Abbott has also been the driving force behind two failed applications to the South Australian government to have the Somerton Man's body exhumed.

The case is also the focus of several informative blogs, including the *Tamamshud Blogspot*, managed by Gordon Cramer. Cramer has exposed micro-coding hidden behind the letters found on the back cover of the Francis *Rubaiyat*, but at the time of writing he is yet to decipher them.

The micro-coding discovered by Gordon Cramer

Cramer has also raised the question as to whether the unidentified man was in fact deported from England early in the 1940s as an undesirable alien and housed in Australia as an internee at either the Hay or Tatura camps.

The Rubaiyat

In 1859, amateur translator Edward FitzGerald published a translation of a series of quatrains by Omar Khayyam, an 11th-century Persian known primarily at the time for his contributions to astronomy and algebra. FitzGerald called his translation *The Rubáiyát of Omar Khayyám*.

The first edition of Fitzgerald's translation went unsold. The following description of its remarkable rediscovery appears in a 1932 version of the *Rubaiyat* published by Walter J. Black in the US. This is an excerpt from the introductory passages by the American lecturer, literary critic and poet, Jessie B. Rittenhouse (1869-1948):

If Dante Gabriel Rossetti, the artist-poet and mystic, had not been lounging one day about the bookstalls of Piccadilly (London, UK), dipping now into the "farthing" and now into the "penny box", in search of treasure, the (sic) "Rubáiyát of Omar Khayyám" would doubtless have sunk still deeper under the dusty piles of unsalable old books and waited another decade for a discoverer.

It was already wearing on to a decade since the little quarto pamphlet in its brown paper wrappers ... had been issued from the press of Mr. Bernard Quaritch at the sum of five shillings, and failing of buyers, has fallen by natural stages to the ignominy of the "penny box".

Rossetti shared it with his Pre-Raphaelite circle, where it received an enthusiastic reception, including from the poet Swinburne (1837-1909) who began to write in Omaric metre.

The reputation of the *Rubaiyat* grew rapidly throughout the nineteenth century as reviews were published and popular poets tried to emulate the stanza format FitzGerald had invented. By the turn of the century the *Rubaiyat* had become a popular sensation; the average American and almost every poet writing in English could quote stanzas verbatim.

The *Rubaiyat* was so widely quoted that more than half of it appeared in *Bartletts's Quotations* and *The Oxford*

Dictionary of Quotations.

By 2007, more than 1,300 versions of the *Rubaiyat* had been published in over one hundred languages.

The Flying Officers

Tom Livesey, Leigh Bowes (the author's father), Doug Vanderfield and Mick Grace served as flying officers in 453 Squadron, based at Sembawang in Singapore in 1941. Grace was the son of one of the Grace brothers, owners of a department store housed on the first two floors of the Grace Building that General MacArthur used as his HQ when in Sydney during the war.

MacArthur also had the keys to a thirty-foot luxury Halvorsen Cruiser, moored at Brooklyn, a small village on the Hawkesbury River fifty-three kilometres from Sydney. This boat was hired by the author in 1979 for a five-mile trip upriver to Milson Island, the site of a lunatic asylum, long since closed. Despite extensive enquiries, the author is unable to discover if the cruiser still exists.

Mick Grace was widely known to wear a money belt containing gold sovereigns, and on his way to Singapore had more success at shipboard poker than anticipated. He was responsible for the pistol shot in the Raffles Hotel (an incident recounted in this book) in the days prior to the Japanese occupation of Singapore in 1942, and was accompanied by Livesey, Bowes and Vanderfield on that night.

The last two aircraft to leave Singapore were piloted by Flying Officer Leigh Bowes and Flying Officer 'Congo' Kinninmont. Both Buffalo aircraft were destroyed by Japanese fighter aircraft from the 64th Sentai on 9 February 1942 minutes after landing at Batavia, a large city on the northern coast of Indonesia. The two pilots were drinking coffee in a hangar when they were surprised by the attack and later that evening, little worse for the experience, they visited the Black Cat Nightclub.

After the war, all four men joined the Tattersall's Club in Sydney and were strongly competitive in the pool and on the handball court, though none swam as fast or played as hard as Leigh Bowes.

Tattersall's, established in 1858, remains one of Sydney's more exclusive clubs and its position in the centre of Sydney, together with its pool, casual dining facility, handball courts, steam rooms and sauna baths, has resulted in a waiting list of several years for prospective members.

The author was a junior member for many years and accompanied his father and younger brother to the club once a month on a Saturday.

Source: War Diaries, F.L. Bowes. Privately published.

The Padre

Padre John Patrick Pierce served as chaplain with the RAAF during the Japanese advance along the Malaysian peninsular at the outbreak of the Pacific War in 1941. He broke into a car dealer's showroom in Ipoh, Malaysia, on 16 December 1941, and commandeered a vintage Bentley to transport a number of wounded and sick pilots to Singapore. Flying Officer Leigh Bowes was among them, suffering another bout of dengue fever.

Once in Singapore, Pierce commandeered a merchant steamer and with over sixty RAAF ground crew escaped to the city of Darwin in the Northern Territory, Australia.

Source: Australian Dictionary of Biography, W.J.McCarthy, and War Diaries, F.L. Bowes.

Meyer Lansky & Charlie Haffenden

In 1942, the American ship SS *Normandie* caught fire and capsized while tied up at Pier 88 in the Hudson River, New York, during its conversion to a troopship. US Navy intelligence initially thought it an act of sabotage but witnesses later came forward saying that a welder working among flammable materials had accidentally started the fire.

Nevertheless, the US Navy decided it was time to improve both the security of the east coast shipping lanes, which were suffering significant losses to German U-boat packs, and take control of the New York docks, which for years had been run by the Mafia.

A meeting was arranged at Longchamps restaurant in New York between Commander Charles Radcliffe Haffenden of the Third Naval District and Meyer Lansky, a senior Mafia boss. When Haffenden put his proposition forward for Lansky's consideration, Lansky responded positively but on the proviso that New York Mafia boss, Charlie 'Lucky' Luciano, be transferred from Clinton Correctional Facility in Dannemora, New York, to the more hospitable Great Meadow Prison in Comstock, Washington County, New York.

Haffenden agreed and a surprised Luciano was moved within days. The agreement between the US Navy Office of Naval Intelligence and the Mafia was known as 'Operation Underworld'.

Meredith Knox Gardner

Meredith Knox Gardner was born in Okolona, Mississippi, in 1912. He was a multi-linguist and codebreaker who started cracking German and Japanese codes in a war-requisitioned girls' school in Arlington, Virginia, in 1941. The historic main building of the former girls' school now houses the classrooms and administrative offices of the Foreign Service Institute.

Gardner was later employed on the Venona Project, deciphering a large accumulation of Russian diplomatic cables. Among his first successes were decryptions of radio cables intercepted by a wireless transmitting station at Gawler in South Australia, a secret facility that began operating on 10 February 1942 and was decommissioned in May 1946.

The English Spies

Roger Hollis has long been suspected of being a double agent. Robert Hemblys-Scales, who accompanied Hollis on his second visit to Australia in August 1948, left after helping to set up the new Australian Security Intelligence Organisation (ASIO).

Hemblys-Scales was posted to Ismailia in north-eastern Egypt; his immediate superior was Kim Philby.

Kim Philby was a well-regarded and influential member of British Intelligence who worked as a double agent before defecting to the Soviet Union in

1963 where he served as an operative for both the NKVD (People's Commissariat of Internal Affairs) and KGB (Russian Committee for State Security). His memoir, *My Silent War*, was published in the UK in 1968. He died in 1988 aged 76 and is buried in Moscow.

The Tass Correspondent

Fedor Andreevich Nosov was the Tass correspondent in Sydney between 1943 and 1950. He succeeded Vladimir Mikheev, who was responsible for setting up a group of well-placed people sympathetic to the Russian communist cause, including Allan Dalziel, Private Secretary to Australia's Attorney-General and Minister for External Affairs Herbert Vere Evatt.

Nosov lived in a flat at Potts Point, frequented the bohemian quarter and was exposed as a spy in the early forties when Ray Whitrod, an ASIO agent, took pictures of Dalziel and Nosov in Nosov's flat.

The Convalescent Hospital

One of the buildings still remaining in what was the Georges Head army base in Sydney was originally built as officers' quarters in WW1 and later converted into a convalescent hospital for wounded soldiers in WW2. The hospital was administered by the Red Cross and staffed by nurses from Sydney's major hospitals.

WW1 converted officers' quarters at Georges Head photographed by JWC Adam.

The CIS

Eric Edwin Longfield Lloyd, director of the Commonwealth Investigation Service (CIS) in 1947, was considered unable to keep up with advances in post-war intelligence methods, in particular the threat to the Australian Department of External Affairs (Foreign Office) from Russian infiltration. The Americans thought Lloyd incompetent and refused to share intelligence with Australia until a new Australian security apparatus (ASIO) had been created and Lloyd replaced. He died in 1952.

In the *Australian Dictionary of Biography*, David Sadlier describes Lloyd as a 'softly spoken, self-effacing, modest and cautious man, and a dependable public servant'.

Patrick Heenan

Patrick Heenan was summarily executed on the Singapore docks by the military police a few days before the Japanese entered the city in February 1942.

On 9 December 1941, at Alor Star, Malaysia, Keenan was caught red-handed communicating with the Japanese on a short wave radio; he had one disguised as a typewriter and the other concealed in a field communication set. He also had incriminating papers and a codebook in his possession. Keenan was sending the Japanese information about aircraft movements on the Malaysian RAF Kedah airfields.

Project Venona and MI5

In February 1948, two senior officers from the British MI5 intelligence agency, Director General Percy

Sillitoe and future Director General Roger Hollis, travelled to Australia's capital, Canberra, with the intention of telling Prime Minister Ben Chifley and Attorney-General and Minister for External Affairs Herbert Vere Evatt that Australia had to improve its national security. They had learned that members of the Australian Department of External Affairs (Foreign Office) were leaking information to the Soviet Union. MI5 claimed to have learned of the leak from a Soviet defector.

Hollis and Sillitoe were surprised to find themselves being forcefully interrogated by Evatt to such a degree that their cover story was exposed as a sham. As a result, the MI5 representatives were forced into a series of humiliating retreats and were compelled to share much more information with the Australians than they originally intended. The fact that they disliked Evatt didn't help.

Hollis and Sillitoe eventually conceded that information about the leaks had come from intercepted Soviet cables decrypted in America by an organisation codenamed Venona, a US intelligence agency based in Arlington, Virginia, and kept secret from both US President Harry S. Truman and the CIA (the US Central Intelligence Agency). This extraordinary secrecy was made necessary because of FBI Director J. Edgar Hoover's belief that Soviet agents had penetrated the CIA.

Meredith Gardner, the Venona Project's head cryptographer, told Peter Wright, author of *Spymaster*

(1987) that the English spy Kim Philby was a regular visitor to Arlington Hall. He observed the strange intensity with which Philby had watched the decryption teams at work: 'Philby was looking on with no doubt rapt attention but he never said a word, never a word.'

The Strathmore Hotel

On 1 December 1982, Tom Loftus, an Adelaide-based journalist, interviewed Ina Harvey who was the Strathmore Hotel's receptionist in 1948. Loftus then ran two articles in *The News* about an unidentified man who had stayed at the Strathmore Hotel in late November 1948 and was possibly linked to the Somerton Man.

Harvey clearly remembered the man who had no baggage other than a small black case such as a doctor or musician might carry. She did not remember him going into the bar at any point. Harvey described him as having an air of general refinement and thought he was possibly a professional man.

She remembered that when he spoke his grammar was 'correct and lucid'. She told Loftus: 'He certainly didn't murder the Queen's English.'

The Strathmore Hotel is still open for business at 129

North Terrace in Adelaide, opposite the Adelaide Railway Station.

The Final Inquisition

On 14 March 1958, the final inquisition under the Coroners Act, 1935 was issued by Coroner Thomas Erskine Cleland:

"AND I, the said Justice of the Peace and Coroner, do say that I am unable to say who the deceased was. He died on the shore at Somerton on the 1st of December, 1948. I am unable to say how he died or what was the cause of his death."

'It's like dropping a long fishing line into myriads of silver fish, every one a fact, and the line is your story. There are a thousand fish in this school and your line has a thousand hooks, and when you've drawn your story on board, hand over hand, right to the very end, all thousand fish are caught.'

PB, August 2016

In Gratitude

Angie, who handed me a newspaper article on 1 December five years ago, thinking I might be interested.

Gerry Feltus. *'No more emails, just write the book!'* Thanks for yours.

My friend and publisher, Deb *Benno* Bennison: she knew there was a story in it.

The University of Adelaide archives.

The National Archives of Australia.

The inquest papers.

The Internet.

Keith Role, Gwen Dundon, Mick, Hilly, and Pete: they picked the flute needle.

The readers of tomsbytwo.com. Thirty a day, every day.

The burrowers: Byron D, Misca *she's a girl*, and Clive, who found Tibor Kaldor.

Gordon Cramer. When this is forgotten his work will remain.

John Bungate: 15 years wrapping his hands around villains' throats and three listening to me over lunch every Tuesday.

Sister Philomena, who insisted I choose better adjectives.

Keith Parker, for reading over my shoulder.

List of Characters

Alex Barrat, Sydney journalist
Ed Baxter, Australian Army lieutenant engineer
Ellse Baxter, Ed Baxter's wife
Rod Beecham, second hand car dealer
Nick Bellantoni, criminal associate of journalist Alex Barrat
John Bingham, director of Australian Signals Intelligence
Mr Buford and Mr Stace, Australian Commonwealth Intelligence Service agents
Nigel Chen, sampan owner
Frank Delaney, FBI agent
Eric, railway porter
Meredith Gardner, Arlington-based cryptographer
Mr George, café proprietor
Commander Charlie Haffenden, US Navy
Harold, senior luggage porter
Jessica Hartnell, trainee nurse
Ina Harvey, hotel receptionist
J. Edgar Hoover, director of the FBI
Val Johanssen, skipper of the *Cycle*
Tommy Keane, seaman on the *Crusader*
Tosya Keyannik, seaman, Russian courier
Meyer Lansky, Mafia boss
Sammy Lee, nightclub owner
George Lorrimer, FBI agent
Private Chat McCimber, Australian Army
John Millar, communist activist
Eddie Mittelhausenn, rag trader

Mordecai, Australian Army Blacktracker
Pete Musgrave, Australian Army lieutenant engineer
Padre Pearce, Catholic priest
David Pym, assistant director of Australian Signals
Intelligence, based at Arlington
Oscar Rostov, Tass correspondent and NKGB agent
Marta Shubin, Russian sorting clerk
Major Bill Stanner, Australian Army
Theresa, missionary sister
Tom, Australian seaman
Otto Trozyth, NKGB agent

Bennison Books

Bennison Books has four imprints:

Contemporary Classics
Great writing from new authors

Poetic Licence
Poetry and prosetry

Non-Fiction
Interesting and useful works written by experts

People's Classics
Handpicked golden oldies by favourite and forgotten authors

Bennison Books is named after Ronald Bennison,
an aptly named blessing.

bennisonbooks.com